THE

POWER
REVEALED

LEAH M. BERRY

ISBN 978-0615898742

To Logan and Rowan,

*for anxiously awaiting each new chapter
and for always being willing
to join in our adventures.*

Chapter 1

JUSTIN STEPPED OFF the dirt path and moved deeper into the forest, unaware of what lay ahead. Weaving between the trees, he soon found his way closed in by a tangle of bushes and grasping vines. He stopped and stared at the living wall. After all that had been taken from him recently, the barrier seemed like one more thing determined to break him down. Fighting the ache inside, he shoved the branches aside and pushed ahead.

A cold wind whipped at his face. The breeze carried the voices of his classmates from down the path near the high school. Justin was tired of the flood of unfamiliar faces and needed some space. He plunged farther into the thick web of undergrowth. But his search for solitude was a vain attempt to escape the memories that plagued him. It had been almost two weeks and he still couldn't accept that his best friend was gone.

After pulling a tree branch aside to create an opening to pass through, Justin came upon a break in the thick undergrowth. The clearing revealed a massive Douglas fir that stood apart by itself. The rest of the forest didn't dare intrude on its space. Justin crossed the unspoken boundary and found a dry spot of ground below its high branches. The bed of spongy earth and fallen needles provided a comfortable seat as he leaned against the enormous trunk. Closing his eyes, he tried to shut out any memories of the car accident. Whenever he thought about the phone call and the look on his mother's face as she received the terrible news that Grandpa had died, Justin's throat would gum up and he'd have to grit his teeth to hold his emotions in check.

An intense vibration shook through the tree he leaned against, tingling along Justin's spine and distracting him from his grim thoughts. Justin opened his eyes and glanced around, but all he could see was an endless panorama of green. He looked up, hoping to see the sun for the first time since moving to Bellingham, Washington a few days ago. But the small openings in the forest canopy revealed only a diffused light filtered through dreary, grey clouds. He missed the wide open skies of Texas.

He was about to shut his eyes when he felt the tremor again. Justin twisted around and touched the trunk. Heat spread across his palm and fingers. He pulled his arm away and stared at his hand in wonder. Doubting the sensation, he touched the tree again. Energy flowed into his body like liquid sugar running through his veins.

A buzz of energy traveled from the top of his head to his toes. He yanked his hand away from the rough bark of the tree, but he could still feel the charge. Justin ran his hand through his wavy, brown hair in an unconscious effort to brush the sensation away. Energy crackled across his palm. He pulled his hand down expecting to see sparks coming off his fingertips, but his hand appeared normal.

"Hello, there."

Justin spun around, but no one was in sight.

"Hello-ohhhh," came the voice again. Justin wasn't only hearing the voice–it vibrated through him like music did when he played it at full volume in the car.

"Where are you?" Justin asked.

The voice chuckled. "The tree, of course. How else could I talk to you?"

Justin felt the energy vibrate through him in sync with the words. It seemed to emanate from the tree and pulse through his entire body. He jumped up from the tree and looked around. "Come on. Who is this?"

"I'm Katie. What's your name?"

Even though he was no longer touching the tree, he could still feel the power pulse with the words. Justin hesitated. Did he really intend to speak to a tree? He'd heard of people talking to their plants. But he'd never heard of plants starting the conversation. He wondered if his inability to accept Grandpa's death had finally driven him to hallucinations.

He heard another laugh. "You know, it's not a difficult question. Why not start with your first name?" Another rush of energy flowed into him seeming to push the answer right out of him.

"Justin." Yep. He did it. He just introduced himself to a tree. He was clearly losing his mind.

"Hi, Justin. I haven't heard of you. Where are you from?"

He couldn't explain why, but he opened his mouth to respond. "I just moved here from—" Justin stopped mid-sentence when he noticed a girl from his science class come around the bend into view.

"Are you talking to that tree?" she asked.

"No!" Justin said quickly, looking around to see if anyone else saw him.

"I saw you talking to that tree." She brushed her long black hair away from her face. For a moment, Justin was distracted by the blueness of her eyes. She was stunning. But she was

3

obviously one of those girls who found it entertaining to make fun of anyone below her social rank, so it didn't matter to him what she looked like.

"No, I don't make a habit of talking to trees. But if you're really desperate for someone to chat with, I suppose you're free to try speaking to that rock over there."

The girl's mouth shot open, but she seemed uncertain what to say. She bit her bottom lip and blushed. The color in her cheeks made her look even more attractive. But hot or not, Justin wasn't going to wait for her to confirm that he had been talking to the local plant life. He marched down the path toward some of his fellow classmates, anxious for the school day to finally end.

Chapter 2

JUSTIN DROPPED ONTO his bed and pulled a pillow over his head trying to silence the arguments fighting it out in his mind. His brain wouldn't stop replaying the events in the forest trying to find a reasonable explanation for what had happened. So far, he could come up with only two possibilities. One, trees could talk. Unlikely. Or two, he was going crazy. More likely. He didn't want the second answer to be true. But he wasn't very excited about accepting the first option either. He desperately needed to clear his head. Throwing the pillow aside, he changed into a pair of shorts and t-shirt, and bounded down the stairs. "Mom, I'm going for a run."

Justin heard his dad call from the den. "Do you have your homework done?"

Justin gritted his teeth. "Yes. You've dragged me a few thousand miles from anyone I know, so what else do I have to do but homework?"

"You didn't finish the dishes from dinner. I shouldn't have to remind you. Wash them before you go," his dad said.

Justin turned around to argue back, but stopped when he noticed his mom and the sad look on her face. She put on a strong show these past couple weeks, but even with all that had happened to him today, Justin couldn't help but notice the red circles around her eyes. She must have been crying again. He wasn't the only one struggling with Grandpa's death. He washed the dishes without argument and headed for the front door. "Be back by nine," his mom gently called to him. Justin gave her a supportive smile, slipped into his running shoes, pulled on a jacket, and left the house.

The air smelled deeply of pine trees and something else. He couldn't put his finger on it. The scent reminded him of camping trips to Colorado with Grandpa. But thinking about his grandpa made Justin even more upset. In less than a month, his parents had told him they were moving to Bellingham, then his grandpa died in a car accident, he had to start at a new school, and now he was hearing voices from trees. He was pretty sure the last thing was due to the first three. He needed to clear his head and the best fix was always running. His feet pounding against the pavement felt good. Each collision of his shoes against the ground usually succeeded in chipping off a piece of his frustrations. The bigger the problem, the longer the run he needed to work things out.

But running alone wasn't enough to make sense of the chaos churning inside of him. There was no way he could sleep until he convinced himself that he had imagined the events of earlier today. He needed answers about what happened in the forest, and the only place he'd find them was at that tree.

He rounded the corner and saw the convenience store located a couple of blocks from his school. He hadn't noticed he'd been running in that direction. As he approached the path leading into the forest, Justin slowed down. The few miles had passed too quickly. He needed answers, but he worried he wouldn't find the answers he wanted.

Walking deeper into the forest, it became even darker, with the moonlight only breaking through occasional openings in the canopy. Rounding a bend in the path, he came upon the tree. It was bigger than he remembered. It rose above the rest of the forest like an imposing tower. Justin approached it. Slowly extending his arm, he placed the palm of his hand against the tree. He braced himself for–something.

After about thirty seconds, he realized that he hadn't been breathing. Sucking in some air he placed his other hand on the tree. He could feel energy, but it had been bouncing around in him for the last few hours. Was it coming from him or the tree? An argument erupted in his head.

See. It's just a tree.

But maybe I need to say "hi" first.

Oh, come on, now you're going to try to start conversations with trees?

I just want to be sure.

Fine!

Justin let go of the tree and looked around. He wasn't going to be caught talking to a plant again. He circled around the trunk and looked carefully in every direction. No one was nearby, so he placed his hands against the tree again. He opened his mouth, but nothing came out. This was just way too weird. He continued arguing with himself.

Oh, just get it over with.

It's a tree. I'm not talking to it.

Why not? You're talking to yourself right now. Why not include the tree in the conversation?

Justin wickedly chuckled. *Fine, I'll do it.* Taking a deep

breath, he whispered a hello. He waited almost a minute, but nothing happened.

See, it was nothing.

Oh, come on. A little louder than that. How could it hear through the bark?

Fine!

The absurdity of the whole situation finally came flooding out and overcame his embarrassment. Sarcasm erupted. "Hello, tree. How are you doing? I'm Justin. I don't normally talk to trees, but I've had a rough month and I'm clearly losing my mind. Do you normally talk to people? Or do you usually just talk to squirrels, birds, and the occasional dog to ask it not to pee on you?" After that little outburst, Justin was done. "See I knew you couldn't talk. Goodbye!" Justin began to let go of the tree when—

"Goodbye? I haven't even had a chance to say 'hello'," came a voice from the tree.

Justin took a step away from the tree, tripped over a rock, and fell backward. The force of landing on his back snapped his head against the ground. Lying on the earth, he gently touched the back of his head expecting a massive bruise, but it didn't feel too bad. The thick layer of moss and pine needles must have softened the collision. Pushing himself up on his elbows, he stared for a long moment in shock at the tree. "Did you talk to me?" Justin asked.

"Yes. I said hello. We haven't met before. What's your name?" the voice asked.

Justin frowned. "How can you not remember me? We met just a few hours ago." The tree had been all he'd been able to think about for the last few hours, but it didn't even remember him. "I know you must be really old, but do all trees have such a short memory?"

"Trees? Why would you think I'm a tree?"

"Uh, you're brown and green and covered in bark and pine needles. What else could you be?"

"Was today the first time you've ever talked to a tree?"

"Yes."

"Did I give you my name when we spoke earlier?"

"Man. I thought *I* was losing my mind. You don't even remember your name?" Justin said.

"Humor me. What name did I give you?"

"Katie."

"Oh, Katie is in so much trouble. Toying with a new Tree Elementer and making him think he was talking to a tree instead of through a tree. What's your name?"

"Justin."

"Justin. I can assure you, you're not losing your mind. My name is Anya Cruz and I am definitely not a tree. Nor is Katie, though she is in trouble for confusing you. We're Tree Elementers, like you."

"Tree Elementers? What are Tree Elementers?"

"Tree Elementers can access the powers of the trees," Anya explained.

"The power of the tr—" Justin thought he heard someone. He froze and listened carefully. A few seconds later he heard a twig snap in the direction of the road.

"I've gotta go. Someone's coming," Justin whispered. "How can I find you again?"

"We're Tree Elementers. Link up through a tree and call. I'll hear you," Anya said.

Justin quickly, but quietly, moved away from the direction where the sound had originated. He circled back through the trees toward the path and ran home.

⟫⟫⟫

9

Raven lounged in her backyard burrowing her feet in the moist soil, drinking in the musty smell of the garden. Her mother didn't like it when Raven disturbed the landscaping, but she was gone on another business trip and Raven needed the peacefulness the garden gave her. She tried to forget about the rude comments the new kid made to her today. Granted, it must have seemed weird for her to accuse him of talking to a tree. Clearly, he wasn't talking to a tree. Normal people didn't do that.

But Raven wasn't normal. So it didn't seem strange for her to think he was talking to a tree. But unless she wanted people to suspect anything about her, she couldn't go around asking people if they were talking to plants, even if they looked like they were doing so.

As her thoughts continued to plague her, she felt a strange vibration against her feet. She sat up straight. This didn't feel normal. Even for an Earth Elementer, like her. She glanced back toward her house then leaned forward to place her hands on the soil.

"Who's there?" Raven asked.

No one answered.

"Can you hear me?" she said.

Still no answer. She dug her hands into the soil and closed her eyes. Concentrating, she tried to determine the location of the energy source. In her mind she traced the strange energy pattern back to the park across from her high school. That was weird. Why would an Earth Elementer be here in Bellingham? Why weren't they answering? Why the unusual energy vibration? She had to know.

Raven walked quickly into the house, called to Marcela, their cook and housekeeper, saying she'd be back soon, wiped off her hands and feet, and slipped on some shoes. Jumping onto her bike, she rode as fast as she could, arriving at the park in a few minutes. She biked up the path till it became too steep and dropped her bike in the bushes. Raven didn't normally do things impulsively. Her father had always taught her to analyze, plan, and then act. But it was lonely being the only Earth Elementer nearby. If another Earth Elementer was in town, she wanted to meet them. Since they weren't responding to her calls, she wanted to find them before they left.

Hearing footsteps, she froze and scanned the forest. Walking in the park alone, at night, definitely didn't qualify as a 'good plan'. Her heart pounded in her chest and she knew that had little to do with the bike ride. She jumped as a small animal skittered in the bushes behind her. Nervously laughing at herself, she looked around, listened, and heard steps moving away from her. Raven walked down the path toward the sound trying to remain quiet. She saw something. A figure moved quickly through the trees toward the path below her. She broke into a run. As she rounded a corner, she caught a clear sight of the person before they disappeared around the next bend in the path.

It was the new kid.

Who was he? What was he doing here? Raven wanted to follow him, but she needed a plan first. As she biked home, Raven decided she'd go to school early the next morning to talk to Mr. Hamilton about the new kid.

Chapter 3

RAVEN WALKED DOWN the deserted hallway the next morning, toward David Hamilton's science classroom. As she entered the classroom, her science teacher looked up from the assignments he was grading and slid his glasses up to rest on his unruly, dirty blonde hair. He sat up straight, stretching out his long, lanky body. "Raven, what are you doing here so early?"

Raven walked past the blackboard that displayed an intricate drawing of a food web. Posters explaining various scientific principles covered almost every square inch of wall space in the classroom. The room was a reflection of her teacher. Mr. Hamilton lived and breathed science and almost nothing else. Raven sat on top of one of the student desks. "I need to talk to you about the new kid. There's something strange about him."

Mr. Hamilton gave her a look of reproof. "Raven, everyone is different. Just like in nature, the biodiversity gives an ecosystem its strength."

"He's different all right. But not the normal kind of different. He's different in the—" She looked through the window in the door to the hallway to make sure no one would overhear. Even then she lowered her voice. "I think he's different in the Elementer sort of way. But extra different in that I suspect he's an Earth and a Tree Elementer."

Mr. Hamilton put his pen down. "It's possible he's an Elementer. But I seriously doubt he's a Double Elementer. There hasn't been one of those for over a hundred years."

"I know the history. You taught it to me. But yesterday, during our class, I'm sure I caught him Tree Talking. I felt the energy increase while looking around. I assumed it was you, but was surprised you'd be using your powers during class so I walked toward the energy source to see if anything was wrong. I found the new kid holding a conversation with a tree."

"What did you do?"

"I asked him if he was Tree Talking, but he just denied it and was really rude. But even stranger, last night, I was outside in my back yard and I sensed an Earth Elementer nearby. I tried to Talk to them, but they wouldn't respond. So I followed the link to the park across from school, and what did I find? No one–except the new kid quickly running away. The coincidence is too high. He must be both. But why is he hiding it?"

"Raven, the Elementer Council would know if there were any modern Double Elementers. He might be an Elementer and simply didn't admit it because he didn't know anything about you. Did you tell him that you're an Earth Elementer?"

Raven looked at him like he was crazy. "No. I don't go around telling total strangers that I can use the earth as a cell phone."

Mr. Hamilton chuckled. "Justin probably felt the same. I'll change the lesson plan today to have the class go outside again.

Do you think you can find a way to determine if he's an Earth Elementer?"

"Sure." Raven seemed to be satisfied. "Thanks, Mr. H."

Chapter 4

MS. CHALMERS, JUSTIN'S English teacher, was far more interested in books than she was in her students. Her short, stubby legs paced back and forth at the front of the room while she glared at the students. "Justin?!" Ms. Chalmers's shrill voice caused everyone to jump.

The guy sitting behind Justin kicked Justin's chair. Justin's chin slipped off his hand where it had been resting when he nodded off. Disoriented, he quickly looked up at the teacher.

"Justin, are you listening?" she demanded impatiently.

"Allegory," the same guy whispered in Justin's direction.

Unsure of what he had missed, he repeated the words hoping that would satisfy the teacher. "Allegory?"

"Correct," the teacher scowled. She seemed irritated that he had answered correctly, but at least she turned her attention back to the class. Justin turned around and whispered a thanks to the guy behind him, but Ms. Chalmers's monologue suddenly stopped. Justin could feel her eyes burning into the back of his head. He turned around to face her. She gave him an irritated look and continued her boring explanation of grammar.

Justin hadn't slept at all last night. After talking with Anya yesterday evening, he was pretty sure he wasn't going crazy. But if his conversation with her wasn't imagined, he needed to know how he could talk through trees. He had spent the night coming up with questions he wanted to ask her. He also tried to come up with his own answers, but every explanation he came up with seemed just as strange as the next. The only thing that kept him from going out in the middle of the night to call Anya from the tree in his backyard was that she was likely asleep. He figured the same basic rules applied for both phone calling and tree calling—if that's what they called it. Calling at three in the morning would probably irritate her. Until he knew her better, he thought it best to wait until he was sure she was awake.

By morning, he had decided what he would do. During lunch time, he would find a secluded patch of trees in the forested park across from the school and try to contact Anya. He didn't want to wait that long, but he figured that was his earliest opportunity. Skipping classes after just starting at a new school would cause more problems with his dad than he cared to face.

The bell rang a couple of minutes later, ending English class. Justin grabbed his backpack and turned to head out the door. The guy who had whispered the answer to him earlier stood nearby. He was tall, with dirty blond hair, and blue eyes. But the rest of his facial features and his skin tone definitely suggested some Asian ancestry. "Hi, I'm Lewis."

"Hi. Thanks again for the help." Justin looked toward the door wanting to make his way to the forest beside the school as quickly as possible.

"No problem. Ms. Chalmers can put us all to sleep." Lewis swung his backpack over his shoulder. "So where are you from?"

Justin began walking to the door hoping to end the conversation without being rude. "Houston."

"Houston? Bellingham must be quite a change," Lewis said. Justin sighed. "Yeah."

As they entered the hallway, Justin was about to make his getaway when a skinny blond with pink and purple streaks in her hair stopped in front of them. Her clothes were even more colorful than her hair. "Hey, Lewis. Are you going to introduce us?"

Lewis turned to his new classmate. "What's your name?"

"Justin."

The girl twirled a strand of pink-streaked hair around her finger. "I'm Amanda. Want to have lunch with us? The weather's nice, so we'll be eating outside." Justin hesitated, trying to think up a good excuse, but Amanda didn't give him any time. "Good. I'll introduce you to the group." She casually placed her hand on the crook of his elbow and led him down the hall. Justin looked back at Lewis, who just shrugged his shoulders as if he understood the difficulty of saying "no" to Amanda. Justin tried to sneak in a few words between Amanda's energetic tour of the school and overview of social life at Sehome High School, but after a while, he gave up trying to get away. He could contact Anya right after school, instead.

Justin's desire to socialize had evaporated since Grandpa's death. For the past week-and-a-half since the accident, Justin had pretty much closed up, simply going through the motions of the funeral, packing up, and saying his goodbyes. But Amanda seemed to do all the work in the conversation, making it easy for Justin to just walk and listen. It kind of felt good to be around someone who didn't know they should be saying they were sorry for his loss.

After buying lunch, Lewis and Amanda led Justin outside past other groups trying to enjoy the rare spring warmth. They sat down at a partially-filled table and introduced Justin to their friends. He listened while the group enjoyed giving him a quick tutorial about social survival in Bellingham. They asked him questions about Houston, which he answered in as few words as possible, but their friendly banter back-and-forth between each other began to ease some of the tightness in his chest that had been there since news of the accident.

Near the end of the lunch break, Justin walked back toward the school with the group. A gathering of pine trees at the edge of the field caught his eye and he wondered how late he'd be for his next class if he hurried over and tried to contact Anya. But, suddenly, he bumped into a wall that he hadn't noticed being there.

"Watch it, loser!" boomed a voice.

Justin turned around and looked up. He hadn't walked into a wall. He had bumped into a beast. The guy was well over six feet tall and half as wide, and the mass seemed to be all muscle. The guy shoved Justin with enough force to send him falling back into Amanda. Thankfully, Lewis grabbed both their arms to keep them from falling. Justin had dealt with enough bullies in the past to recognize one on sight. Once his blankouts had started happening in fifth grade, he had become something of a target for bullies. He stood up to the jerks, often just making things worse, but he didn't care. He wasn't going to be a pushover. Besides, the blankouts weren't his fault. Unfortunately, that didn't stop some kids from making fun of him and most of his teachers from accusing him of not paying attention.

A ball of anger burst inside of Justin. "Back off. It was an accident."

"You're telling me to back off?"

The huge, football lineman narrowed his eyes and took a step toward Justin, but someone nearby quickly grabbed the guy's arm. "Hank, forget about him. You could be suspended from the team if you're caught fighting again."

Hank's feet stood still, but he leaned forward and glared much like a bull preparing to run at the bull fighter. "Do that again, and it's your funeral."

Wrong expression. The word 'funeral' caused something to snap inside of Justin. The memory of standing in front of a closed casket flashed in Justin's mind. The casket had to be closed because of the car explosion. Grandpa had always been so full of life, and suddenly, he was gone with only his remains locked away in a long, brown box. All the pain Justin had been feeling for the past ten days yearned to erupt. It felt like a tornado of fury swirling inside of him with nowhere to go.

Amanda must have noticed the change because she gently grabbed Justin's arm and pulled him toward the school doors. "Come on, Justin." He allowed Amanda to lead him away, but he could feel the storm of energy ricochet inside of him, struggling to burst free.

Crack! A loud ripping sound caused everyone to turn to see a large tree split in half down its trunk and smash into a nearby empty patio table sending pieces of the tree and the table flying in all directions. Amanda gasped, while numerous more enthusiastic exclamations erupted from students nearby. A blast of nausea rushed through Justin and he staggered back. The splintered tree looked like it had exploded from the inside. A disturbing thought entered his mind, suggesting that his pent up energy had gone into that tree. But that was absurd.

He stared at the tree until Amanda pulled on his arm again. "Come on. Let's get out of here before Hank decides to show off. He's a hothead. Just ignore him and stay away from him."

"I'm not very good at ignoring stupidity," Justin said.

"But your face won't look nearly as cute as it does currently if Hank covers it with bruises." Amanda smiled playfully and let go of his arm.

Justin was much better at coming up with insults for jerks than at responding to compliments from girls. Thankfully, as they neared the school doors, Lewis started talking to Amanda about a movie he saw last night. Justin walked beside them wondering silently to himself what had caused that tree to fall.

Chapter 5

"WE'RE GOING TO begin working on a research project," Mr. Hamilton announced to his science class later that afternoon. "You'll be working on the assignment in pairs." Whispers and movement rippled across the room as the students quickly tried to claim a partner.

Mr. Hamilton spoke over the noise. "I'll be choosing the groups for the project." Silence cut in for a moment and then moans and complaints arose. "As I was saying, I have selected the partners, so listen carefully as I read out the names. Raise your hand when I call out your name."

While the names were read out, a mixture of cheers and groans were heard. Finally, Justin's name was called. But to his surprise he was paired with Raven, the girl who accused him of talking to the tree. He couldn't believe his bad luck. He had planned on staying away from her, hoping that she would simply forget about the tree event yesterday. So much for trying to avoid her.

Mr. Hamilton gave the instructions for the research project and dismissed them to go outside to the neighboring park to gather the items they would need to begin phase one of their project. Raven walked over to Justin's desk. "Come on. I'll show you the way."

Justin reluctantly followed her down the hallway, out the door, and toward the park across the street. He didn't want to start talking to her and have her accuse him of talking to a tree again. So he walked behind her, letting her chatter with another classmate about the upcoming basketball game. Once they reached the park, Raven led him away from the rest of the students.

"Why don't you start clearing out a spot on the ground while I go get some tools from Mr. Hamilton?" Raven suggested, promptly walking away before he could argue.

Justin was stuck with her, so he'd deal with it, but there was no way he would let her catch him talking to, or through, a tree again. He made a point to keep space between him and any plant life larger than a bush. He bent down and began brushing away various rocks, leaves, and pine needles to clear a two-foot circle of ground for their project. Just as he finished clearing the circle, energy rushed from the ground into his hands and throughout his body. He froze in place. He wasn't touching any trees. What was going on?

"Hello," a voice called to him.

Once again, he spun around to find the source of the voice. And again, no one was in sight. Justin groaned. This couldn't be happening to him! And if it was, why did it need to happen right now? His science partner would return any moment, and he couldn't let her catch him talking to the ground this time.

"Justin. Are you there?" the voice spoke up again.

Justin's eyes darted around making sure no one was near. He whispered, "Yes, I'm here. Is that you Anya?"

"I knew you were an Earth Elementer!" the voice exclaimed.

"I'm a Tree Elementer, not a—" Justin's forehead furrowed and he shook his head. "What did you call me? An Earth Elementer?"

"Of course. You have to be an Earth Elementer. You're Earth Talking with me right now."

"Wait," Justin paused and looked around again. "You're not Anya. Who is this?"

"Come on. You haven't guessed yet?"

"How should I know? You haven't told me. And how do you know my name?" Justin's forehead furrowed from the headache caused by the million questions pressing against his brain.

"It doesn't take much detective work when I find you talking through a tree."

Justin snapped up his head and looked around for his research partner. "Raven?!"

Raven came walking from behind a tree toward Justin. Her arms were folded across her chest and she had a satisfied smile on her face. "I knew you were the Earth Elementer I sensed the other night."

Justin's mind reeled. "Uhh. No, I'm not. I'm a Tree Elementer." Oops. He didn't mean to say that.

"If you can Earth Talk, you shouldn't be able to Tree Talk."

Justin had enough of all this craziness. He wanted answers. Standing up he took a step toward Raven. "Then how did I talk to Anya last night?"

Raven stopped walking forward and bit her lip. "You know Anya?" She hesitated and her eyes grew wide upon realization. "That's why I sensed you last night but couldn't Talk to you. It's because you were Tree Talking. How can you Tree Talk and Earth Talk?"

"What's Earth Talking?" Justin asked.

"Talking is simply using the elements to communicate with

other Elementers. Don't you know anything about Elementers?"

"Excuse me, but the first time any of this freaky stuff started happening to me was when you interrupted me yesterday. What's wrong with this place?"

Raven's back straightened. "There's nothing wrong with Bellingham. It has nothing to do with where we are. Earth, Tree, Wind, and Water Elementers have existed for millennia all over the world. But Elementers aren't supposed to cross boundaries."

"Oh, so now you're going to tell me I'm not only a freak, but a freak who isn't following the rules. You sound just like my dad."

Raven shook her head. "It's not about breaking any rules. No one has had the power of two elements in a very long time." Raven paused. "Wait. So yesterday was the first time you ever Earth or Tree Talked?"

"Yes."

"Wow. So are you completely freaked out?" Raven said.

"No," Justin looked at the ground and dug his hands into his pockets. "Maybe a little." Justin looked up at Raven trying to decide how to respond to all she'd said. Finally, his curiosity won out over his desire to not embarrass himself in front of her. "So, if you know so much, I have some questions."

"I'm sure you do. What do you want to know?"

"What's happening to me?" Justin asked.

"You're beginning to Earth Talk—and Tree Talk."

"I figured that much. Why am I Earth and Tree Talking?"

"Some people are just born with the gift."

"A gift? To talk through trees? If I want a gift, I'll ask for a trip back home to see a Houston Texans football game. And if I need to talk to someone, I'll use my phone. I can carry that with me. A tree isn't very portable. Besides, if I was born with this ability, why couldn't I use it until yesterday?"

"The ability can't be controlled until you're a teenager," Raven said.

"How long have you been doing this?"

"About a year."

"How old are you?"

"Fifteen," Raven said.

"So am I. Why have you been doing it longer?" Justin asked.

Raven smirked. "Haven't you heard? Girls mature faster than boys."

Justin chose to ignore her comment. "So does everyone know you can Earth Talk?"

"Are you kidding? I can just imagine what Eric would think if he knew I was a walking metal detector and could predict earthquakes."

"Who's Eric?"

The color in Raven's cheeks suddenly became a much deeper red. "Come on. We need to talk to Mr. Hamilton."

Chapter 6

"WHY DO WE need to talk to the science teacher?" Justin said.

"Mr. Hamilton is a Water Elementer. He can help," Raven said. "Let's go see him,"

But Justin wouldn't budge. "What? How many of you are there?"

"Not many. But new Elementers are always assigned a Guide. There weren't any Earth Elementers available when I gained my powers so they assigned Mr. Hamilton to move here last year to be my Guide. You're just lucky to be near others. Come on! Mr. Hamilton can answer all of your questions." Raven led the way toward some of the other students and Justin eventually followed.

They stopped about thirty feet away from Mr. Hamilton and waited until he had finished helping some other students. Once he saw them, Raven motioned with her head for him to meet them away from the rest of the students. As Justin followed Raven, he kept looking back and forth between Raven and his science teacher, trying to find some visible evidence of their strangeness. But they looked as normal as anyone else. As normal as him, so appearances clearly didn't mean much. Justin noticed Mr. Hamilton looking at him. Was he trying to determine the same thing?

"Raven. Justin. How can I help you?" Mr. Hamilton asked as if they simply needed help with their research project. But Raven got right to the point.

First, looking around to be sure no one was near, Raven announced, "Mr. Hamilton, Justin is both an Earth and Tree Elementer."

Mr. Hamilton looked at Justin again, with an obvious air of concern. "Raven, are you sure?"

"I just Earth Talked with him and he Tree Talked with Anya yesterday."

Mr. Hamilton's eyebrows rose. "How would the Council not know about him?"

A smile rose on Raven's face, and she paused before announcing the big news. "He started accessing his powers only yesterday during science class."

"Excuse me! I'm here and can talk," Justin said.

Shaking his head in disbelief, Mr. Hamilton looked again at Justin. "Sorry. This must all seem a little strange to you right now."

"A little?"

"Okay, more than a little strange. You must have a lot of questions," Mr. Hamilton said.

"To say the least," Justin agreed. Now he finally had someone who could provide him with answers. He shot a barrage of questions all at once at Mr. Hamilton. "Why is this happening to me? What does it mean? How does it work? Why do I feel energy when people talk to me? Why is it suddenly happening to me now? Why haven't I ever heard of this talking before? And what did Raven mean when she said I shouldn't be able to do both Earth and Tree Talking?" He paused to talk a breath.

"It's going to take time to answer all of your questions. But as to why it is happening to you, being an Elementer is a very rare gift. It's simply how you were born, but it takes maturity till you can control it," Mr. Hamilton said.

"What do you mean? I've never felt it before."

"Oh, I'm sure you have. Do you ever feel like you can barely sit still because the energy inside of you is building up? Have you ever had fainting spells?" Mr. Hamilton asked.

Justin thought of his blankouts but didn't say anything at first. He called them blankouts instead of blackouts, because he didn't experience darkness when they came; instead, he felt like he was drowning in light and energy. He would lose consciousness for a minute or two and sometimes he'd get the shakes. He had always struggled sitting still all day in school. By third period, he felt like he was going to explode through his skin. Doctors wanted to put him on Ritalin but Grandpa convinced Justin's mom to skip the medications. He taught Justin how to mentally focus the energy building up inside. It wouldn't release the energy, but at least it helped keep the pressure in check until he could get active again to release it.

"I don't have fainting spells. But I do have blankouts," Justin said.

"What do you mean?" Mr. Hamilton stepped closer.

"I don't fall over, like people do from passing out. I just kind of zone-out for a couple minutes at a time and I sometimes get the shakes. It's like I've hit overload and my brain has to reboot"

Trying to prevent a blankout took concentration, so he often got in trouble for not paying attention in class. But even when he did focus, the technique didn't always work. When he couldn't hold it in any longer, he sometimes skipped class. His dad always freaked out when he learned Justin had cut class, but that was better than having an episode right in front of everyone at school. Justin would take off and run miles upon miles until he had released all the pent up energy. Mom said he was just an energetic boy, but Justin had always known it was more than that. There was something wrong with him, at least something different, and maybe this explained it all.

"Interesting," Mr. Hamilton said. "Fainting is normal for Elementers before their powers manifest, but maybe it's different for you since you can access two elements. Don't let it bother you. It should stop happening now that you're accessing your powers. You've always been connected to your element, but until you develop the ability to harness it, the energy can overload your system sometimes."

Justin didn't altogether believe what they were telling him about Elementers. Part of him wanted to walk away from the insane conversation. But, he didn't know how else to explain what had been happening to him these last two days. He desperately wanted answers to the questions keeping him awake all of last night and the thought of never having another blankout was a very appealing thought. He needed to know if this was for real.

"So how many Elementers are there? And how many types of Elementers exist? Raven said you're a Water Elementer."

"I am. There are only a few thousand Elementers in the entire world. As far as types go, there are four types of Elementers: Water, Earth, Tree, and Wind. Normally, an Elementer can only access one element. It is very rare to access two elements," Mr. Hamilton explained.

"How rare?"

"The last Double Elementer lived over a hundred years ago."

"A hundred years ago?!"

Justin looked between Mr. Hamilton and Raven trying to see if they were just playing with him. But they seemed serious. Once again, his curiosity overcame his disbelief. "So how do I know if I can also Water Talk?"

"You can't Water Talk," Mr. Hamilton said matter-of-factly.

Justin tried to control the ball of anger that erupted in his stomach. He hated only one thing more than someone picking on him because of the blankouts. And that was someone telling him what he could or couldn't do. "Why not?" Justin said.

"No one has ever been able to access more than two elements," Mr. Hamilton said.

If this was for real, Justin wouldn't have anyone telling him he couldn't do it. "How do you know I can't Water Talk until I try?" Justin argued and walked toward a small pond of water that must have formed from the last rainfall. Reaching the edge of the water, Justin looked up at Mr. Hamilton, who seemed to have a know-it-all smile that reminded Justin of the one his father often wore when Justin wanted to try something new. This simply drove Justin all the more to prove he could Water Talk.

He stood over the water by balancing himself on a few partially-submerged rocks. Crouching down, he shoved his hands into the cool water. His anger caused him to forget about trying to use the water to talk to anyone. Instead, he focused his irritation at the water and began to feel the energy coming from the water into his hands. But in his irritation, he pushed the energy right back at the pond.

The water started swirling around his hands. It started bubbling. Finally, a stream of water shot straight up toward his face. Justin yanked his hands out of the water in an attempt to use his arms to balance himself. He stumbled back off the rocks and eventually steadied himself on the dry ground.

Looking up, he saw Mr. Hamilton's bottom jaw drop nearly to his feet. Justin waited a few moments for Mr. Hamilton to say something, but his teacher just stood there looking at Justin as if he were from another planet. Normally, Justin would have felt satisfied proving he could do something new. But Mr. Hamilton stared at Justin as if he was from another planet. The frozen stare began to make Justin uncomfortable, so he turned to Raven. Her response was much different. A huge grin spread across her face as she tried not to laugh. But after a few more seconds she broke out in giggles.

"What?" Justin asked.

Raven finally stopped laughing. "I think you'll need to learn better control of the water."

"What do you mean?"

Raven tried not to smile as she pointed at Justin's jeans.

Justin looked down. "You've gotta be kidding!" The blast of water had done more than just hit him in the face. It also sprayed the front of his jeans, making it look like he had wet his pants.

Raven's laughter had jarred Mr. Hamilton out of his shock. He still shook his head, but at least he seemed to be processing the implications of this new discovery. Mr. Hamilton took a deep breath. "Justin. I don't know how this is possible."

"I don't understand what the big deal is. If I can do two, what difference does it make if I can do three?" Justin asked.

"Justin. No one has ever been able to access three elements. Ever."

"What? I'm sure some people have done it if I can," Justin responded casually.

"No. The Elementer Council has written records going back more than two thousand years and there is no record of any Elementer accessing more than two elements." Mr. Hamilton took another deep breath and shook his head in disbelief. "You are the first."

Justin thought Mr. Hamilton looked like a bobble-head with all of his head shaking. But his teacher finally seemed to come to grips with the idea. Mr. Hamilton took a step closer to Justin. "If you can control three of the elements, we should check to see if you can also access the fourth."

Justin nodded his head glad to see Mr. Hamilton believe in his possibilities far faster than his dad ever would. "How do we do that?"

"Accessing the wind element is a little more tricky and dangerous than with the other elements. So let's not try to influence the element. Just stick with Talking. Agreed?"

"Okay," Justin said. He was intrigued by Mr. Hamilton's description of the wind element, but figured he could get to the more interesting parts later. "So how do I do it? With Tree, Earth, and Water Talking, I touched something to communicate. How do I touch the wind?"

"Technically, you don't need to touch the elements. It just makes it easier to hold the connection. You just need to feel the energy around you and find the connection," Mr. Hamilton explained.

"Oh, thanks. Feel the energy and connect. That's a lot of help," Justin looked at him skeptically.

"Why don't you focus on Talking to a specific Wind Elementer? I know two in Texas."

Justin asked, "Texas? How am I supposed to reach that far?"

"Wind Elementers can reach greater distances than other Elementers. If you can Wind Talk, the distance won't be a problem."

"Okay. I'll give it a shot. Who's this Wind Elementer?"

"His name is Henry O'Malley," Mr. Hamilton said.

The smile on Justin's face immediately disappeared. It took

him a few moments to get out his next question. "Where does Henry O'Malley live?"

"He lives in Baytown, Texas. But don't worry. You don't need to know his exact location to reach him. Just connect to the wind and send out a greeting."

The color had drained from Justin's face and he stumbled back a few steps away from his teacher. Justin mumbled, "I can't Wind Talk to him."

"Why not at least give it a shot? If you can access three elements, there's a possibility you can access all four. Just give it a try," Mr. Hamilton encouraged.

"No. I can't Wind Talk with Henry O'Malley because," Justin finally choked out the rest of the sentence, "he's dead." Justin began breathing deeply, as if the air had thinned and his lungs couldn't obtain the oxygen they needed.

"What?!" Mr. Hamilton said, "I haven't heard any such thing. How could you know that?"

Justin fought to dislodge the lump in his throat. Finally, he choked out, "He's my grandpa."

"Your grandpa? Oh, Justin. I'm so sorry!" Raven blurted out.

"But how? When? I just talked to him in March. That was barely a month ago," Mr. Hamilton stumbled over his words.

"He was in a car accident two weeks ago," Justin said.

"Justin. I'm sorry. He was a great man." Mr. Hamilton took a step toward Justin.

The pain was too much for Justin. His grandpa had been his best friend and the accident had ripped him away. Justin still had a hard time believing he was gone. It wasn't fair. During the last month, Justin's heart couldn't decide what to do. Did it prefer to wallow in sadness or boil in anger at the injustice of it all? And to top it all off, his dad still decided to take this new job and move them across the country.

Suddenly, the storm inside Justin switched from sadness to anger. Anger at the stupid gasoline truck driver who collided into his grandpa's car and exploded. Anger that his parents dragged him across the country and abandoned his grandma at such a time. Anger that he wouldn't see any of his friends again. Anger about a lot of things.

But then something else occurred to Justin.

"Wait. So you're saying my grandpa was a Wind Elementer?"

"Yes. One of the best," Mr. Hamilton confirmed.

"Why didn't he ever tell me? We never kept any secrets from each other. We told each other everything."

"Justin, Elementers can't tell anybody about their powers. It's simply too dangerous," Mr. Hamilton gently explained.

"I wasn't anybody! I was his grandson and his best friend! How could he lie to me?" Justin fumed. He loved his grandpa and his anger wasn't really directed toward him. But he couldn't hold the hurt inside any longer, and he had to lash out somehow.

"Justin, he wouldn't have told anyone, not even his wife."

That didn't make Justin feel any better. Sure, he hadn't spent as much time with Grandpa this last year. He'd been busy with school and friends. But that didn't change the fact that they were still close. His grandpa was the only person who had ever really understood him. The sadness began to win out, but when he thought of his grandpa keeping such a big secret from him, the anger built up even more. Justin felt like he had to fling his anger at someone before it exploded. "I have no interest in being any kind of Elementer if it means lying to those you care about. I'm outta here!"

Justin spun around and began to storm away from them, but then he halted and turned around. He refused to look at either Mr. Hamilton or Raven in the eyes, but he said, "I can't go walking back into the school with wet pants. Raven?"

Raven took her school jacket off and tossed it to him. "Justin—" she began to say, but before she could utter anything more, Justin quickly walked in the direction of the school holding Raven's jacket in front of him.

Chapter 7

RAVEN COULDN'T DECIDE if she was more irritated with Mr. Hamilton, Justin, or herself. Mr. Hamilton had flown to New York City to meet with the Elementer Council. Justin refused to speak to her. And she was the fool that promised Mr. Hamilton she would convince Justin not to communicate with any other Elementers until her teacher spoke to the Elementer Council. But each time she tried to talk to Justin today, he either shushed her in class or simply headed in the opposite direction. Now it was the end of the school day and she still hadn't been able to talk to him.

The only choice left was for her to show up at his house, but there was one problem with that option. She had no idea where he lived. She made up a white lie to one of the office secretaries explaining why she needed Justin's address, but the grumpy, gray haired woman stubbornly refused to give Justin's address to Raven spouting privacy rights of the students. Raven considered giving up. She had done her best. What more could she do without his address? But her conversation with Mr. Hamilton replayed in her mind.

"I'm concerned how Elementers are going to react to the news about Justin," Mr. Hamilton said.

"What do you mean?" Raven asked.

"Some Elementers believe the universe gives this ability to Elementers to help maintain balance in the world. If there's an unprecedented Triple—or Quadruple—Elementer, I can see some Elementers thinking that Justin is a sign of a terrible imbalance which can only be corrected by a Multi-Elementer."

Raven hadn't thought of that before. "Do you think that's true?"

"No. There's absolutely no proof that we have this ability because of anything other than some physical anomaly. The same is true for Justin. But I'm more concerned that others might fear Justin, rather than what they may think he represents. No one knows what having access to three or four elements will do to Justin. Will it be too much for him to harness so many elements? If his powers become out of control, either our secret could be exposed or he could cause real damage to himself or others."

"I'm sure he'll be able to harness his powers with practice. There's nothing to worry about," Raven said.

"If he can harness all the elements, than that might be some Elementers' most serious worry."

"That's crazy. Why would it be a problem if he has his powers under control?"

"The Elementer records say that Double Elementers didn't have twice as much strength and power than regular Elementers. The combination of the two elements gave them much greater power. If that's the case, how much power will Justin develop with three or four elements?" Mr. Hamilton asked.

"But think of all the good he could do."

"Yes, but what if he abused his powers. What–"

"Of course he wouldn't abuse his powers!" Raven interrupted fervently, "He may be a little rude, but he isn't bad. I can sense that much from him."

"Yes. Yes. I agree. But some members on the Council may not be comfortable with the fact that they might not be able to control him if necessary."

"He's not theirs to control!"

"Raven, you know the main purpose of the Council is to make sure that all Elementers obey the rules so that none of us are discovered. They rarely have to play the role of enforcer, but many on the Council take that responsibility very seriously," Mr. Hamilton gravely reminded her.

"What are you going to do about it?"

"I'm going to explain the situation to the Council and try to assure them that I'll train and keep a very close eye on Justin. Hopefully, that will satisfy them for now. In the meantime, I need you to ensure that Justin avoids speaking to any Elementers until I meet with the Council."

Raven stood in the hall trying to convince herself that she had done all she could do. If she couldn't get Justin's address from the school, how was she supposed to find him? She was great at feeling Elementers' energy signature, but Justin was new and thus he had a weak, sporadic connection. The internet wouldn't be much help. His address wouldn't be listed online yet since he had moved here just a few days ago.

Just then, from around the corner, Raven heard one of the two office secretaries. "Helen, I need to take these forms to Mr. Young's classroom. I'll be back in about 10 minutes. Can you watch the office for me?"

"Sure. Go ahead. I'll cover you," the other secretary said.

The thought of stealing Justin's address popped in Raven's

head. Maybe she could get a glimpse at Justin's records if she could just distract the remaining secretary. She knew the records were in one of the side rooms off of the office. She had seen one of the secretaries bring her records out when Raven had brought in a form from her mom. Raven's heart rate suddenly quickened. Was she seriously considering breaking into the office? No. She couldn't be. Could she? She had never been in trouble for anything at school in her entire life. And now she was suddenly considering breaking into the office? Well, she had never before had a good enough reason to do such a thing. She trusted Mr. Hamilton's judgment about the importance of keeping Justin quiet for now. Having another Elementer around seriously complicated her life.

Raven nervously looked down both directions of the hall. Most of the students had already left. Only students with cars or those in after-school activities remained. The nearest student was at the other end of the hallway. But how could she distract the other secretary? Raven knew she needed a plan and a quick one before the other woman returned.

She could set off the fire alarm, but that was drastic and she'd be in trouble if anyone found her still in the building. What about locking the woman temporarily in one of the office side rooms? Raven had learned how to manipulate locks when she forgot her house keys one too many times and hadn't placed the spare key back under the red flower pot. After the third time, she became pretty good at manipulating the metal and rotating it to the right location to unlock the door.

Raven nervously checked the hall one more time and decided that if she was really going to do this, she'd better do it now. She peeked around the corner so she could see into one of the side office rooms. A plant sat on top of a large metal filing cabinet. Raven took a few deep breaths. To manipulate the elements, she had to connect and feel the energy. That was difficult with her heart behaving like she had just run a 400 meter run. Calm down. Calm down. She repeated silently to herself. Her heart slowed and she began to feel the energy flow through her.

She reached out toward the filing cabinet and used the energy to move it. First, it was just a minor vibration, but soon, the cabinet began shaking as if it were in the middle of a major earthquake. The cabinet already made a racket, causing the secretary to look up from her desk in the direction of the noise. But from her angle she couldn't see the filing cabinet. A couple seconds later, the plant atop the cabinet had been jostled to the edge and fell off producing a crashing sound as it hit the desk below breaking into many pieces. The woman got up and hurried to the room as fast as her old legs would carry her.

Once the woman was inside the room, Raven reached out with the energy to gently rotate the door hinges until the door closed. She tried to do so quietly hoping the woman would remain distracted by the broken pot and resulting mess to not notice the door. Next, she focused the energy at the door knob. The inner portion of the door knob heated up and melted, deforming it just enough to prevent it from rotating to open the door, but not so much that it would be too hard to reform it. Thankfully, the door didn't have a window. Raven hoped the secretary would be busy dealing with the mess for at least a couple minutes before she noticed she was locked inside and began calling for help.

Taking one last glimpse down the empty hallway, Raven hurried into the office and to the door of the student records room. Placing her hand against the door's lock, she reached out with the energy toward the metal elements. It was like she could see the pieces inside the lock, but she visualized it with senses other than her eyes. She could see it in her mind. Having practice, she could unlock her house door in seconds, but this one wasn't familiar and thus she rotated some sections too far. The nervousness certainly wasn't helping either. Any sound she heard caused her to jump making her move pieces too far.

Finally, she unlocked the door, quickly slid inside the room, and closed the door behind herself. The door had no window so no one would be able to see her. But she also wouldn't be able to see anyone coming. Thankfully, she had a gift for sensing other people's energy. Mr. Hamilton claimed her ability was very rare, but it seemed to her to be a fairly boring and unimpressive talent. Elementers had different gifts even within the same element, and simply being able to sense other people keenly seemed like a rather lame talent. But at least it might prove helpful here.

Raven suddenly realized that she didn't know Justin's last name. Argghh! What was wrong with her? This is why she never did things without a plan. Well, never, until Justin showed up. She couldn't possibly scan through all of the files. Her heart pounded so hard she felt like it would jump right out of her chest. What to do? "Breathe. Breathe," she whispered to herself. "Think. Think." Raven realized that Justin had been introduced in her science class just two days ago. What did Mr. Hamilton say Justin's name was? "Come on. You can remember." Raven pictured Mr. Hamilton introducing Justin at the front of the class. She remembered Justin's smile and wavy brown hair. He did have cute dimples. She shook her head. Dimples were irrelevant right now. She needed a name. Justin? Justin? Justin Wood? No. Justin Winters? No. What is it? Why couldn't she remember?

She was running out of time, so in desperation she used her powers to unlock the cabinet with the W's. Halfway through one of the drawers she found it. Wilder! Justin Wilder. Quickly pulling out the folder, she opened it up and laid it on top of the other files. His main contact information was stapled to the left side of the folder.

41

Raven was too nervous to count on her brain remembering the address, so she quickly pulled out her phone and took a photo of Justin's contact information. Her hands were shaking as she closed the folder causing her to drop the papers. The sheets spilled across the floor. She forced her nerves to calm down and quickly picked up the pages. Too much time had passed, so she shoved the folder back in the drawer at the front. It wasn't in the correct alphabetical order, but that wasn't a high priority for her right now. Quietly, she slid the drawer closed, relocked the cabinet, and tip toed toward the door.

She leaned her ear to the door and heard some rattling. The secretary tried to open the door Raven had jammed. It probably wouldn't be long before she began calling for help. Raven began opening the records room door when she sensed someone coming around the corner and into the office. She quickly closed the door hoping she hadn't made any noise.

"Helen?" a voice called out.

Great, Raven thought, the other secretary was back. How would she get out of here now?

"Cathy? Is that you? Help! I'm locked in here!"

Raven heard more jiggling of the door handle, but she knew they wouldn't be able to open the door.

"Helen. I'll go find someone who can help. I'll be right back."

Raven waited until she could sense the woman had left and she slid her door open. Her nerves were shot as she ran around the office desks and toward the front office door. But just as she reached the door, she collided with someone coming around the corner.

Stunned, Raven looked up. It was one of the vice-principals. "Mr. Weizman. I'm so sorry."

He seemed to have a look of chastisement, but with amusement hidden beneath it. "I think we all know not to run in the halls, especially not in the office. What's your hurry?"

Raven's mind went totally blank. "Uhh. Uhh."

The door handle rattled again. Thankfully, Raven's brain seemed to restart. "Well, I was going to try to get help. Someone seems to be locked in that room."

Mr. Weizman looked at Raven and then at the shaking door. "Someone is locked in my office?"

"Oh, is that your office? Well, then yes. Should I go get someone to help?" Raven asked.

"No. I have a key and can open the door to see who is in my office. But thank you."

"Okay. Bye." Raven forced herself not to bolt down the hallway. Instead, she rounded the corner and stopped to listen to the activity in the office. Raven knew his key wouldn't be able to unlock the door as it was. If she didn't reform the knob, the poor woman would be locked in there for quite some time. The woman may not have been helpful, and the ordeal nearly gave Raven a heart attack, but the woman didn't deserve to be locked in the office for hours. Raven calmed herself down just enough to reach out to the metal in the door knob. Melting it was easier than reforming it well enough to allow the door to open smoothly.

"Raven, there you are."

Raven jumped and her hands instinctively went to her chest in a subconscious effort to ensure her heart didn't actually leap out of her rib cage. Spinning around, Raven saw Eric walking up to her. "Oh." Raven clasped her hands behind her back so Eric wouldn't notice they were shaking. "Hi, Eric."

"Where have you been? I thought you said you were going to come watch our practice today."

"I'm sorry. Uhh." Raven avoided his eyes. "My mom just called me and needs me to help her with—" Raven swallowed. She hated lying, but telling others about the Elementers wasn't an option. "—a meeting she's planning,"

Eric frowned. "Isn't she out of town?"

"She is. Uh, that's why she needs my help. She's gone and can't do it herself. She doesn't like leaving things to chance, so she needs me to double check on the arrangements today before she gets back."

"I thought we could grab something to eat after practice."

"Sorry. She insisted I hurry home to help. Maybe I can watch tomorrow. I'll see you later, okay?"

Eric leaned in to give her a kiss goodbye, but Raven had already turned and was walking down the hall and out of the school. That was the last time she was going to do something to risk detention, arrest, or serious bodily harm. It was too much stress. But at least she found what she needed. Now she just needed to convince Justin to listen to her.

Chapter 8

RAVEN SLOWLY WALKED up the steps later that afternoon and hesitated before ringing the doorbell. What would she say to convince Justin to listen to her? Her dad always taught her to have multiple plans in place, but she wasn't confident any of them would work. Raven held her breath and rang the doorbell.

A woman answered the door. "Hello. Can I help you?" Raven figured it must be Justin's mom. She shared the same hazel eyes and wavy brown hair with Justin. The woman had a playful look that danced in her eyes. It made Raven wonder if Justin shared that same look when he wasn't being bombarded with strange news about Elementers.

Raven exhaled. "Hi, my name's Raven. I'm a friend of Justin. Actually, we're partners for our class science project. I'm here to work on our project with him."

"Oh, Justin must have forgot. He went out for a run, but he'll be back soon. You're welcome to come in and wait for him." Justin's mom pulled the door open further and motioned graciously with her hand to welcome Raven inside.

"Thank you." Raven followed the woman into the living room. It wasn't fancy, but even with all the moving boxes strewn about, it felt warm and inviting.

"My name's Mary. I'm Justin's mom. Please have a seat," Mary said. Raven sat down on a simple, but very comfortable couch, across from her. "Excuse all the boxes. We just arrived on Monday and still have a lot of unpacking to do. Would you like something to drink?"

"Water would be great."

Mary soon returned from the kitchen with two glasses of water. "So, Raven, tell me about yourself."

Raven was surprised by how much easier she could talk to Justin's mom than her own. But that probably had something to do with the fact that Mary was probably more interested in her than her own mom. Having to keep secrets, Raven had become accustomed to keeping things to herself, so it surprised her that Mary learned so much about her in the short ten minutes before they heard someone come in through the front door.

Raven turned to see Justin enter the living room and stop suddenly when he saw her. His shorts, shirt, and hair were completely drenched. It made Raven smile. She loved to walk in the rain, but she could never get anyone to go with her. She always received the same response when asking someone to come with her: "It's raining." To which Raven would respond, "I know, that's why I want to go." They'd just look at her strangely.

But Justin wasn't looking at her strangely. Upon seeing Raven, Justin's body tensed up and he folded his arms across his chest. "What are you doing here?"

"Justin, don't be rude. Raven is here to work with you on your science project," his mom interjected.

Justin stood there looking at Raven as if trying to make a decision. Finally, he dropped his shoulders and tugged on his wet shirt. "Just give me a minute to change. We can work in the backyard. Don't worry. The rain stopped."

It wasn't a welcome from Justin, but at least he hadn't kicked her out the door. Raven waited for Justin to return downstairs wearing a Texans sweatshirt and jeans. She noticed the waviness in his hair was more pronounced when it was wet. She liked it. He led her to a small gazebo in the far corner of their back yard. He sat down on the bench and looked at Raven. "How did you find me?"

"I got your address from the school office."

"Yeah, right. They wouldn't have given it to you," Justin said.

"Well, I didn't say they gave it to me. I needed to talk to you so I had to...get it myself."

Justin tilted his head slightly and the corners of his mouth lifted slightly. "You stole it?"

Raven stared at her grey and blue running shoes, nudging a small rock with her foot. "Well, I needed to talk to you, and they wouldn't give it to me, so I snuck into the records room to get it."

Justin's smile broadened and he seemed to look at Raven with even greater curiosity and respect? Raven noticed that her suspicions were correct. Justin did have that same playful look in his eyes as his Mom. "Really? I've never had a girl break the law just to get my phone number or address."

"Very funny. I came to help you with your powers," Raven said.

Justin's smile faded. "Who says I need help?"

"Just because you're beginning to connect with the elements, doesn't mean you have control over them. When Elementers begin to connect, the elements have a way of erupting around them. It's dangerous not only to yourself, but to others around you. Such outbursts can also expose our—

your—secret," Raven continued, hoping to get as much in as she could before he stopped her. "You can't turn your back on this. You're connected, whether you like it or not. If you don't learn to control your powers, you'll quickly become a danger to yourself and others."

"I just moved the water yesterday on my first try. It can't be that hard," Justin said.

"Justin. You created a little water spout. That's nothing. Experienced Water Elementers can build bridges of ice, shoot water cannons, and much more. Besides, controlling it is way more difficult than simply moving it. Do you want to spray water on your pants again? Much worse things can happen if you can't control the elements. Especially for you."

"What does that mean, 'especially for you'?" Justin crossed his arms in front of his chest. "I can do this just as well as you can."

Raven took a breath. She had to find the right words to say. "If Mr. Hamilton is right, you'll be doing it better than me or any other Elementer—ever. Previous Double Elementers were way stronger than other Elementers. So Mr. Hamilton believes a Multi-Elementer, like you, may be many times stronger than a Double Elementer."

"Really?" Justin unfolded his arms.

"But that also means it's probably going to be equally difficult for you to learn to control your powers. It was hard enough for me to learn basic control over the Earth element last year and I'm still working at it." Raven paused when Justin lifted an eyebrow. She knew she had to convince him of the necessity of her request, but he didn't seem to appreciate the danger. "You're going to have to learn to control three, possibly four, elements all at once. Manipulating each element is different. Each has a different frequency and flow. We think that's why Elementers can usually only access one of the elements. Each element is so different. Learning them all at once will be like learning multiple languages at the same time. Add on the fact that your magnitude of power will likely be much greater. The point is, it won't be easy so you are going to need some help."

Raven braced for another argument from Justin, but instead he just looked at her and finally said, "If I need so much help, why don't you start teaching me something useful?"

Raven didn't expect that response. She looked down at her shoes again. "Uhh, I would except Mr. Hamilton doesn't want you Talking to any other Elementers until he gets back." She glanced up to see his response.

Justin's back stiffened. "Why not? Wait—back from where?"

"Well, he just flew to New York City to meet with the Elementer Council tomorrow."

"The who?"

"The Elementer Council. They're thirteen Elementers, three from each element, plus the Chairperson. They're responsible for making sure Elementers obey the rules," Raven said.

Justin gritted his teeth. "What rules?"

Justin's irritation was clear, so Raven chose her words carefully. "Nothing that doesn't make sense. We aren't supposed to use our powers in ways that would cause non-Elementers to find out about us. That's all."

"I can do whatever I want. Some Council can't tell me what to do. It's none of their business!"

"Well, it kind of does matter to the rest of us. If someone finds out about you, they could use you to discover the rest of us."

"What?"

"Because we're connected to the energy, we can sense when other Elementers are using the energy. That's how I knew you were Tree Talking during science class. So a single Elementer could expose all of us."

"Expose us to who?"

"Everybody. Do you really think people are just going to accept you as the new guy at school if they find out you can create a tornado which could wipe out the school? What's the point of schools checking for weapons if they knew we could level the school with an earthquake? People would see us as freaks, weapons they'd want to control, or threats they'd like to eliminate. I don't know about you, but I don't like any of those options."

"Oh, come on. It wouldn't be that bad."

"Really? Have you ever heard of the Salem witch trials? A few Elementers lived there. People found out and called it witchcraft. One of the Elementers was killed, though two of them got away. But the hysteria was so great that many innocent people were accused who had nothing to do with Elementers or witchcraft. And that's only one example that we haven't been able to cover up. There are plenty more."

"Fine. But why do we need to wait till Mr. Hamilton gets back? You must know some interesting things to teach me," Justin said.

"He doesn't want any Elementers to find out about you until he tells the Council."

"Now we're hiding from Elementers too?"

"Only until the Council has been informed. Justin, you're, umm, special. If Mr. Hamilton is right, you may become stronger than any Elementer ever before. That's going to make some people nervous, even Elementers. Mr. Hamilton just wants to let them know he'll take responsibility to teach you so that you can learn control as quickly as possible. That's all." Raven wished she knew what Justin was thinking. "So are we good? Are you okay with not using your powers until Mr. Hamilton returns on Saturday?"

Justin paused, but finally spoke. "He said I shouldn't talk to other Elementers. But he didn't say anything about using the powers. Why don't you show me how to do something?"

"Justin, it's dangerous for you to try using your powers until someone trains you."

"What harm is a little spray of water?"

"It can be far worse than that."

"Like what?" Justin asked.

Raven hesitated before answering. "Did you eat outside at lunch yesterday?"

Justin's forehead furrowed. "Yeah. How did you know?"

"I didn't. But you were out there when the tree crashed. Weren't you?"

"So?"

"You did it, didn't you?"

"What are you talking about?" Justin said.

"You caused the tree to crash."

"What? Of course I didn't. I wasn't anywhere near it." But he looked away and seemed to be replaying the events in his mind. He finally looked at Raven again. "That's impossible."

"I heard about Hank giving you a hard time," Raven said.

"Yeah, I told him to back off and then he told me it was my funeral."

Raven saw the anger and pain in Justin's eyes. "Hank has a big mouth. But Justin, that's why we need to learn to control our powers. When we get emotional, they can get out of control."

"How does getting angry have anything to do with the tree?"

"What did you feel just before the tree crashed?"

Justin stood up from the gazebo bench and began pacing back and forth in front of Raven. "What do you think?" he stopped and stared at the ground. "I was angry."

"But what else did you feel?"

Justin shrugged. "I just felt the anger swirling inside of me. That's all."

"Swirling?"

"Yeah."

"Then what?" Raven asked.

"I don't know." Justin looked back up at Raven. "It just—left."

"Before or after the tree crashed?"

Justin didn't seem to want to answer the question. "Just before. So?"

"I was inside the school at the time, but I felt a surge of Tree energy right around that time. I wondered if it was your energy, but I didn't hear about the tree until today. That wasn't just anger swirling inside of you, it was the elemental energy you released on that tree. Someone could have been seriously hurt. That's why you need to be trained before you start using it anymore."

Justin didn't say anything right away and Raven chewed on her lip while she waited for a response. Justin finally spoke. "At least tell me how this all works. Everything is essentially made up of energy, and Elementers must be manipulating that energy. How do we convert potential energy to kinetic energy?"

Raven's tilted her head and looked closely at Justin.

"What?" Justin asked.

"It's nothing." Raven bit her lip.

"Come on. Tell me."

"You seem to know science pretty well, so how did you get a D in biology?"

Justin's face darkened. "How do you know I got a D?"

"Well, when I was looking for your address I dropped your file your transcripts spilled on the floor. Sorry. But seriously, you seem too smart to be failing biology."

"Grades are about impressing teachers and parents. But it doesn't matter what I do, I can never measure up to Graham.

Dad always reminds me that Graham got straight A's. Graham never got into fights. Graham is perfect."

"Who's Graham?"

"My older brother. He's off on a full scholarship at Stanford."

"Why did you get in fights?"

"At least you asked why. Dad never did. But there are always jerks who want to remind you that you're different. Dad never had blankouts, so he has no idea what it's like," Justin said.

"They picked on you because of your blankouts?"

"Yeah, but I could handle myself. But other kids got picked on too and needed help."

Raven looked at him more intently, reaching out with her energy to sense his. "You stuck up for others? That's great."

Justin shook his head. "My dad sure doesn't think so. But anyway, the point is that I'm the irresponsible, under-achieving, problem child and Graham is the perfect son. That's just how it is, so I don't see why I should work hard to impress anyone when I'll always be second best."

"He's really not that bad, is he?"

"Worse."

"Well, at least he notices you."

"I wish he didn't."

"Don't be so sure about that," Raven whispered. Justin looked at her questioningly, but she didn't feel like explaining, so she quickly changed the subject. "But what about your grandpa?"

"Henry? He was incredible."

"You called your grandpa by his first name?"

"Yeah, ever since I was seven. He said we were best friends and that best friends call each other by their first name. He was just that way. Everyone loved him, even my friends. He was the only person who ever got me. I mean, my mom and grandma are nice, but Henry accepted me for me. But I guess that's because he really did understand what I was going through. I wonder if he knew I was a Elementer too."

"I think he probably suspected it. Though I'm sure he would have been stunned to find out you could access multiple elements."

"Yeah. I wish he could have been here to find out I was a Elementer too. I think he would have liked it." Justin had a smile on his face, but his eyes looked sad.

"I think he would have been really proud of you."

Justin looked up at Raven and seemed to suddenly decide the conversation had become too serious. "I'll tell you what. I'll try to hold off on any power explosions till Saturday, if you'll show me what you can do."

Raven hesitated, but Justin didn't seem the kind of person to just do things because he was told to do them. She figured this was her best chance at keeping Justin under the radar until Mr. Hamilton had time to talk to the Council. "Okay. But only a couple of small things."

The tall bushes surrounding much of the gazebo gave sufficient privacy to use her powers without being seen. Raven closed her eyes and let the energy begin to vibrate within her. Then she opened her eyes and focused on a handful of small, lose rocks scattered near their feet. She reached out to them and sent them rising and spinning in a circle above the ground between Justin and herself.

"That's cool. What else can you do?"

Raven let the rocks drop to the ground. "Uh, how about this?" She shot up a lop-sided rock the size of a golf ball and focused a strong pulse of energy into the center of the rock. Boom! Pieces of rock shattered in all directions causing both of them to pull their arms in front of their faces to protect them from the fragments.

Justin stared wide-eyed at Raven. "Wow! That's cool. Remind me not to get you angry."

Raven smiled. Hiding who she was from others made it difficult to really connect with people. It felt good to just be herself around Justin. It would be nice to have him around.

"Well, I'd better get home. I have homework I still need to finish," Raven said.

Justin stood up with her. "Yeah, does Ms. Chalmers always lay on the homework that thick?"

"Usually. But it's worse right now because you have to catch up on the assigned book. I can give you my notes so far if you'd like."

"Thanks. That'd help," Justin said. They were walking through the kitchen and heading toward the front door. "Oh, I need to give you your jacket. Just a sec." Justin leapt up the stairs two at a time and quickly returned with the coat. "Is this your jacket?"

"No. It's a friend's. How did you know?"

"I didn't figure you had lettered in football. Or do you have other talents you haven't told me yet?"

Raven laughed. She was amazed at how comfortable she felt around Justin. Admittedly, it helped that he was also an Elementer, but she knew it was more than that. She couldn't seem to suppress a smile around him.

"So who's is it?" Justin asked, clearly trying to sound as nonchalant as possible.

"Uh, Eric Johnson."

"So why were you wearing it?"

"He and I are kind of seeing each other," the words stumbled out of Raven's mouth. They also brought her back down to earth.

"Hmm. Lucky guy." Justin's smile was still there, but it seemed to disappear from his eyes.

To end the uncomfortable silence, Raven said, "Well, I guess I'll see you tomorrow?"

"Sure. See you,'" Justin said as he stood in the doorway watching Raven leave.

Raven took a few steps and turned around. "Thanks, Justin."

"For what?"

"Just, thanks. See you tomorrow." Raven climbed on her bike and waved at Justin as she headed down the road.

Chapter 9

MR. HAMILTON WIPED the sweat off his palms as he walked into the Council Room. The ceilings were almost two stories high and the sound of the secretary's high heels echoing on the inlaid marble floor made the room feel even more intimidating. Murals covered the four walls representing each of the four elements and converged on the ceiling near the chandelier making it look like the source of energy for all four elements. The scene distracted him, but as soon as he looked down and saw the faces of the Council members, he immediately remembered the daunting task ahead of him.

The secretary's loud steps stopped near the far end of the room. She placed her left hand on the back of an ornately carved seat at the end of the Council table. Mr. Hamilton unconsciously took in a deep breath and sat down.

Twelve Council members flanked the long, rectangular table. Three Water Elementers and two Wind Elementers sat on Mr. Hamilton's left side. An empty seat reminded him of Henry's

O'Malley's absence. Three Earth and three Tree Elementers occupied the right side of the table. Facing Mr. Hamilton at the opposite end of the table sat Charles Wittington, the Council Chairperson, with his dignified air.

Mr. Hamilton only knew five of the Council members personally. They were from around the world, so he hadn't even met some of them. He was just lucky they were here in New York City this week. Naturally, he knew the three Water Elementers. He also knew the Council Chairperson and Rex Dryden, the Wind Elementer from Texas. The other Elementers represented a diverse group from every continent except Antarctica.

"David. How can we help you today?" the Chairperson asked with his Oxford educated English accent.

Mr. Hamilton had memorized his speech, but for a short moment, he thought he had forgotten what to say. He fidgeted with his glasses for the third time in a minute. Taking a deep breath, the words returned to his mind. "Council Members, I'm here today to share some important news. While it is unexpected, if we keep an open mind, I believe we can discover new and interesting possibilities never known in the history of Elementers." A few of the Council Members turned to him with skeptical looks, but Mr. Hamilton continued, "A few days ago, Raven, my apprentice, discovered a new Earth Elementer."

"How would a new Earth Elementer affect the history of Elementers?" Rex Dryden impatiently asked in his heavy Texan accent. He leaned forward placing his muscular forearms on the table. Mr. Hamilton knew Rex's arms were that size from calf wrestling and serious labor on his ranch. It reminded Mr. Hamilton that he was glad he wasn't a calf.

"It's because we quickly discovered that he is also a Tree Elementer," Mr. Hamilton explained. The Council Members' reactions varied from reserved raised eyebrows to concerned looks and mumbles of disbelief.

Rex Dryden spoke up again. "Even if what you say is true."

"It is," Mr. Hamilton responded in a quiet voice.

Rex continued as if Mr. Hamilton hadn't spoken. "A Double Elementer is rare, but definitely not unprecedented. You're exaggerating things," the Texan criticized.

"True, a Double Elementer is not so unusual," Mr. Hamilton said trying to be agreeable. Taking a final deep breath, he dove into the deep end. "But we discovered he's also a Water Elementer."

"What?! That's impossible!" Rex exclaimed.

Mr. Hamilton's eyes fell to the floor dreading the task of arguing with one of the Council Members, particularly Rex Dryden. "I've seen it with my own eyes."

"Are you certain?" the Elementer to the right of him asked.

"What does this mean?" one of the Tree Elementers questioned as they nervously watched the responses of the rest of the group.

"Council Members. We clearly have some questions for Mr. Hamilton so let's give him the opportunity to explain himself." The Chairperson interrupted firmly, but calmly. Turning to Mr. Hamilton he asked, "Are you certain about the Elementer accessing three elements?"

"Yes, I'm sure he can access three. Raven Earth Talked with the boy. Katie Powers and Anya Cruz have Tree Talked with him briefly." The Tree Elementers raised their eyebrows at that information so Mr. Hamilton quickly added, "But those were his first brief Talking experiences so Katie and Anya don't yet know he can access other elements. Then he channeled water and created a water fountain in a creek right before my eyes."

"Why were you encouraging him to already influence the elements?" Rex demanded.

"I didn't. When I explained to him that Double Elementers

were unusual, he wanted to know if he could access the water element also. I told him that no one could access three elements, but he wanted to see if he could do so."

"So he doesn't listen," Rex said.

"I wouldn't say that. It was all so foreign to him that accessing three elements seemed no more strange than accessing two elements," Mr. Hamilton said.

One of the other Wind Elementers spoke up. "So, are we certain he can't also Wind Talk?"

All eyes turned and focused on Mr. Hamilton. This too was a bit of a sensitive subject. "I did suggest that he try Wind Talking to answer that same question. But unfortunately, I suggested he attempt to connect to Henry O'Malley."

In response to the name, many lowered their eyes or turned their heads toward the empty chair. Mr. Hamilton gently continued. "I hadn't yet heard of his tragic accident. The young man informed me of the news."

The Chairperson spoke up. "Why would this boy know about Henry's accident?"

Mr. Hamilton hesitated. He had been hoping to keep Justin's identity private until he knew the Council's reaction to the news. But that no longer seemed possible. "The boy knew about it because he's Henry's grandson."

The Chairperson's bluish-gray eyes opened wide and he ran his hand through his thick, silver hair. "The Triple Elementer is Justin Wilder?" he asked in surprise.

"You know the boy?" the woman from Zimbabwe asked.

"Yes, Henry and I were very close friends so I've met the boy a number of times through the years."

"And what do you think of him?" she asked.

"Henry adored him. Justin always seemed like a decent young man. A little rambunctious, much like Henry, but good," the Chairperson said.

"Do you think he's up to handling three channels?"

"I haven't seen him in almost a year. Henry often bragged about the boy. Hopefully, his judgment wasn't too biased. But none of us know what it will be like harnessing three elements." The Chairperson turned to Mr. Hamilton. "You still haven't answered the question whether the boy can Wind Talk."

"Sorry. I don't know."

Rex jumped back into the conversation. "You didn't think it important to find that out before bringing us this news?"

"When Justin learned about his grandfather keeping the secret of being a Wind Elementer from him, he was quite upset. That happened on Wednesday. He wasn't ready to talk the next morning before I flew out here to meet with you. I thought it wise to inform the council as soon as possible."

"I'd say the first thing we need to do is to make sure he can't Wind Talk," Rex stated.

"Yes, I agree it would be best to know before we make any decisions. Rex, would you attempt to Wind Talk with him?" the Chairperson requested.

"Right now?" Mr. Hamilton swallowed.

"Yes. Now," the Chairperson responded in a tone that removed any argument.

The room turned their eyes to Rex who leaned back in his chair and focused his eyes on a spot on the far wall. Mr. Hamilton could feel the slight energy vibrations coming from the other side of the table.

Chapter 10

MR. HAMILTON'S SUBSTITUTE teacher turned on a boring film about the structure of atoms leaving Justin plenty of time to catch up on his near non-existent sleep.

"Justin Wilder. Justin Wilder." A voice woke Justin up and he shot upright in his seat. He quickly looked at the teacher's desk assuming the substitute had caught him sleeping. But the substitute teacher seemed pretty close to dozing off himself.

"Justin," the voice called again. He felt the energy buzz through his body when his name was called. He turned to look at Raven who likewise stared at him with wide eyes. The look on her face suggested that she was just as surprised as he was by the incoming energy.

"Justin, are you there?" the voice called out to him again.

"What?" Justin whispered under his breath. The guy in front of Justin turned around to look at him, but Justin immediately directed his eyes elsewhere and shrank down into his seat.

"Justin. My name is Rex Dryden. I'm a Wind Elementer. I knew your grandfather."

In response, Justin mumbled "mmm hmm" under his breath.

"Justin. Is that you?"

Justin leaned forward placing his elbows on the desk and propped up his head by cupping one of his hands in front of his mouth. He whispered, "Can't talk now."

"Justin. I'm here with the Elementer Council and we need to ask you a few questions."

"Call later," Justin mumbled again in frustration.

"This is an important matter and we need to speak to you now."

The irritating voice clearly wasn't going to leave so Justin put up his hand. Thankfully, the teacher looked his way and Justin asked if he could go to the bathroom. Quickly exiting the classroom, Justin rounded the corner and looked to make sure no one else was in the hall. "Uh, Mr. —whoever you are, what are you doing in my head?"

The voice responded, "My name is Rex Dryden. I'm here in a meeting with Mr. Hamilton."

"This really isn't a good time. I'm in school right now and I look like an idiot talking to the air."

"Justin. This is very important. I'm here with the Council." The voice invading his mind wouldn't shut up.

"Tell Mr. Hamilton that I'm in the middle of his science class and his substitute teacher is going to wonder where I am if I don't return soon." As he spoke, a girl rounded the corner in front of him and looked at Justin like he was a little unbalanced. An idea came to Justin. While quickly walking down the hall and around another corner he pulled out his phone and pressed it against his ear. He'd rather get in trouble for talking on his phone during class hours than have people think he wandered the halls talking to himself.

But as Justin rounded the corner, he swiftly ran into someone. He looked up and realized it was the same guy he bumped into the other day. Great.

"Hey, you're the loser who mouthed off to me the other day. There are no teachers nearby to stop me from teaching you a lesson," the guy sneered.

Justin wasn't afraid of taking a punch. He'd had his share when standing up to bullies. But this guy was huge and Justin had enough sense to avoid pain if he could. He began backing away from the enormous guy trying to think of a tactic to get away from him. But his backward progress was halted by something. He peeked behind himself to notice he had backed up into a drinking fountain. It gave him an idea.

"Justin, we need to talk." Justin ignored the Elementer speaking to him and tried to connect to the water. He put his phone in his front pocket, placed his arms at his sides and subconsciously stretched out his fingers as if trying to touch the water. Reaching out his fingers likely didn't make a difference, but it helped him mentally. Despite his efforts, he couldn't make the connection. Maybe he needed to be touching the water. But that would look suspicious. The bully had a sadistic grin on his face as he closed the gap between them. He seemed to be taking his time, as if he enjoyed seeing the fear he induced in people. Just as the guy reached out to grab Justin's shirt, Justin took a step to the left leaving the monster standing square in front of the drinking fountain.

With every ounce of desperation Justin truly felt, he urged the energy from his arms into the pipes of the fountain. Suddenly he felt something different. The energy flowed back. Without wasting a moment to think, or be punched, he envisioned or willed the water to burst forth out of the water fountain and toward the bully. The only problem was that it worked better than he expected.

Water first shot up toward the ceiling. Justin redirected it toward the guy, but the extreme water pressure caused the ceramic drinking fountain to begin rattling. Suddenly, it shot off its foundation like a cannon. Launching across the hallway, the large ceramic projectile missed the bully's midsection by a few inches and smashed into the opposing wall. With the plumbing out of the way, the agitated water shot out like a fire hose directly at the football player. It flung the guy against the wall, landed him on his butt, and continued to pummel him with a steady jet of water preventing him from being able to stand up or even control himself enough to roll out of the way.

"Justin! Did you just channel one of the elements?" The Elementer seemed to yell at him in his head.

Justin backed away from the explosion of water. "How did you know?"

"That doesn't matter. You need to be trained before you try using the energies. It's dangerous."

"Yeah, that's what I heard. But it's also dangerous to be pulverized by an oversized football lineman. Your call caused me to run into, and aggravate, the meat head, so I needed to do something. I told you it wasn't a good time to talk."

"You can't go around flashing your powers."

"I didn't flash anyone. There was simply a small malfunction with the drinking fountain and the jerk happened to be near it at the time. He's not going to think I magically made the drinking fountain break. He's not that stupid. Well, probably not."

Teachers and students were beginning to come out of the nearby classrooms to discover the cause of all the noise. "Look. I need to get back to class before I really get in trouble. Bye." Hurrying down the corridor and around the corner, Justin quietly slipped back into his classroom. As he walked to his desk he could feel Raven's eyes boring into his head. He didn't bother looking her way. If the Wind Elementer had sensed his use of energy, he was sure Raven must have also. Great! He couldn't wait till after class to hear it from her too. But a realization crossed Justin's mind. Mr. Hamilton's question had been answered. He was a Wind Elementer. Just like his grandpa. That could be interesting.

Chapter 11

JUSTIN WATCHED RAVEN'S long black hair swing behind her as he followed her and Mr. Hamilton through the forest Monday after school. A bird swooped down out of a tree and caught his attention. "Are we there yet?"

"Not much farther." Mr. Hamilton turned his head back toward Justin while climbing over a fallen tree so thick that would take at least two people to wrap their arms around it. "Not many people come to this part of Larrabee State Park, but I want to hike in just a little further off the trail to find a good spot where we don't have to worry about anyone seeing us practice."

It wasn't easy climbing over and around fallen trees, overgrown bushes, branch blockades, and more. But Justin enjoyed the hike, absorbing the rich scents and mosaic of sounds and carrying on casual conversation with Raven. Just when he thought he could do this all day, Raven suddenly stopped in front of him.

"There he is," Mr. Hamilton said.

Justin noticed a small creek bubbling nearby and meandering through the forest. But he was surprised to see a man with a cowboy hat and huge silver belt buckle standing there in a clearing of the trees.

"Rex, I'm glad you were able to find my coordinates." Mr. Hamilton walked up and shook the man's hand. Then he turned to Raven and Justin. "Rex, this is Raven." Raven waved. "And this is Justin Wilder. Raven and Justin, this is Rex Dryden."

Justin remembered the name. "Yeah, we talked on Friday."

"Hardly. You refused to talk," Rex said.

"Only because you interrupted me in the middle of class. What was I supposed to do? You nearly got me beat up in the hallway."

Rex stepped toward Justin. "So you went and used your powers right in front of someone. Your impulsiveness is a danger to us all."

Justin took a few steps forward leaving only a couple feet between them. Despite having to look up at Rex, Justin glared at the man with clenched fists at his side. Mr. Hamilton nearly choked from the tension, but he nervously spoke up to redirect the discussion. "Justin. Rex is going to help you train today. He's a Wind Elementer, so we'll focus on Wind training today."

"Fine." Justin turned away from Rex and saw Raven smile in encouragement. If he had to be around some pushy wannabe cowboy, at least Raven would be there also.

Rex circled around Justin with an expression that seemed to be a mixture of irritation and anticipation. The way the Texan sauntered while wearing that cowboy hat made Justin think of a Wild West gun fight. Justin couldn't suppress a chuckle. But from the look on Rex's face, the Texan didn't appreciate Justin's light heartedness. Justin really wanted to tell the guy to ease up, but figured it would just make the guy more uptight.

A sudden gust of wind blew at Justin from behind nearly knocking him off his feet. He regained his balance and looked at Rex who stood there with a satisfied grin on his face. Justin tried to reach out to the wind energy, but he couldn't seem to connect. It felt like grabbing air with his hands. It didn't work. He wondered if it was the air's lack of firm substance that made it hard to connect to it.

Another wind gust rushed him from behind and this time it threw him to his knees. His right knee screamed out in pain as it struck a large, sharp rock which cut through his jeans and into his knee. Justin pressed his lips together to prevent any sounds of pain from escaping his mouth and used his arms to help push him up and hide the fact that he was favoring his leg. There was no way he was going to give Rex the satisfaction of seeing he'd been hurt.

Angrily reaching out, he tried again to connect, but he couldn't figure out how to grab hold of the air. A buzz of energy seemed to come at him a third time. Justin shot a huge wall of water at the oncoming wind. The liquid and wind collided causing an explosion of water in all directions.

"We're training with wind, not water," Rex said.

"Maybe you need to actually bother teaching me how to connect instead of just blowing hot air!"

"You know how to connect to earth, tree, and water. Connect to the air."

"It's not the same. You can't grab hold of air, so how do I reach out to it?"

"You don't grab hold of wind energy. You open yourself up to it and let it flow into you. Open up."

What a useless teacher, Justin thought. Taking a deep breath, he tried to relax. At least as much as he could while waiting for

Rex to pelt him with a wind cannon at any moment. He felt the desire to reach out again, but resisted the urge, closed his eyes, and tried to open himself to the wind energy. It wasn't long before he felt goose bumps spread across his arms. A coolness poured into his chest like thick syrup. It expanded within his rib cage and he waited to feel the pressure build up. Instead, he felt like his body had become part of the world around him and the energy continued to expand within him.

"That's right," Rex said.

Justin opened his eyes oblivious to the goofy grin on his own face. Seeing Rex in front of him wasn't even enough to wipe it off his face. "Wow. That's cool." Justin thought he saw Rex's face soften and almost smile. But he blinked and the stone face had returned. Maybe he just imagined it.

"Now that you're connected, let's get to work. I'm going to send some more wind your way and unless you want to be on your knees again, you'd better deflect it."

Justin tried to push back the next blast, but it was like holding up a pillow in defense during a pillow fight. Sure, you didn't get hit directly, but the force still pushed you around. After being knocked around five or six times, Justin had enough and decided to go on the offensive by hijacking Rex's connection. He hoped it was similar to forcing a fumble in football. Rather than directing a gust of wind at Rex, Justin shot a burst of energy at Rex briefly disrupting Rex's connection to the wind element. Justin picked up the wind gust at that moment and sent it barreling right back at Rex. The surprise and force combined to hit Rex firmly in the gut and throw him back against a large tree.

"Wow," Raven said. Mr. Hamilton choked back a laugh.

Rex grimaced and didn't respond to the comment. Instead, he stood back up and said, "Again."

This time, wind wasn't the only thing heading Justin's way.

The faster wind picked up some small branches which were flying toward him. Justin tried to force another fumble, but Rex was prepared for it and Justin's attempt to steal his connection failed. With the branches only a few feet away from him, Justin shot a perpendicular wind gust which collided from the side with Rex's force and pushed the branches enough to the side so that only one hit him. He was pretty sure it'd leave a bruise on his shoulder, but it could have been worse.

Rex clearly wanted to force Justin to give up. He didn't even start a new gust. He simply turned the existing one around, which picked up more debris along the way, and directed it back at Justin. This continued for what felt like a few hours, when in reality it was less than thirty minutes. In the midst of just surviving, somewhere in the back of his head, Justin wondered how many cuts and bruises he'd have and how he'd explain them to his Mom.

"Are you done yet?" Rex asked.

Despite having never been more exhausted in his life, there was no way Justin would ask for mercy from this creep. While thinking about the refusal, Justin must have lost some of his concentration because he didn't notice the coming gust until a large branch hit him solidly in the back. As he dropped to the ground from the force and pain, his vision blurred and sounds seemed to be muffled. A small part of his mind could hear his name being called and steps running toward him. But all he could really sense was the anger burning inside him and the need to defend himself from this jerk. He didn't send a wind gust. Instead, he closed his eyes and pushed the energy out in all directions as if to create a protective barrier.

He heard what sounded like a bunch of fireworks go off almost all at once in the distance and, in the midst of it all, a scream. He opened his eyes, but things were a blurry for a moment and he wasn't sure where he was. The forest seemed to be gone. He saw Mr. Hamilton and Rex standing near each other looking at the same spot on the ground. Anger erupted in Justin at the sight of Rex and he thought about using the wind to throw Rex in the creek, but he followed where their eyes were focused. Raven laid on the ground with her eyes closed, blood on her forehead, and a fallen tree across her legs. The anger was suddenly forgotten.

"Raven!" He shook the fog and anger from his mind and leaped up to cross the twenty feet to reach her. Dizziness tried to pull him down but he stumbled across the distance and dropped to his knees next to her, oblivious of the pain in his sliced up knee. "Raven. Are you okay?"

Justin touched Raven's arm, but when he did so, a spike of energy rushed into him. It was like an electric shock, but many times stronger. He automatically pulled back his hand and noticed that Raven jerked in pain at the same time. Sure that it was a freak occurrence and wanting to help Raven, he reached out to her again and they were both jolted again. Raven's body shook in response.

"Stop touching her you fool!" Rex yelled at Justin as he rushed toward them.

Raven slowly opened her eyes, but she squeezed them shut again as she grimaced in pain. "What was that? What happened?" Raven mumbled.

"I'll tell you what happened!" Rex shouted. Before he continued his tirade, he paused to use the wind to carefully lift the tree off of Raven. Luckily, one side of the tree had fallen on a nearby boulder so it hadn't crushed Raven's legs. "What happened is this boy clearly has a dangerous power he can't control! He's a danger to himself, and to others, as he has so plainly demonstrated just now."

Mr. Hamilton knelt on the other side of Raven. "Raven,

where does it hurt?"

"Oh, I think it's just my forehead. It really isn't that bad."

"Raven, I'm so sorry," Justin said looking down at her.

"What did you do?" Mr. Hamilton asked Justin.

"I—" Justin tried to remember what he did, but all he could recall were images of bright light and a rush of fury. He did his best to push the feelings aside. "I don't know what happened. I just pushed the energy out to protect myself. My eyes were closed so I didn't see. What happened?"

"I've never seen one in person, I've only read about them, but it looks like you created a microburst. The wind was so fast and powerful that it flattened all the trees around you. Rex only had time to raise a defense right in front of him just before it hit. I was behind him so the two of us were protected, but Raven was running toward you to see how you were doing after the branch hit you. She's lucky she fared as well as she did. That boulder protected her from being crushed," Mr. Hamilton said.

Justin looked up at Mr. Hamilton and saw that his teacher seemed to be concerned about him too, but he also seemed hesitant, or maybe even just a little afraid of him.

"David, I told you he's dangerous," Rex said.

Justin glared at the Texan. "If you had backed off, I wouldn't have felt the need to defend myself."

"Against this girl?" Rex said.

"No! I didn't mean to do that," Justin said.

"If you didn't intend to create this level of damage and it just happened accidentally than that's all the more proof that you're dangerous."

"I said I was sorry," Justin said. He felt the urge to put Rex in his place, but he suddenly felt drained and didn't have the energy to argue.

Mr. Hamilton spoke up. "I think Raven is safe to move so

we should be on our way. Others will have heard the noise and we don't want to be found in the middle of this."

"We are going to have to do something about this boy," Rex said to Mr. Hamilton

"You can't tell me what to do," Justin gritted his teeth wanting desperately to shut Rex up.

"Rex, can we talk about this later?" Mr. Hamilton said.

Raven assured them that she was okay, but Rex easily picked her up as if she were a small child and carried her back to the jeep. Justin followed the group back to the car with thoughts burning through his mind of how best to humble Rex.

Chapter 12

JUSTIN SHOVED THE hotel's bathroom door with far more force than necessary, taking his frustrations with Rex out on the door. Mr. Hamilton had dropped Justin and Rex off at Rex's hotel before driving Raven home. Justin turned down a ride home preferring to run to his house to help clear his head.

Justin had popped into the hotel to use the bathroom before heading out. Walking down the hallway to the lobby, Justin recognized Rex's voice. The jerk was arguing with someone. No surprise there. Justin slowed as he listened in on the conversation. But his feet came to an immediate halt when he heard a certain name. Wanting to catch more, he backed up against the wall of the hallway to make sure Rex wouldn't see him, and slowly slid along the wall to get closer to better overhear the argument.

Not only was Justin stunned to hear his grandpa's name, but it seemed even stranger that the man Rex argued with had a Russian accent. "It must be so much easier to get what you want with Henry gone. Look what you've gained. With Henry dead, I hear you were even made Head Wind Elementer on the Council.

How convenient for you."

"Maybe we didn't agree on everything—"

The Russian interrupted. "The two of you never agreed on anything."

"Just because we disagreed doesn't mean…" Rex's voice was drowned out by some bossy woman at the other end of the lobby telling her husband what to do. Justin inched closer to the lobby while still remaining hidden. The woman quieted down and Justin caught Rex's voice again. "… can't prove Henry's death wasn't an accident." Rex's words hit Justin like a train at full speed. He felt like he had been punched in the stomach. Justin choked and had to fight to prevent his knees from buckling underneath him. He tried to focus back in on the conversation, but it was difficult because his head spun like the time he rode the Mad Tea Party cups at Disneyland.

"Rex, as always, it was a pleasure seeing you." Justin could recognize the sarcasm even with the Russian accent. A set of footsteps that sounded like Rex's large cowboy boots stomped off toward the front doors. Justin peaked around the corner and saw the man with the Russian accent walking toward the elevator. He had dark brown, wavy hair that hung to his shoulders. His clothes looked expensive and flashy. He must have been in his early thirties.

After watching the man enter the elevator, Justin thought about leaving, but he felt numb all over. His legs wouldn't move. Instead, his body involuntarily lowered itself until he sat on the floor with his back against the wall. Rex's words kept repeating in his head, "Henry's death wasn't an accident. They can't prove Henry's death wasn't an accident." Justin closed his eyes and took a few deep breaths. Could it be true? Had Rex murdered his grandpa?

Chapter 13

JUSTIN DIDN'T KNOW how long he sat in the hallway trying to absorb what he had just heard. It wasn't until someone nearly tripped over him coming around the corner that he came out of his daze. Pulling himself up off the floor, he made his way through the lobby and out to the parking lot. Justin looked up for any trace of the sun, but the grey clouds did all they could to block out the light. He began crossing the parking lot, when he heard someone call out his name. Justin turned in the direction of the voice.

The Russian man that had been arguing with Rex walked toward him. "You're Justin Wilder, aren't you?"

"How do you know my name?"

"I'm Alexei Novokov. News has spread fast and everyone is talking about you, Justin. I saw David Hamilton drop you off so I figured it had to be you," Alexei said.

"Who's talking about me?" Justin asked.

"Everyone. Everyone in the Elementer community."

"Why would they be talking about me?"

"Are you serious?" The man walked next to Justin and lowered his voice. "Justin, you're the only known Elementer to ever be able to control all four elements. You're not just famous now. You'll be famous for centuries to come. Don't you realize how special you are?"

Justin shrugged. "Mr. Hamilton told me no one else can access all four, but I've just spent the afternoon with Rex treating me like I have a terrible curse that threatens to destroy humanity."

"Rex is just jealous that he doesn't have your talents. You're going to become the most powerful Elementer ever. Rex only wishes he could have that power." Alexei looked at his watch. "You know, I was going to go for a drive before meeting someone for dinner. Do you need a ride home?"

"That's okay. I was going to run home."

"I think you'll change your mind when you see my car. Why don't you at least come over and see Alina?" Alexei started walking toward the far end of the parking lot and motioned for Justin to join him.

Justin wanted to learn more about the conversation he just heard between this man and Rex so he followed Alexei across the parking lot. Justin's jaw dropped when Alexei stopped next to what was clearly Alina. Despite his current mood, the sleek, fire red sports car took his breath away. "What is it?"

"The Ferrari Italia 458. Isn't she a beauty? Come inside. You haven't experienced her until she's wrapped her arms around you."

The guy clearly liked his car a little too much, but Justin walked around the car and opened the door. As he slid into the soft leather seat that seemed to fit him perfectly, Justin immediately took back his judgment about Alexei and his car. This wasn't a car, it was a creation. Every detail was sleek and graceful. "Wow," was all he needed to say.

"Are you sure you don't want a ride home?" Alexei asked, enjoying Justin's appreciation for the car.

Justin thought about all the questions running through his mind needing answers. He needed to find someone who could help answer them. "I guess I can go running later."

"Want to take a spin before I drop you off?"

"Sure."

Justin closed his door and buckled up before Alexei peeled out of the parking lot like a horse at the start of a race. By the time they reached the empty rural roads at the northeast side of town, Alexei was flying around corners at crazy speeds. Justin expected the car to tip over from turning so fast, but the car hugged tightly to the road. Alexei often swerved into the opposite lane with complete abandon to pass cars causing Justin to unconsciously grab tightly onto the door handle. But despite his fear, Justin couldn't help but enjoy the thrill just a little.

Suddenly, Alexei turned the car sharply in the middle of the road spinning them 180 degrees so that the car stopped in the other lane ready to head in that direction. Justin's heart pounded as quickly as if he had been running home. A grin spread across his face. "Wow. That was something else."

"You liked it?"

"You're a great driver."

"I'd better get you back home so that I'm not late for my meeting. I'm in town just for the day so I can't miss it. Where do you live?"

As they headed back into Bellingham at somewhat less dangerous speeds, Justin took the opportunity to try to get answers to his questions. "Alexei, did you know Henry O'Malley?"

"Every Wind Elementer knew Henry. He was the Head

Wind Elementer on the Council. He was your grandpa, wasn't he?"

"Yes. What do you know about his death?"

"What?" Alexei seemed to stiffen up for a moment, but then his smooth demeanor quickly returned. "I heard he died in a car accident."

"Yes. It's just that I've heard things."

"Things?"

Justin didn't want to sound ridiculous suggesting some conspiracy theory that his grandpa had been murdered, but the conversation he overhead certainly suggested he had been. "Did anyone not like my grandpa?"

Alexei looked at Justin for a moment and then back at the road. "He was a brave and brilliant man. He always stood up for what he believed in even when others disagreed with him. Even those in power."

"What do you mean? Who did he stand up against?" Justin asked.

"Oh, they won't want me talking about it," Alexei said.

"Who won't? I need to know about my Grandpa," Justin insisted.

"Some of the people in power wouldn't want me talking about this. You've already met one of them."

"You mean Rex, don't you? I don't care what he wants. They can't push me around."

"Ah, you sound just like Henry. He wouldn't let Rex or any of the other Council members tell him what to do or say. I can't help but think that his accident was—" Alexei turned away from the road and looked at Justin.

"What? What were you going to say?" Justin asked.

"I'm sorry, Justin. It's just speculation."

"Tell me," Justin said.

"There's just been talk about the fact that Henry and Rex

had been at serious odds about some issues important to the Council. Your Grandpa had half of the members behind him and Rex had the other half. Rex 'The Tex' doesn't like people getting in his way."

"Yeah, I can see that."

"So the thing is, they were going to be having an important vote coming up and it looked like Henry's position would win by a single vote. The day before the vote, your Grandpa agreed to go to a meeting at Rex's ranch. The story is that Henry and Rex had a huge argument, Henry left, and he had the accident after leaving Rex's ranch," Alexei said.

"What are you saying? You don't think my grandpa's death was an accident?" Justin asked nearly choking on the words.

"I'm not saying anything. But other people are talking. A Wind Elementer could easily create a gust strong enough to push that gasoline truck into Henry's car in the oncoming lane. It must have happened very quickly because otherwise Henry would have diverted it away with his powers. He was one of the best Wind Elementers I know. But even though people are saying these things, I question it. I don't like Rex, but I have a hard time believing he'd do such a thing. It's probably just talk. I'm sorry. I've upset you. I shouldn't have said anything." Alexei pulled up in front of Justin's house.

"I'm glad you did. I want to know the truth," Justin said.

"I'm sure we'll see each other again soon." Alexei pulled a business card out of his wallet and handed it to Justin. "Here's my card. Give me a call if you need anything."

Justin took the card. "Thanks for the ride. It was wild." He climbed out of the soft, leather seat and leaned down to see inside. "And informative. I hope we see each other again soon."

"I have some business I'm doing up here in the area, so I'm sure we will. Enjoy yourself and watch your back," Alexei said and then sped away.

Justin watched the car speed around the corner wondering if there really was a need to be careful.

Chapter 14

JUSTIN TOLD HIMSELF he shouldn't feel nervous. He was just bringing Raven notes from class. It was no big deal. But he couldn't stop fidgeting as he stood waiting at the door. He had been comfortable when he called her at lunch after not seeing her in English class. He wanted to make sure her injury from the microburst yesterday wasn't worse than she let on. She assured him she was okay, but Marcela, her cook-housekeeper-fill-in-mom, had insisted she rest today.

A short, older Hispanic woman opened the door. "Ah, you must be Justeen. Adelante." She ushered him into the entry room and smiled warmly. Turning toward a large, ornate circular staircase, she called out, "Raven. Justeen is here for you."

Justin scanned the massive living room and the stunning view of the ocean and the San Juan Islands that the floor to ceiling windows afforded. A door opened upstairs and the sound of footsteps approached. "Hi, Justin." Raven seemed to fit in with the amazing surroundings as she descended the staircase.

"Hi. How are you doing?" Justin asked.

"I'm fine. It's nothing but a little headache. But my sweet Marcela is such a mother hen." Raven sidled up next to Marcela and gave her a hug. "She kept me prisoner in the upper tower all day long. Admittedly, I don't know many prisoners who get fed treats and are forced to watch movies all day long."

"This is an amazing house."

"Thanks. The view is nice, but my favorite part is the garden on the side of the house. I'll have to show it to you sometime when I'm allowed outdoors," Raven said.

"You kids sit down. I bring drinks."

"Thanks, Marcela," Raven led Justin into the living room and sat down on a couch motioning for him to join her. "So how was the charming Ms. Chalmers?"

"Boring as ever. But I took decent notes since I knew you'd need some." Justin unzipped his backpack and rummaged through it till he pulled out a few papers and handed them to Raven.

"Thanks, Justin. Not only do I get notes, but I get them hand delivered instead of by email. That's service."

"I guess I wanted to make sure you really were okay and not just saying you were fine to make me feel less guilty. I really am sorry for tossing that tree at you."

Raven chuckled.

"What?" Justin said.

"I may be the only person who has ever heard that apology. Life is going to be more dramatic with you around, isn't it?"

"Hopefully, in a good way. I promise to never again need to apologize for throwing a tree at you. Deal?"

"Deal. So anything interesting happen while I was under house arrest?"

The conversation he overheard at the hotel between Rex and Alexei came to Justin's mind, but he didn't know how to tell Raven about it. While he didn't hear the whole conversation, the pieces he did catch were pretty clear. But accusing Rex of murdering his grandpa seemed a few levels beyond melodramatic. During his run over here, he thought about how he could tell Raven about what he heard, but for every scenario he came up with, he quickly considered all the things someone would say to counteract his accusations. All he had were a few broken sentences and some gossip from Alexei. But deep down, Justin felt like there really was something suspect about Henry's death and Justin could believe Rex would do just about anything to get what he wanted. Justin simply needed some proof first.

Marcela came in and handed them both some lemonade. She seemed to give Justin a quick examination, smiled with approval, and left without saying anything. Justin turned his attention back to Raven. "No, nothing too exciting. I did meet Alexei Novokov, a Wind Elementer that's here in town on business. Do you know him?"

"I've never met him, but I've heard of him."

"What do you know about him?" Justin tried not to seem too interested.

"I've heard he's one of those Elementers that are always crossing the line. The Elementer Council doesn't like him. That much I know. I'd be careful around him."

"I don't think the Elementer Council likes me either. At least one of the Council members doesn't," Justin didn't need to say Rex's name.

"I know Rex was being a jerk yesterday, but please try to get along with him."

Yeah right, Justin thought. *Like I'm going to hang out and be buddy-buddy with my grandpa's killer, or at least possible killer.*

When Justin didn't say anything, Raven continued, "The

Council could make life difficult for you. I just don't want to see you hurt. Please try. Okay?"

Justin didn't want to talk about Rex anymore. As he looked away, he noticed a group of photos on a nearby table. He stood up to get a closer look. He picked up a frame containing a picture of a man and a little girl with two long black braids sitting in a two-seater bi-plane. "Is that you?"

Raven smiled shyly, "Yes, that's me and my Dad. I was seven. The picture was taken the very first time I got to help fly the plane."

"You flew a plane at age seven?"

Raven stood up and came over to view the picture. "Helped fly a plane. My dad is a pilot and I always begged him to let me come up with him. That's how I got my nickname."

"What? Raven isn't your real name?"

"No, it's actually Raylen. But between my black hair and my love of flying, when I was six, my dad started calling me Raven, like the bird, and it stuck."

"You like to fly?"

"I love it!" Justin noticed that Raven's face lit up. "There's nothing like soaring like a bird."

"And you're the one telling me to be careful?"

"Flying is very safe as long as you have a plan and follow it."

"Come on. Weather is seriously unpredictable. Even my grandpa, who I called the walking weather vane, couldn't always predict it. And you're not a Wind Elementer, so you can't influence it."

"A good pilot has a plan for every possible situation. I'll be getting my pilot's license soon. I can't wait. If I pass and get enough flight time in, Dad promised to get me a share in a plane when I turn seventeen."

"A plane? Most kids get a car."

"Well, I do get one of those soon when I turn sixteen. But

the plane is way more exciting."

"Must be nice," Justin said looking again at the fancy furnishings in the house.

"Don't be jealous. I get a car and part of a plane, but that's it. I met your mom. I'd trade with you any day, even if it meant giving up the plane."

"What do you mean?"

"My dad lives down in California and I see him once a year and my mom plays at being a mom. She's gone half the time on trips or helping with one of her causes. Even when she's here, she's not really here. Marcela is the closest thing I have to family," Raven looked down at the carpet.

"Yeah, but think of all the freedom you have. No parents around to tell you what to do. Marcela seems like a softie. She isn't much of a prison warden, is she?"

Raven looked up and gave a one-sided smile. "Okay, so she really is a bit of a push over. She is good at sending me on guilt trips when she's worried about me. But freedom isn't that great. You'd grow tired of being able to do whatever you want. It loses some its value without having people to share it with."

Justin looked concerned and Raven seemed to realize she had shared a little too much. "Anyway, once I get my pilot's license, I'll have to take you up some time. Well, once you've gained greater control of your Wind powers. I wouldn't want your powers causing too much drama while we're up in the air."

"Oh, thanks for the vote of confidence."

"I said *when* you gain control, not *it*. I know you'll learn to manage your powers and you're going to be amazing. My particular talent is being able to acutely sense other Elementers. But it isn't just sensing when they're nearby. I can sense their strength—and other things—within them." Justin could feel a slightest buzz of energy. Was she sensing him now? After a short moment she considered him intently. "Mr. Hamilton is training us tomorrow and I know you'll do great. Just wait and see."

Justin knew Raven meant what she said. Her complete confidence in him made him feel stronger than he had felt in a long time. Other than Henry, no one had ever believed in him like Raven did. His mom definitely loved him, but she loved him despite his problems. He had only known Raven for about a week, but he was beginning to feel closer to her than anyone else. He took a step closer to her. The urge to touch her face suddenly surfaced, but he quickly pushed the thought away. She had a boyfriend. But the impulse returned. He figured it was time to leave.

"Well, I'd better be going. The prison warden will probably kick me out if I go past visiting hours. So I'll see you tomorrow?"

"Yes, our training session will be great. You'll see."

Chapter 15

"JUSTIN, WE'RE GOING to send some things your way. I don't want the seats in my jeep to get dirty on the ride home, so deflect them."

"Why do I need to be the target? Rex treated me like a bull's eye too," Justin said.

"Sorry, but thousands of years of training have proven that the most effective way for Elementers to learn control is in defensive mode. Rex took it too far earlier this week, but your powers are a danger to yourself and others if you don't learn control quickly, so we have to use the quickest method. Ready?"

"Ready?" Mr. Hamilton asked.

Justin wasn't sure what was coming, but with Mr. Hamilton being a Water Elementer, he had a pretty good guess. "Sure."

"Okay, stop whatever I send your way."

Justin connected to the water element and felt the energy flowing through him. He could sense Mr. Hamilton connecting also. It felt like they had each thrown a rock in the water and the ripples from each rock were colliding with each other. The energy waves Justin affected were also being influenced by Mr. Hamilton. Following his teacher's gaze, which moved toward the creek, Justin saw a sphere of water the size of a baseball lift up out of the creek and fall back down. "Sure you're ready?" Mr. Hamilton asked.

Justin focused on the area where Mr. Hamilton had moved the water and simply nodded a yes to his teacher. Another ball of water shot out of the creek and toward Justin's chest. The speed surprised Justin so much that he forgot about using the energy and instead quickly dropped to the ground to avoid being hit by the water ball.

"You stayed dry, but the purpose of this lesson is for you to develop your Elementer abilities, not your athletic ability," Mr. Hamilton said.

Justin stood up and dusted off his pants. "Yeah, yeah. It just surprised me. Do it again."

"Be ready this time," Mr. Hamilton raised another ball of water out of the creek and shot it toward Justin. He tried to push the oncoming energy to the left, but that just seemed to stretch the ball out into a long strip of water making it a wider obstacle to avoid. Justin had to lunge down to the right to avoid being hit.

"Another one's coming," Mr. Hamilton warned. Justin jumped back up on to his feet. This time, he maintained the ball's shape and began to move it, but not enough. At the last moment his arms instinctively shot up in front of him as a barrier to block the water. He got sprayed, but at least it wasn't a direct hit. By the fourth and fifth balls, Justin finally began developing a feel for manipulating the water and redirected the balls away from him. "Well done," Mr. Hamilton said. Justin began to relish in his triumph, but realized Mr. Hamilton wasn't stopping. "Get ready!" His teacher warned.

This time, three water balls rose up out of the creek.

"Three?" Justin exclaimed. The balls suddenly exploded into mist above the creek. Justin hadn't done it. He looked at his teacher. "How'd you make them explode?"

"I just directed the water molecules apart because you seemed scared of three little balls of water. If this is too much for you, we can stop," Mr. Hamilton teased.

"Bring it on!" Justin said with confidence, but his eyes grew wide as the three new water bombs shot toward him. Justin only had time to deflect one of the balls. The other two hit him in the stomach and chest. "Not fair. I can't connect with three balls at the same time."

"Don't try to connect to them separately. They're all part of the same energy. Connect to the water element as a whole. You can theoretically influence all of the water around you at once," Mr. Hamilton said.

"Theoretically? Can you do it all at once or can't you?" Justin asked.

"It's possible. You're only limited by the amount of energy you can manage. Some Elementers can handle more than others. I suspect, with training, you'll be able to manage quite a bit. Now let's do that again," Mr. Hamilton said.

Justin continued to serve as target practice for Mr. Hamilton until he could regularly deflect five water balls at once. He ended up being hit by seven or eight, but at least his shirt was the only thing really wet.

"Okay, Raven. Now I need you to see if Justin can stay clean. Why don't you send him some mud pies?" Mr. Hamilton said.

Raven stood up with a hesitant look on her face. "Are you sure?"

"He needs more practice with the earth element."

"Okay." Raven turned to face Justin and asked, "Are you

ready?"

Justin nodded and noticed the mud near the water's edge begin to move. It reminded him of a big brown slug. A lump of the mud seemed to leap up and fly toward him. He focused on the energy and pushed it to the side so that it landed a couple feet away from him. Raven lobbed a few more mud pies toward Justin, but he easily protected himself by pushing them to the side.

"Raven. He's ready for the next level. Send more at once and shoot them faster," Mr. Hamilton said.

Raven didn't say anything. But she clearly was uncomfortable throwing mud at him. Justin found her hesitation funny and couldn't help but tease. "I thought you were experienced at this, Raven. But I guess that's all a girl can do."

Raven's eyebrows raised and she smiled, "Oh, I'll show you what a girl can do." Without warning, four lumps of dripping mud shot out one after another from the creek's edge aimed directly at Justin. He quickly pushed the first one back in the direction from where it came causing it to collide and stop the next two shots. He just barely redirected the fourth causing it to careen within inches of his waist and hit a tree a few feet behind him. But before he had time to gloat another pack of mud bombs shot toward him. He stopped the first four coming at him, but the fifth large glob of mud hit him. The surprise caused him to lose his concentration and also his connection making him temporarily defenseless against three new mud pies already heading straight for him. He dodged the first, but that just placed him in the precise position to catch the second with his face and the third with his chest. The shock of the hits caused him to lose his balance sending him to the ground.

"Justin!" Raven immediately ran over and knelt next to him, "I'm soooo sorry. I didn't mean to hit you in the face. Are you okay?"

Justin wiped the mud from his cheek. Her face stopped close to his, reminding him of his desire yesterday to touch her. Part of him wanted to reach out and stroke her cheek, but the mischievous part of him had something else in mind. That part won. He directed a stream of water from the creek dumping it on Raven.

Raven just knelt there with her mouth wide open gasping for air from the shock of the cold water. "I said I was sorry."

Justin stood up and reached out his arm to help her up. The look of shock on Raven's face caused him to start laughing. Suddenly, he felt the earth shaking beneath him. Did they have earthquakes here? Justin reached out to grab the branch of a nearby tree, but another furious shake caused him to lurch forward and fall onto his hands and knees.

"Raven. Stop that. We're here to practice," Mr. Hamilton said.

Wide eyed, Justin stared at Raven. "You created that earthquake?" Raven nodded. "Cool!" Justin said. Raven's frown slowly turned into a smile.

"Justin and Raven, we need to get back to practice," Mr. Hamilton said.

Justin looked at his teacher and whispered to Raven. "I'm thinking Mr. Hamilton is looking far too clean. We need to fix that."

Raven's jaw dropped and her eyes opened wide. "You wouldn't."

Justin smiled mischievously. "Wanna bet?" He turned toward the creek and simultaneously shot a stream of water and mud balls at Mr. Hamilton. His teacher deflected the shots of water, but he yelled as the globs of mud hit him.

Raven just stood there with her mouth wide open waiting to see how Mr. Hamilton would react. He just stood there with mud dripping off of him staring at his two students not saying a word. Finally he spoke. "Justin Wilder," Mr. Hamilton paused, causing Raven to cringe and suck in her breath, "very impressive. I expected it to take some time for you learn how to control two elements at once, but it seems that it won't be difficult after all. All you needed was the proper motivation."

Raven exhaled her breath and her shoulders relaxed. Admittedly, even Justin was relieved and grinned. He often did impulsive things and they sometimes got him in serious trouble. But he couldn't seem to resist despite the consequences.

"Raven?" Mr. Hamilton said in a serious voice causing her to cringe again.

"Yes?"

"We came here to learn. Did we not?"

"Uh, yes."

"Well then, why don't you teach Justin how to reverse this mess?"

Justin watched wide eyed as he saw the mud on Mr. Hamilton seem to lift off from his skin and clothes and fall to the ground.

"Wow! How'd you do that?" Justin asked.

"It's all earth, just spread over a larger area. It's really no different than what we just did before. Try it."

Justin envisioned all of the mud molecules vibrating and lifting free away from his skin and clothes. It took a few tries to get all of the dirt off of his clothes, but he did it. Next, he did the same with the water. It was a little trickier, but after a few tries he was fairly dry.

"Umm. Can someone help me?" Raven asked shivering now in her wet clothes.

Mr. Hamilton nodded toward Justin. "Go ahead. This is practice time."

Justin connected and agitated the water molecules trying to separate them from Raven's clothes. Some of it separated, but he caused much of the water, including Raven's clothes, to vibrate. Raven started to twist around giggling. "Ahh! Stop that."

"What?" Justin asked.

"That tickles."

Justin grinned, "Really?"

"Don't you dare! Just get the water off of me."

Justin was tempted, but he figured he had already pushed his luck dumping water on her. He focused on pulling the water away from her and let it fall into puddles around her feet.

After practicing for about an hour, Mr. Hamilton stepped toward them. "Okay, that's enough for today. We'd best head out while we're still clean."

Raven picked up her jacket off of a fallen log and began to walk in the direction they came from when she paused and turned to Justin. "Race you back?"

"You're on," Justin said. With that, Raven bolted, taking advantage of her head start. She scrambled over large boulders and fallen trees. Justin's footsteps were closing in on her, but then she thought she heard him slip. There was no time to turn and look, so she continued forward. A massive fallen trunk, whose diameter was as high as her chest, blocked her path. She decided to climb over it rather than take the time to run around it. She saw stubs of old branches that would provide footholds and decided to go for it. The improvised steps allowed her to reach the crest of the log rather quickly, but after sitting on the top and swinging her feet over, she saw that there were almost no footholds on the far side for climbing down. Analyze, plan, then act. Raven heard her dad's voice in her ear.

Twigs broke to the left signaling to Raven that Justin was about to pass her. She stepped on the best foothold she could find and leaned forward, but a loud crack sounded and Raven slipped. With nothing to grab onto except wet, slimy moss, Raven tensed herself for the worst. But before hitting the ground, she collided with something else and she grabbed on tight. It was Justin.

He must have run around the tree and reached the bottom of her makeshift slide at the same time as herself. Her heart was racing from the run and scare, but suddenly a spike of energy drove into her with such intensity that it pushed the air out of her. The energy frequency was unfamiliar and alarming. She would have let go of Justin due to the shock, but she held onto him to keep from falling over.

The power passed through her and then she felt another kind of energy rush into her, but this one pulled her toward Justin. She felt drawn toward him like negative and positive charged atoms. Raven looked at Justin's face and the pull felt even stronger. She couldn't look away. She didn't want to look away. She noticed how much she liked his smile. The urge to run her fingers through his brown, wavy hair was nearly irresistible. She stepped closer to him and released her grip on his arm to reach for his hair, when suddenly, she felt like she had been caught up in a river and had washed up on shore. The hold was gone. She gasped in a breath and noticed how close she stood next to Justin. Their faces were only a few inches apart. She quickly stumbled backward to re-establish more personal space and noticed that Justin had a dazed look on his face.

"Uh. Um." Was all either of them could say for a few moments.

A twig snapped nearby causing Raven to look away. "Raven? Justin?" Mr. Hamilton called out.

Rave sucked in a breath and responded, "We're over here." When she looked back at Justin, he had taken a few steps away but looked at her with a question in his eyes.

Chapter 16

"RIIINNNGGG." MOST OF the students snatched up their books and darted for the hallway, but Raven hesitated.

"Justin. Can I talk to you for a moment?" Mr. Hamilton called out over the sound of the school bell.

Raven fidgeted with her books as she watched Justin walk to the front of the classroom. She had spent much of science class trying to figure out how to talk to Justin. For the last few days since training in the forest with Justin and Mr. Hamilton, she felt that Justin had been avoiding her. Not so much physically. She saw him in three of her classes and he said hi. They had even talked about their science project today during class, but that was the focus of class today so he didn't have much of a choice. She couldn't quite describe it, but it felt like he had distanced himself from her ever since their training in the forest. She didn't know how to describe it and she wondered if she had simply imagined it.

When she had touched Justin in the forest, first a bolt of

energy shot through her. But after that, she had felt something else entirely. She felt a pull toward Justin that she had never experienced before. It wasn't the energy. It wasn't even what she had felt with Eric or any other guy. It was—much more. But why would she be having these feelings? She wasn't even sure what she had felt and it didn't make sense. She barely knew Justin. Maybe it was just a result of the fear and adrenalin from falling off the tree.

But why was Justin suddenly avoiding her? At least emotionally avoiding her. She wanted to ask, but what would she say? Nothing came to mind that wouldn't make her feel ridiculous. At first she thought Justin had felt it to, but he'd been so uninterested in her since then, that she was sure it was one-sided. She tried to forget about it, but she completely failed at such efforts. She just wished she knew if it was all in her head. Then she could put it behind her.

That's what she needed to do. She needed to prove to herself that it was just some freak occurrence and there was nothing between them. Then she could get back to regular life. She had struggled acting normal around Eric for the last few days and she needed to do something about it.

She slowly placed her books in her bag trying to time things so that she left the classroom when Justin finished talking with Mr. Hamilton. As Justin turned away from Mr. Hamilton's desk, Raven stopped fidgeting with her backpack and slung it over her shoulder. Justin looked up and hesitated in his step when he saw her, but she wasn't going to be deterred. It was time to get this over with and put things back to normal.

As they approached the door to the hallway, Justin halted as if he didn't want to be in close vicinity with her. The feeling of rejection hit Raven, but she steeled herself and walked into the hallway determined to put an end to this craziness. She slowed down forcing Justin to catch up to her. As they turned down a nearly empty hallway she took action.

Justin said something about their science project when she placed her hand on his arm as casually as possible. Considering the fact that her goal was to prove to herself that nothing would happen, the rush of energy took her by surprise again. This time, her knees started to buckle causing her to instinctively grab tighter onto Justin's arm to avoid falling. She felt his hand grab her other arm helping to stabilize her. Like the previous time, a rush of emotions flooded through her, but this time the buzz of energy remained and grew stronger. Somewhere, in the wash of emotions, she recognized the familiar earth frequency, but so much rushed through her that she struggled to think straight. Part of her knew she needed to let go, but another part of her couldn't resist the pull toward Justin.

She thought he leaned in closer to her, but she wasn't sure if she imagined it. Even with all the energy and emotion swirling inside of her, she noticed her heart pounding. She took a deep breath to calm herself, but she breathed in his citrus-woody scent. It reminded her of walking in the rain and the image of Justin with his wet hair and shirt coming into his living room after running in the rain flashed across her mind. She tried to say something, anything, but she couldn't find her voice. Instead, she heard a different voice. It seemed to be in the distance and calling her name, but the sensation overload prevented her from making sense of it. It called out her name a second time, much louder causing Raven to turn her head.

"Oh!" Nikki, Raven's best friend, halted a few steps away from Raven. Her jaw dropped open upon seeing Raven in such close proximity to Justin, and not Eric. Justin pulled his arms away and the rush of—whatever it was—drained away from Raven again. She wanted it back. "I, uh, was looking for you. I thought we were going to go to the game." Nikki said. She paused and looked at Justin and then back at her friend with a sly smile. "But if you're busy."

Raven blushed. "No. I—we—were just talking. Nikki, this is Justin. He's my science project partner."

"Oh, that's right. You two are studying biology together." Nikki smirked and raised her eyebrows.

Raven knew that look and grabbed Nikki's arm. "Come on. We're going to be late." She turned to Justin who stood there with his hands now in his pockets. She wanted him to pull his hands out and touch her, but not with Nikki standing there. "I'll see you tomorrow?" Justin simply nodded and Raven walked away desperately wanting to know what was going on inside his head.

Chapter 17

RAVEN ZIPPED HER jacket, pulled up her hood, and shoved her hands in her pockets. She normally loved walking in the rain, but it lost some of its appeal when the temperature dropped and the wind picked up. "Where did Mr. Hamilton say we're going to practice today?"

"What?" Justin asked.

Raven repeated louder to be heard over the howling wind. "Do you know where we're going? Hopefully, somewhere warmer."

"I vote for Texas. You need to get your pilot's license soon so we can escape to the heat when it gets like this."

Raven was relieved to have Justin cracking jokes and being more like his normal self with her again. But she made a point not to come in contact with him. After touching him yesterday, she knew the events in the forest weren't from her imagination, but she had a boyfriend and Justin hadn't shown any interest in being anything other than friends. She just needed to put it behind her and accept being just pals.

"Mr. Hamilton seriously needs to hurry up," Justin complained while walking toward Mr. Hamilton's jeep. "I'm freezing. Is it always this cold in April?"

As they neared the edge of the parking lot, Raven sensed a strange energy source nearby and halted mid-step. She tried to focus on the source but the energy pattern was muffled and unusual. It reminded her of a radio station that she couldn't tune in clearly.

"Raven?" Justin came to a stop and called her name. "Raven?" After a few moments, Raven gently shook her head and her eyes refocused on Justin. "What's wrong?" Justin asked.

Raven looked around them. "I'm not sure, but I thought I could sense a Wind Elementer nearby. But the link became fuzzy. It was strange."

"You felt another Elementer?" Justin said.

"I thought I did. I can usually sense them pretty far away, even when they're not using their powers. But this time it felt like the link was just smudged out. I've never felt that before. Weird." She rotated in a circle looking around, even though the Elementer wasn't likely to be within sight if she was struggling to sense him or her.

"Huh. Maybe they're just too far away," Justin said.

"Maybe."

Justin looked at his watch as he walked toward Mr. Hamilton's jeep. "What's taking Mr. Hamilton so long?"

"I don't know, he said he'd be done by–" Raven stopped again sensing the energy, but this time it was much stronger. She could feel someone connecting to the wind energy nearby. The wind quickly picked up greater force roaring at the top of its lungs. Her hood blew off her head and the force of the wind caused the rain to begin pelting her face. The energy started vibrating all around her. Spinning around, she squinted through the driving rain and blowing debris, but there was no Elementer in sight except Justin.

"I can feel it too. What's going on?" Justin yelled over the noise of shaking trees. Everything not tied or rooted down and smaller than a basketball started being picked up and turned into painful projectiles.

"We'd better get back inside," Raven hollered back.

"What about this Elementer?"

"I don't know if they're causing it, but we need to get indoors. Come on!"

Justin scanned one last time and then nodded in agreement. Raven turned to go but she froze when she heard a loud crack that could be heard even over the noise of the storm. She spun around in the direction of the sound to see the power pole at the edge of the parking lot falling directly toward Justin and herself.

She instinctively connected to the Earth element and with all the force she could muster yanked at a huge section of earth creating a massive pile of dirt nearly twice her height between herself and the falling pole. She pushed Justin and herself to the ground behind the temporary protective barrier. Pieces of asphalt flung themselves everywhere. She covered her head with her arms trying to protect herself from the rocks that hit her. The pole struck the pile of dirt with a loud bang. The force of the collision shook through her.

Raven looked over at Justin and he seemed to be fine. Relief poured through her, but then she heard what sounded like bacon being cooked on a human sized frying pan. Unfortunately, it was her bacon that was in danger of being cooked. Her eyes grew wide as she looked up to see that the power line had snapped and the exposed end flung itself toward them like a whip.

Before she had time to stop it, she felt the rush of energy beside her. "Got it!" Justin yelled. Another pile of dirt and asphalt leapt up from the ground, as if shot from a gun, and landed on the exposed end of the power line burying it safely under a large pile of dirt. Raven turned her head to find Justin's face only inches away from her own. It caught her breath for a moment.

"That didn't fall on its own, did it?" Justin said.

Raven slowly shook her head. "I don't think so."

Justin looked around. "Do you still feel the Elementer?"

"They're no longer connected, but I can kind of sense them."

"Where are they?"

Raven pulled herself away from Justin and crouched, slowly rotating in a circle. She stopped once she faced the forested park across the street. "Somewhere over there. I think."

"I'll be back." Justin jumped up and immediately sprinted for the park.

"Justin! Wait! It's not safe!" Raven stood up and stared agape at Justin as he ran toward the threat. She knew it was foolish to go running into the forest if this tempest was caused by someone and their attacker waited for them. But she thought about Justin facing the danger alone and began racing after him. She waited for a car to pass, that seemed to be oblivious to the fallen pole, and then ran across the street. As she headed up the path leading into the forest she heard a loud crack. "Justin!" Raven called out, running in the direction of the sounds.

She rounded two more corners in the path and still couldn't find him. Her heart beat rapidly, more out of fear than exertion. The forest hung heavy with moss and undergrowth. She slowed down trying to listen for Justin. Suddenly, a twig snapped causing her to jump. She shook her head when she realized that she was the one who stepped on the twig. "Justin," she called out in a loud whisper.

"Over here," Justin said.

She quickly rounded a corner in the path and almost ran into him, but she screeched to a halt to avoid connecting with him again. She didn't want to be losing her focus if there really was someone nearby trying to harm them.

"Can you sense where they went?" Justin asked.

Raven reached out, but like before, it felt like the energy vibration had been covered up or somehow muffled. She didn't understand it. "No. It's like they're hiding, but Elementers can't do that. I've—" Raven stopped and turned. "Do you hear that?"

Justin spun back toward the school and listened carefully. "Is that Mr. Hamilton calling us?"

"We'd better head back."

"Raven, we need to find who did this."

"I can't sense them so we don't know where to search. Besides, Mr. Hamilton might also be in danger. We need to warn him."

Chapter 18

JUSTIN SCANNED THE forest one last time and turned. "Okay. Let's go." Jogging back to the school, they called out to Mr. Hamilton who was clearly concerned about the ripped up parking lot and his two missing students. He stood near his jeep viewing the disaster area. They ran over to him and explained what happened.

"Are you sure it wasn't just an accident? The weather is terrible right now. Maybe the power pole was old and weak," Mr. Hamilton said.

"We sensed a Wind Elementer. Didn't we, Raven?" Justin said.

Raven nodded. "We felt someone connect to the Wind energy just before it crashed down toward us."

"Are you absolutely certain it was a Wind Elementer?" Mr. Hamilton turned to Raven.

Raven bit her lip. "Pretty sure." Mr. Hamilton raised his eyebrows at both of them.

Justin stepped forward. "Pretty sure? We felt him!"

"It didn't feel like a normal Elementer. The energy signature became kind of muffled—and then it just disappeared. I thought it was an Elementer when the wind picked up and the pole fell, but after that, it wasn't what I usually sense around an Elementer. I'm just not sure."

Justin folded his arms across his chest in defiance. "Somebody tried to fry us. It wasn't an accident!"

"Be reasonable. Why would anyone want to hurt the two of you?" Mr. Hamilton asked.

Justin wanted to tell them that it must have been Rex and the Council, but he knew what Mr. Hamilton would say. How to make it sound like he wasn't paranoid? "What if they're not happy that I can control multiple elements?"

Mr. Hamilton looked at Justin with a look of care, but coated with a patronizing air. "Justin, they're concerned. That's all."

"Rex said, right in front of me, that the Council is going to have to do something about me. Maybe the easiest thing to do is to get rid of me." Saying the words out loud sent a chill down Justin's spine.

"Justin, they're simply concerned about your safety. They'd never try to hurt you and they'd definitely never resort to murder."

Justin knew he should keep his mouth shout, but thoughts of his Grandpa forced the words out. "They have before." It felt good to say it, but as soon as he saw the look on Mr. Hamilton's face, he knew his theory would never be taken seriously. Mr. Hamilton was part of the establishment. Maybe not behind it, but definitely linked to the Council. If he was going to find the truth about Henry, he needed to look elsewhere.

"What are you talking about?" Mr. Hamilton said.

Justin simply shook his head. "It's nothing. Forget it."

Mr. Hamilton seemed to want to push the matter more, but after a few seconds, he sighed. "We'd better clean things up a bit and then get out of here."

Justin wanted to keep looking for their attacker, but since Raven couldn't sense them anymore, he figured they must have taken off. He and Raven followed Mr. Hamilton's instructions for making the scene look slightly more natural and soon they were driving east of town to find a secluded spot to train.

Chapter 19

SCHOOL WAS A waste of time. He couldn't remember a thing any of the teachers said. He had bigger things to worry about than Romeo and Juliet or what some famous person did a long time ago. At least it was the weekend. As he dropped his backpack on the living room floor and walked into the kitchen, he found his mom sitting at the kitchen table with her head in her hands.

"Mom?" Justin placed his hand on her shoulder.

She looked up and put a forced smile on her face. "Oh, sorry. I guess I didn't hear you come in. How was school?" As she turned toward him, he saw the photo of Henry and himself at the Grand Canyon sitting on her lap. A stab of pain shot into his chest, but he forced a smile too.

"Oh, fine." Justin sat down beside his mom. "School." As if that said it all.

"Grandma sent you a package." She nodded toward a large cardboard box with 'Fragile' written all over it and one corner dented in.

Justin found a pair of scissors sitting on an unpacked box and opened the package. He pulled out his white dress shirt. He must have left it at their house after the funeral. Underneath was a note. He read it out loud for his mom's benefit.

Justin, inside are a few of Henry's things that I think he would have wanted you to have. I miss you a lot. I'll try to visit this summer. Take care of yourself. Love, Grandma.

Justin pulled out Henry's binoculars, ham radio, Swiss Army knife, and the walkie talkies they always took while backpacking. Protected in multiple layers of bubble wrap was Henry's antique storm glass. Justin pulled it out and inspected it. He remembered Henry telling him stories of how Admiral Fitzroy used a storm glass just like this one while traveling aboard the HMS Beagle during the historic voyage with Darwin. Justin showed it to his mom. "It didn't break."

The final item was a box filled with some photographs and papers. He piled the items back in the box. "How are you doing?" Justin asked his mom.

She looked into his eyes and Justin knew the answer. But then she glanced away and said, "Fine. Your dad called and it looks like he'll be a little late, so we won't have dinner till around six."

"Okay, I'm going to put these away," Justin picked up the box and carried it upstairs to his room setting it on his desk next to his bed. He grabbed the pile of photos and sat on his bed. They were photos of Henry as a young man in his late teens and twenties. Justin had seen pictures of Henry when he was young, but he didn't recall ever seeing these specific photos. Halfway through the pile, he froze and stared at the picture in front of him. It was more recent than the others. Grandma and

Henry were sitting in their back yard with a group of friends. Judging from their age, the photo must have been taken about fifteen years ago. Justin recognized Mr. Wittington, an old friend of Henry's. There were two others he didn't recognize. But the guy sitting on the far left wore a cowboy hat and looked very much like a younger version of Rex.

Mr. Hamilton said Henry wouldn't have told Grandma about his powers, but Justin wondered now if that was true if Rex had been hanging out at their house. Justin needed to find out the truth about Rex and Henry. Even if Grandma didn't know about Henry's abilities, she might still know something that could help him. Justin pulled his phone out of his pocket and dialed his grandma.

"Yes, Grams, I've made some friends. Yes, some of them are girls." Justin shook his head. Grams loved to be a match maker for everyone around her, but this was the first time she tried to play that role with him. "But I called because I wanted to thank you for the package."

"Oh, you're welcome. Henry would be happy to know you will use them," she said.

"Thanks also for the photos. I don't think I've ever seen some them before."

"I went through his things and came across the photos in an old box. They reminded me so much of you that I thought it would be nice for you to have some of them."

"Do you remember the photo of the two of you with four other guys in your backyard? Mr. Wittington was there. It must have been about fifteen years ago."

There was a pause. "Oh, yes. We were sitting around the patio?"

"That's the one."

"Did I send you that one? I only meant to give you ones from when Henry was a young man. You wouldn't be interested in a picture with a bunch of old people."

"One of them wasn't that old."

"No, I suppose Rex would have been in his twenties back then."

"Rex? Who was he?" Justin asked.

"They were all friends of Henry."

"Friends?"

"Henry and Charles had been friends since before I knew Henry. The others Henry came to know through the years. They all shared a sort of kinship," Grandma said.

"Kinship?"

"It sounds ridiculous to say it out loud."

"What?"

"It's just—oh, I don't know how to explain it." Grams paused. "There was something special about Henry. I always had a feeling that these men and a few others I occasionally met understood it better than I did. I know that sounds silly."

"I don't think that's silly. What was special about Henry?" Justin leaned forward.

"That will sound even more absurd. I've never said anything to anybody. Henry made me promise. But now that he's no longer here, I suppose it wouldn't hurt if I told you."

"Told me what, Grams?" Justin nearly bounced through the roof in pent up anticipation.

"There was this time that—"

"What?" Justin had to resist not shouting.

Grams sighed. "Okay. When your mom was four, we took her river rafting with us down a section of the Colorado River. I had been a little hesitant to take her, but she was never quite as curious as you were, so I thought she'd be safe with the help of her life jacket and our constant watch. But, at one point, we sighted a pair of Bald Eagles overhead. We looked up for only a few moments, but when we looked down—" Justin could hear Grams voice choke. He'd never heard this story before. "When we looked down, your mother was gone. We scanned the water and Henry spotted her at least fifteen feet behind and to the side of us in the rushing water. The current was stronger in that spot and the river pulled her toward a section of rocks. My heart almost stopped. There was no way we could reach her before she smashed into the rocks."

Justin gripped his phone, unwilling to say anything as his grandma paused, transfixed by the story and not wanting to interrupt her. His grandma hesitated, but then continued. "Suddenly, a huge gust of wind blew into the canyon right toward the spot of the river where your mother struggled. I've never seen anything like it. The wind was so focused and strong that it reminded me of what it looks like when you blow on hot soup. The wind pushed the water and Mary to the side away from the rocks and then directly toward us until we could reach in to pull her out."

Grams sighed. "Henry knew better than to try to convince me it was a freak gust of wind. There had been a few strange things I'd seen around him before, but I had passed them off as the unpredictability of nature. But I knew Henry had saved Mary. I know it sounds crazy, but I just knew it in my bones. He wouldn't admit to anything, he said he couldn't talk about it. For the next couple days, I was upset with him because I was sure he was keeping secrets from me. But he finally came to me and admitted that he had helped Mary, but he said he couldn't tell me how. He asked me if I loved and trusted him. I did. So he asked me to not ask for an explanation and to never tell anyone what happened that day."

"What does this have to do with the people in the photo?" Justin said.

"I just told you this story and you're asking me about a photo? Were you listening?" Grandma said.

Justin was so intent on learning the truth about Rex, he wasn't being careful about how things appeared to his grandma. It was clear she didn't know about Elementers. "Yes, I heard. If you say that's what you saw, I believe you."

"Thank you, Justin. It was hard knowing Henry kept something from me, but I believe in my heart that it was something he had to do. But I sometimes felt that others knew his secret. Whenever Charles and a few others were around, including the men in that photo, I couldn't help but feel like an outsider. A special bond existed between them. Honestly, I felt like he shared that bond with you too. I didn't resent it. I loved the fact that the two of you were so close, but I couldn't help but wonder if—"

"Wonder what?" Justin said.

"If he had told you his secret."

It was the first time that Justin was glad Henry hadn't told him the truth. At least it made it possible for Justin to tell the truth to Grams. "No, he never said anything to me. But you're saying the guys in the photo were his close friends?"

"Charles, yes. But the others—it was more like they belonged to the same club. Henry and Rex were simply too different. I once asked Henry why he invited Rex over when they so often disagreed on just about everything. Henry just shook his head and sighed. They were kind of like brothers who didn't get along. They seemed to stick together out of requirement rather than choice."

Justin sat up straighter. Rex had always been against Henry. He replayed the conversation between Rex and Alexei in his mind. This all confirmed what Alexei said.

"But what's the interest in an old photo?" Grams asked.

Justin nearly jumped in surprise. He was so absorbed in thoughts about Rex's guilt that Justin forgot that he was still on the phone with Grams. "Oh, nothing. I was just curious who Henry's friends were." Justin thought that this all just further proved that Rex had always been against Henry. Justin would prove Rex's guilt and avenge his grandpa.

Chapter 20

ON TUESDAY, JUSTIN threw himself onto his bed exhausted after his training session with Mr. Hamilton. It wasn't nearly as much fun without Raven. Mr. Hamilton pushed him hard, but Justin knew he made a lot of progress. Other than a few uncontrolled flying ice shards that didn't hit either of them, he'd kept his powers from causing any major disasters. He needed progress if he was going to stand up against Rex and his friends on the Council. That had been almost all he had been able to think about. Well, everything except maybe Raven.

She hadn't come to training today and wouldn't be available for Thursday's training either. Justin knew why. It was Eric. She invited Justin to come along on Thursday to the movies with a group of her friends. But Justin knew Eric would be there and the thought of hanging out watching another guy with his arm around Raven didn't sit well with Justin. Besides, someone was trying to hurt or kill him. He needed to focus on learning how to protect himself.

During training, Mr. Hamilton taught him how to turn

water into ice by slowing down the particles until they froze. Justin began cooling water and built up to slush balls. He struggled getting the right consistency for snowballs. Either they were too wet or he turned them into blocks of ice. Not the safest projectile. Finally, he succeeded in building an ice bridge over a small creek. The poor construction and his inexperience in walking on ice were not a good combination. He gently touched his bruised hip where he fell on his ice bridge. At least he was still in one piece. Not something he could say for the bridge.

After getting the hang of freezing water, Justin asked Mr. Hamilton about doing the opposite--speeding up the particles until they started boiling. It seemed simple enough, but a serious look spread across Mr. Hamilton's face.

"Justin, it's time to talk about fire."

"Yeah, why isn't there a fire element?" Justin asked.

"Justin, fire isn't an element like the rest. Fire is a chemical reaction between oxygen and fuel. It's a force of destruction. When we use the elements to destroy life, doing so destroys something within us. There are two main rules for Elementers."

"Two now? I thought there was only one: avoid doing or saying anything that would expose our secret. How many more are you going to dump on me?"

"This is important. You can't use the elements to destroy life. Not only because you shouldn't damage nature or people, but also because our connection to the elements goes both ways. We can affect the elements, but that connection affects us too. If we use the elements to destroy life, that destructive energy reflects back into us. It affects us deeply. Elementers have gone mad by using their powers in destructive ways."

"Then why do you use me as target practice during training?"

"I might have given you a bruise or two, but I have never

destroyed life during our training sessions."

"Raven exploded rocks."

"It's only a problem when you destroy living things."

"But what about when I created that microburst?"

"Exactly. Why do you think Rex was so angry?"

"Rex is always angry."

Mr. Hamilton shook his head. "How did you feel after the microburst?"

"Nauseous and dizzy. But that's because I used a lot of energy."

"Using lots of energy at once can be dangerous and it will wear you out, but the destruction you caused to all those trees, other plants, and possibly a few animals reflected back on you. How did it make you feel? I'm not talking physically."

"Angry. But that's because of Rex."

"It wasn't just Rex. It's hard to explain, but when an Elementer destroys life, it begins to destroy their soul. That's why using fire isn't allowed. It creates destruction both in the world and in the Elementer."

"But I feel fine now," Justin said. "It hasn't affected me."

"I'm certain it affected you, but the real damage comes from repeated use."

"So it can be used occasionally?" Justin asked.

"No!" Mr. Hamilton lowered his voice, but the intensity was still there. "Never. Elementers have thought that in the past. But as they used fire, it affected their soul and perspective to such an extent that they couldn't even see the change in themselves. They were blind to the decay inside of them, kept doing it, and soon it took them over. It always does."

"So I can't even boil water?"

"No, there's nothing wrong with boiling water. I can make the quickest hot chocolate around. But if I boiled water to destroy some animal or person, that destructive action would reflect back at me."

"So what other rules are you going to throw at me?"

"Only those two. But bad things will happen if you break them."

Chapter 21

JUSTIN FORCED HIMSELF to run down the dark road and resist looking behind to see if the white car still followed him. He didn't want to let on that he knew they were trailing him until he found a good spot to lose them. Clouds blocked out much of the light from the full moon leaving only the glow from houses and sparse street lamps to scan for an escape.

He took a turn at the end of the block and discreetly turned his head to look down the road from where he came. The white car passed under the light of a street lamp and continued to drive slow, hanging back at least sixty feet. Justin picked up his pace. After passing only five more houses, he reached another cross street and turned left trying to escape the twisted maze of residential streets.

He wasn't familiar with this neighborhood, so he hoped he was heading toward the main road. If he could reach a place with lots of people, Justin hoped he could lose himself in the crowd. He listened for the unwelcome purr of the car behind him, but he only heard his own ragged breathing and the distant ghostly chorus of hundreds of frogs.

At the end of the next block, Justin took another left and looked behind again. The white car was nowhere to be seen. Justin halted and peered down the dark, lifeless road. A break in cloud cover illuminated the street in an eerie glow. The road was empty except for a few solitary cars left in front of houses. He wasn't sure how long he stood there, but the barking of a dog pulled him out of his daze. The car didn't seem to be following him. Justin shook his head embarrassed for letting his imagination run away on him.

He resumed his normal running pace and tried to think of something other than Elementers. But one Elementer kept invading his mind. Raven. Part of him tried to push her out of his thoughts. After all, she had a boyfriend. But another part of him wanted to keep thinking about her, especially when he remembered what he felt when they touched at the park and then in the school hallway. He had replayed it dozens of times in his mind. The moment she touched him, he felt her tug on him. But even after she let go, he was still drawn toward her. He told himself to forget about it, but he couldn't.

Justin was so immersed in his thoughts that he didn't notice a car cross the same street a block down the road. When the car was nearly through the intersection, it took a wide turn at the last moment and headed in Justin's direction. The sharp turn caused the wheels to squeal and grab Justin's attention. His mind lurched back into the present, he saw the white car, and darted away.

He needed to lose the car. But how? He was fast, but not that fast. He could use his powers, but he didn't know how many people were in the car. And why hadn't they used their powers on him already? Justin didn't know, but he didn't care to stop and ask them the question.

He just hoped they didn't know where he lived. The car started following him after he had stopped at a secluded park to practice his wind energy. He hoped they sensed his use of energy and found him that way. If they knew where he lived… A chill filled his chest. No matter how irritated he was with his Dad, Justin would protect his mom and dad. They had no ability to defend themselves from these kinds of people. People like Justin. Reaching another corner, Justin turned and noticed a small park up ahead. Upon reaching it, he ran across the grass, past the playground, and reached the other side of the park leading to another part of the subdivision. The car would either have to drive across the grass through the park or travel far around to reach the road Justin was now on. The white car slowed slightly as it passed the park, but it continued on and Justin could hear the engine gun and pick up speed once it was out of sight.

Justin wasn't sure how much time the shortcut would give him, but he knew he'd better make good use of it. The street curved to the left and as Justin came around the corner, he saw it terminate in a dead end. He thought this might be his dead end if he didn't find a way out and fast. All the houses lined up in a circle cornering him in. But then a small opening came into sight. The gate to the backyard of one of the homes remained open. Justin hoped that meant the yard wasn't holding a large dog that wouldn't appreciate visitors. Lights were on in the nearby living room, so Justin carefully snuck across the lawn, but when heard the sound of a car closing in on him his concern about the house's occupants disappeared and he sprinted into the backyard.

Half way to the back fence Justin tripped on something in the dark. The collision sent him sprawling to the ground and rolling into the side of a metal storage shed causing a loud clatter. Justin scampered behind the shed and waited a few moments in the dark to make sure the home owners didn't open the back door to check on the noise. He scanned the yard and groaned when he noticed that the back fence stood as tall as himself.

When no one came out of the house, Justin stood up, eyed the fence, and took a run at it gaining enough momentum to successfully pull himself up and over the wall. Unfortunately, the landing wasn't as successful. He dropped on top of a large, hard object and rolled to the ground. Something hissed behind Justin. He spun on his knees only to discover he had fallen on a dog house. Justin jumped to his feet and backed up. Another hiss came out of the dog house. He stopped. Dogs don't hiss.

A set of whiskers and pointed ears peered out from the dog house. Justin laughed. It was just a cat. The orange and black striped face emerged and hissed again. Justin's shoulders relaxed and he whispered, "Hey, kitty." The feline stepped out of the shadows of the dog house. "Holy hugeness. Who's been feeding you?" The cat was easily as big as most medium sized dogs. The feline took a couple steps toward Justin, made an unearthly shrieking sound, and swung her claws at his leg. "Watch it!" Justin took a step back but she continued to approach and swung again scratching his shin. "Ow!" A light in the house turned on. Justin glared at the temperamental, overgrown feline and then turned and ran away along the side of the house, opened the gate, and sprinted down the street telling himself that he wasn't running from the cat. He just didn't want to be seen by whoever lived in the house.

He made it the next few miles back to his house without seeing the white car again. Upon finally reaching his house, he closed the front door behind him with a sigh of relief. He said a quick hello to his mom, hurried upstairs to his bedroom, shut the door, turned off the lights, and closed the curtains. In the dark, he sat by his bedroom window peering through a slit in the curtains into the night keeping an eye out for the white car or any other Elementers. He sat there, keeping watch for hours. He wanted to talk to Raven or Mr. Hamilton, but during the last few weeks he had never asked for their phone numbers since he could always reach them with Earth or Water Talking. He didn't dare use his energy to Talk to them right now since that could lead the people in the white car to his house. Instead, Justin camped out by his window, trying not to spend his time thinking about Raven being out at the movies with Eric. Justin finally gave up the watch by midnight, pumped out a bunch of pushups to expend some energy, and dropped onto his bed hoping that no one showed up while he slept.

Chapter 22

JUSTIN SHOVED HIS English book into his backpack and looked up to see Raven standing beside his desk. "Hello," she said.

"Hi. How was the movie?" Not that Justin really wanted to know about her 'not-a-date'.

"It was pretty good. How did practice go?"

"Good. There were no–" Justin almost said 'no explosions', but he remembered his classmates nearby, so he rephrased his response. "No accidents. I learned a lot. You're coming with us on Saturday to meet with Anya right?"

"Definitely. She's great."

"Want to practice again after school on Monday?"

Raven bit her lip. Justin was beginning to recognize that look. "Monday? How about Tuesday instead?"

"Don't tell me, Eric again." Justin didn't hide the irritation in his voice.

"No, not Eric again. Nikki and I are going to watch the basketball game," Raven said defensively.

"That Eric is playing in, right?"

"Justin, it's a basketball game. They're fun. Why don't you come with us?"

"I think we have other things we need to be doing right now after the," Justin lowered his voice, "attack."

"Justin, I know it's important, but I can't put my entire life on hold."

"I'm not asking you to." Justin wanted to tell her about the white car from last night, but the conversation was going in the wrong direction. "It's just that someone—" he stopped and glanced at his classmates who hadn't yet rushed away for lunch. It was so easy to be with Raven when they were alone. But how was he supposed to talk to her with others around when nearly everything they had to say was secret? "Last night—"

"What?" Raven said.

Justin shook his head. What was the point? She had her own life. "Forget it. I can take care of it myself."

Raven just stared at him for a moment. "Fine." She took one last look at him and then picked up her backpack and walked past him and out the door.

Justin wanted to kick something, but satisfied himself by saying, "Fine!" Not that Raven could hear him.

"I overheard your conversation," Lewis said.

The comment made Justin jump. "What?" Justin's heart sped up as he tried to recall exactly what he said to Raven and how to make it sound like something else.

"I heard what you said," Lewis repeated. "Are you completely insane?"

"Uh, what do you mean?" Justin was pretty sure he'd been careful. What had he said about the Elementers?

"Raven asked you to go to a game with her and Nikki

Valentino and you said no. Are you an idiot?"

Justin laughed. He'd much rather be insulted than have Lewis find out about his powers. "Why am I an idiot?"

"You said no to going out with Nikki Valentino. That has to be the surest sign of an insane brain."

"You like Nikki?"

"Don't you?" Lewis said.

"Not my type."

"What, Raven's your type?"

"Raven? No. Besides, she already has a boyfriend," Justin said.

"Then why did she ask you to go to the game with her?"

"We're just friends."

"Wait. How have you already buddied up to Raven, one of the best looking girls in the school, when you've only been here a couple weeks? I've been here almost a year and can barely get Nikki to say two words to me."

"Women can't resist me," Justin joked.

"Yeah, right."

"We also happen to have been assigned as partners for our science project."

"She has to talk to you. Now that makes more sense." They had reached the cafeteria and joined the long line to buy lunch. "So, you need to tell Raven you'll go with her to the game."

"Why?"

"Because Nikki will be there and I'm coming with you."

"I don't know. I think Raven is pretty irritated with me right now. She probably doesn't want me coming any longer."

"Oh, that's right. The women can't resist you because you're so smooth with them."

"Whatever. I don't see Nikki over here asking you to go out tonight."

"That's because I'm busy. A bunch of us are going out

tonight to eat downtown and afterward we're going across the street to go bowling. Want to come?" Lewis asked. He added with a mischievous smile, "I know Amanda wants you to come."

He still didn't entirely feel like being social, but he figured it was better than sitting at home while Raven was likely out with Eric. "Yeah, I could use some down time."

Chapter 23

JUSTIN SAT DOWN in the booth of the diner and Amanda scooted in next to him.

"You're Mom's really talkative," Justin said as he turned to Lewis across the table.

Lewis laughed, "Yeah, sorry. She's a reporter and wants to know everything about everyone. I always get drilled with questions about my day. Just be glad you're not the topic of some story. She never stops until she has all the answers. She can be a real bull dog."

"Like you're all that different," Amanda said.

"Me?" Lewis said.

Amanda turned to Justin. "Lewis can find anything online. It's a game we sometimes play. We ask him to find any bit of information, and he tracks it down in no time. I don't think it's always legal how he does it." Amanda gave Lewis a look. "But it's amazing to see. Besides, Lewis' mom is super nice."

"I suppose. But you've never been between her and what she wants to know. She never lets up. Anyway, she'll pick us up down the street at the bowling alley at nine. So be prepared to give a play by play of the night," Lewis said. Amanda and Joyce just shook their heads.

The food arrived while the girls were telling Justin about Ms. Chalmers falling off the stage at the last school assembly. Justin thought about how good it felt to laugh and feel like a regular teenager. He hadn't laughed since— He realized he hadn't laughed since Henry's death. But during that thought he looked up to see Raven and a few of her friends walk in the door to the restaurant. Raven was wrapped up in a conversation with someone. Justin figured it must be Eric. The group sat down at a table on the other side of the restaurant.

Throughout the meal, Justin tried to ignore the other table, but every once in a while, his ears would catch Raven's voice and he'd force himself to not look over there. As his friends were finishing up their meal, Justin felt a buzz of Earth energy. He automatically looked over at Raven's table but she and Nikki weren't there.

"Justin? Earth to Justin. Are you ready to go?" Lewis asked.

"Oh, yeah," Justin shook his head to clear his thoughts of Raven.

"Let's head over to the bowling alley," Lewis said.

As they began to get up from their seats, they hear a scream from the kitchen followed by the sound of numerous kitchen pots crashing to the ground. Justin turned to look through the large window opening into the kitchen and saw huge flames engulfing half of the kitchen. A fire alarm began blaring throughout the building and a few kitchen employees climbed over the counter, trying to swiftly escape the fire behind them.

All at once, everyone seemed to launch from their tables

and catapult for the front door. The doors couldn't fit the mob all at once, resulting in a frenzied shoving match. By the time Justin and his friends made it out the door, Justin noticed the guy Raven had been walking with standing amongst the crowd, but Raven wasn't with him. A heavy rock seemed to plummet to the bottom of Justin's stomach. Where was Raven?

Justin rushed over to the guy Raven came in with. "Where's Raven?" Justin demanded.

"She and Nikki went to the bathroom. They must be around here somewhere," the guy stopped and looked at Justin like he was a lower life form. "Who are you?" Just then the guy's phone rang. He pulled it out of his pocket, looked at the screen, and answered, "Raven? Where are you?"

"Where is she?" Justin asked.

The guy listened to his phone for a moment. "If there's a fire in the hallway, sit tight in the bathroom. I'm sure the fire engines will be coming soon."

Justin didn't wait to hear more. Without thinking, he hurried over to one of the employees. "There must be a back door. What's the quickest way to it?"

The guy pointed to the right. "Go past the stores, take a left, and turn into the alley." Justin bolted in that direction.

"Justin, where are you going?" Lewis called after him, but Justin didn't take time to answer. He knew he had found the back door when he came upon a few more diner employees standing in the alley involved in a heated discussion about what happened. Justin immediately headed for the door.

"What are you doing?" yelled an older man who must have been the manager.

Justin quickly realized that it would be faster to get rid of the guy rather than argue with him about the wisdom of entering a burning building. "Um, I was looking for the manager. There are a bunch of official people out front asking for the manager," Justin said.

"Oh, thanks," the man hurried in the direction Justin came from with the rest of the employees walking behind. With his audience removed, Justin carefully touched the door handle to make sure it wasn't too hot. That was the only caution he felt he had time to indulge in. He yanked open the door and waved his hands through the smoke in a vain attempt to see better.

"Raven!" Justin yelled. But he heard no response. "Raven!" he hollered again as he walked further into the smoke filled haze. His nose and throat began to burn from the smoke inducing an involuntary coughing fit. With his throat on fire, yelling was difficult, but he realized he didn't need to yell. Lowering himself to his hands and knees to get below the worst of the smoke, Justin connected to the earth element and reached out. "Raven! Where are you?" he called.

"Justin? Is that you?"

"Yes, where are you?"

"We're in the bathroom at the end of the hallway along the right side of the restaurant. We can't get out because there's a huge fire at the end of the hallway. What's going on?"

"I'm not sure what happened, half the kitchen is on fire. Can you use your powers to get out?"

"No. I don't know how I could. I'm in here with Nikki." Raven stopped and her connection got a little fuzzy. "Uh, no, Nikki. I didn't say anything. Please stay at the back of the bathroom. I'm just plugging the bottom of the door with wet paper towels." She paused again and the connection cleared up. "Sorry, Justin. I'm in here with Nikki. I don't know how to stop the fire and I can't very well use my powers to break down a wall with Nikki here. She's not going to believe that happened naturally unless I create an earthquake and that might cause the roof to come down on us. Please tell me you're here to help."

"Of course. Just stay away from the door and give me a minute."

"Thanks."

"No problem," Justin spoke with far more confidence than he felt. He dropped the connection with Raven and focused his concentration on stopping the fire. He crawled forward until he could really feel the heat against his skin. He reached out to the water element and focused on the sinks to the right of him. Much like the water fountain, he urged the water out of the tap, but made sure he used a little less pressure to avoid uprooting the sink. Directing the water toward the fire near the hallway, Justin expected the fire to go out easily, but instead the water just strengthened and spread the fire. It dawned on him that this must be a grease fire. Duh! He just made things worse. So much for being the hero.

Flames began taking over even more of the kitchen and attempted to engulf him. Justin backed up slightly and tried to figure out how to put out the fire. Peaking over the counter, he caught sight of a fire extinguisher. Unfortunately, it was near the kitchen doorway leading to the bathrooms and the intense blaze completed surrounded it.

Justin mentally did an inventory of the elements available to him. Water wasn't going to work. Trees certainly weren't much help. They'd just serve as fuel for the fire. The Earth element? No. Not unless he wanted to bury the restaurant in dirt. All he had left was wind. But wouldn't that just make it stronger like when he blew on a campfire to get it started? Arghh! Something had to work. Wait. Candles can be blown out. They just needed enough wind force relative to their size. Justin thought that maybe hurricane force winds might be able to blow out the fire. He worried about making things worse. But he had no time to argue the matter in his head. Wind it would be.

Opening himself up to the Wind element, he could feel the energy swirling around him. The fire had a chaotic effect on the air around him, making it difficult to focus and direct the wind. He realized he needed to create some hard core air current and that would require a clear path. Quickly accessing the earth element, he used the energy to yank open the back door, but in his urgency he ripped the door right off its hinges. Oops! Oh well, Justin thought, it was out of the way. Focusing again on the air he began pulling in the wind from behind the restaurant, through the kitchen, and out through the front of the building.

The flames seemed to enjoy the fresh source of oxygen and burned even stronger. For a moment, a very brief one, Justin considered defeat since everything he tried seemed to make the fire more dangerous. But his stubbornness, the thought of Raven in danger, and his desire to be able to help Raven even though he hadn't been able to prevent his grandpa's death, all combined to overcome his doubts. He thrust all of the energy he could control into the air. The wind picked up so quickly that it flung him forward, but he caught himself before face planting the floor. Pots, cupboard doors, and anything loose began rattling and as the wind continued to pick up. A spatula flew forward, hit him in the back of his head, and continued hurtling past him. Suddenly, a slew of other items became dangerous projectiles shooting toward the front of the restaurant. Justin dropped to his stomach and instinctively placed his arms over the back of his head.

It was hard to will the wind forward while it posed such an immediate danger to him, but he knew he needed faster speeds so he stayed down and directed it onward. As the howl of the growing wind rushing through the kitchen replaced the sound of rustling knives, Justin lifted up his head. The flames were struggling against the strong wind, but they still burned. Justin needed more.

POWER REVEALED

Sweat poured down his face. He mentally reached out far from the restaurant and willed the air toward him. He heard a deep roar from far away, then it grew louder. Suddenly, the wind rushed with so much force through the back door, into the kitchen, and past the seating area that it caused some of the front windows of the restaurant to explode outward. Justin could feel the wind pushing him along the floor and nearly lifting him off the ground for brief moments. The gale shoved him toward the front of the kitchen, the area under fire. Justin reached out to a cupboard handle and held on tight to avoid moving forward. He couldn't feel the blistering heat on his skin anymore, but that might be simply because of the speed of the wind rushing past his body.

He needed to know if the fire was out because he couldn't keep this wind up much longer or he'd endanger more people from the gale force winds. Justin couldn't see the hallway from behind the counter, but if he let go of the cupboard handle, he knew he might be pushed into the fire. Turning his head to look toward his feet, he couldn't see any flames in that area, so he released his grip on the handle. The wind propelled him along the floor and shoved him against a cupboard near the sinks.

Hoping to see all the flames gone, he was distraught to see the fire burning in the only place he absolutely wanted to extinguish it, the hallway to the bathrooms. The hallway was a dead end. The wind must have flowed in the direction of least resistance, toward the front of the restaurant. He was about to try and raise another wind gust, but his eyes fell on the fire extinguisher which had previously been blocked by the fire. Justin released the wind energy, jumped up, ran over, and grabbed the extinguisher. "Owww!" Justin dropped the extinguisher and it crashed to the floor. Justin's hands burned from touching the fire heated metal. *Way to use your brain,*

Justin thought. Pulling off his jacket, he used it as makeshift oven mitts to handle the hot exterior of the fire extinguisher. Hurrying over to the hallway, he squeezed the handle and hoped it would work. The foamy mixture sprayed on the flames and Justin inched forward as the flames were extinguished.

Finally, Justin couldn't see any flames amongst the smoke filled building. He dropped the extinguisher and hurried forward and knocked hard on the women's bathroom door. It hurt his hands, but he didn't care. "Raven! Are you okay? The fire's out. Raven!" He pushed at the door which resisted as if it were stuck in mud.

"We're here. Just a minute. Let me move the paper towels." Hearing Raven's voice, Justin's heart skipped a beat. He took a deep breath of relief but coughed from the smoke. Raven's face appeared in the opening door. Justin's throat felt like it had been rubbed with sand paper, his eyes burned, his skin felt like he had a bad sunburn, and everything stunk like burned toast. But the sight of Raven's smile was all that registered to him at that moment. Raven reached out and grabbed his arm. Her touch sent a bolt of energy through Justin. Like before, all four energy forces seemed to combine and pull him toward Raven. Their eyes locked and he felt like he was connected not just to Raven but to the universe.

His hand involuntarily lifted to touch her face when the door opened wide and something leapt out at him. "Thank you!" Justin staggered back as arms encircled his neck. Long, blonde hair flew into his face and he was pushed him back breaking his hold on Raven's hand. The rush of energy cut off and Raven crumpled to the ground. Nikki, the owner of the blonde hair, noticed her friend fall and spun around to help her. "Raven!"

Justin dropped down beside Raven and reached out to help lift her up. As he touched her, Raven's body shuddered. He pulled back immediately. He wanted to help her, but he suspected he was the reason she was on the floor. Did she feel the same things he felt when they touched? But why did it seem to jolt her worse? Justin knelt beside Raven, but made sure he didn't touch her. "Are you okay?" Raven looked up at him searching his eyes. Justin wondered if she was asking the same questions, but he wouldn't ask with Nikki nearby.

Before he could say anything more, a deep voice boomed out. "Is anyone in here?" All three of them turned to see a large fireman coming around the corner. "Are you guys okay?"

As the fireman carried Raven out of the building, Nikki sprung into a long dialogue of the trauma she and Raven experienced and how Justin heroically saved them. Justin did all he could to downplay his involvement. He explained that by the time he entered the back of the restaurant, the flames were all out except in the hallway and all he did was use the fire extinguisher to put out the fire near the bathrooms. The fireman was impressed with Justin's courage, but scolded him for entering a burning building since that was the role of firefighters.

When Raven noticed Justin favoring his hands, she absolutely refused to be examined by a medic until someone began treating the burns on Justin's hands. While experiencing the pain of the ointment application, he overheard numerous comments within the crowd about the strange wind that seemed to miraculously put out the fire. Justin was thinking about the earth energy he felt before the fire ignited. He kept trying to feel if he could sense other Elementers nearby, but he couldn't feel a thing. Justin needed to talk to Raven. Finally, he found a moment when the medics and Raven's friends were all occupied. Justin walked over to Raven who sat in the back of the ambulance.

"Sorry, Raven." Justin said it quietly, trying to avoid anyone hearing him.

"Sorry for saving my life?"

"No. I'm sorry for being a jerk earlier."

"Well, I suppose saving my life is one way to make up. I just hope you don't have a habit of doing such grand apologies. I don't want to go through that again."

"Raven, I felt some earth energy just before the fire. Was that you?"

"No. I noticed it too, but when you showed up to rescue us, I figured it was from you. It wasn't?"

"No. I think an Earth Elementer started that fire," Justin said.

"We're not allowed to use fire."

"I know. But I think whoever attacked us last week and followed me last night, probably isn't very concerned with following the rules. They could have killed you. Twice."

"Followed you? Who did? Why didn't you tell me?" Raven asked.

"I tried to this morning, but I couldn't with others nearby and then I went and made you mad at me."

"I'm sorry. Who followed you?"

"I don't know. They didn't do anything but trail me in their car," Justin said.

"Justin. What are we going to do?"

Justin could see the anxiousness in her eyes. "We'll figure it out," Justin said with far more confidence than he felt. "Remember. You said yourself that I have more power than anyone else. I'll just send another microburst if I need to protect us."

"I don't want you to hurt yourself using destructive energy," Raven said.

"It'll be okay. We're meeting with Anya tomorrow. Maybe she has some information that can help us. I won't let anything happen to you. I promise. You're still coming, aren't you?" Justin asked.

"Definitely. Besides, I've always wanted to see her house."

"What's special about her house?" Justin asked.

"You'll see."

Chapter 24

MR. HAMILTON DROPPED the newspaper on Justin's lap as he sat down in the jeep. "So how's the hero this morning?" Mr. Hamilton asked.

Justin looked at the newspaper and gaped at the headline: "Boy Rescues Friends from Fire." Below the bold text sat a photo of him standing next to Raven being treated beside the ambulance.

"You've had your powers less than three weeks and you're already front page news. That has to be some kind of record. I'm sure this will help convince the Council I can help keep your powers under control and a secret," Mr. Hamilton shook his head.

"All you care about is what the Council thinks of you," Justin turned toward his teacher.

"No, it's not about me. It's about you. And it's serious, Justin. If the Council doesn't believe I can help you manage your powers and maintain our secret, they will step in and I'm not sure what they'll do to you."

"They don't own me," Justin said.

"What were you thinking using your powers like that?" Mr.

Hamilton asked.

"It's not my fault. I think another Elementer started the fire. Both Raven and I felt the earth energy just before the fire started."

"Another Elementer? Not that again."

"We both felt it. There was a burst of Earth power right before the fire started."

"Are you sure it wasn't your own powers?"

Justin glared at his teacher, "I did not start that fire. I suppose you're also going to suggest I imagined the car that followed me last night."

"What car?"

"Last night, after you dropped me off, I noticed a white car tailing me. It kept pursuing me. I finally had to cut through some yards and jump fences to lose them. I was worried they were going to show up at my home."

"Why didn't you call me?"

"I didn't have your phone number and I was worried that I'd lead them to my house if I used the energy to Talk to you."

Mr. Hamilton glanced over toward the forest contemplating something. "What did the driver in the car look like?"

"It was dark. I couldn't see them."

"Did you see who started the fire?"

"No," Justin stared at his lap.

"Did you even try to find them?"

"Excuse me. I was busy. Raven was stuck in the middle of an inferno and I didn't want her to die."

"Justin, I'm glad Raven is safe, but you can't go around risking the safety of other Elementers by parading your talents so publicly," Mr. Hamilton said.

"If I hadn't used my powers, it would have meant the likely death of one Elementer, and I don't care what the Council has to say. Raven's safety means a whole lot more to me than their little secret."

"Justin, that secret isn't just protecting their lives. It's protecting your life too."

"It's my life to risk. Raven was in danger. I wasn't about to let her be hurt," Justin said.

Mr. Hamilton looked past Justin, "Oh, good morning, Raven."

Justin spun around in the passenger seat to find Raven step forward and place one of her hands on the open window of the jeep next to Justin. "Hi, Mr. Hamilton," she nodded at her teacher, but she was staring at Justin. "Hi, Justin."

"Hi," Justin's face heated up.

"How are your hands?" Raven said looking from his face to his hands.

"Your hands?" Mr. Hamilton asked.

Raven looked up at Mr. Hamilton. "He burned them picking up a hot fire extinguisher when coming to help Nikki and I." She reached out to lift Justin's hands to look at them, but just before touching him she suddenly stopped and pulled back her arms. "How are they feeling?"

"They're fine. It's no big deal." Justin's hands actually woke him up a couple times during the night when he rolled over and bumped them. But he wasn't going to admit that and make Raven feel guilty.

"At least you used the fire extinguisher near the end," Mr. Hamilton said. "The news article just makes you sound like a foolish hero, instead of someone with supernatural powers."

"They said I was foolish?" Justin said.

"No," Raven spoke up. "I read it this morning. They said you were a hero. Thanks again for saving our lives."

"Oh, no big deal."

"It was my life and I consider that a very big deal. But Mr. Hamilton is right. You shouldn't have risked exposing yourself."

"What? Do you think I was going to just stand there and hope the firemen arrived before you burned to a crisp?"

"That's what everyone else did." Raven looked down.

"I'm not everyone else."

Raven lifted her face, looked intently into Justin's eyes, and smiled. "Yes, I've noticed. I'm glad you're—you." Raven's words struck Justin deep. He couldn't say a word and just looked at her trying to determine her sincerity. But it was clear she meant it. No one had ever said that to him. Not even Henry, though Justin knew he felt that way. Justin was brought out of his thoughts by Raven's voice. "But you can't give the Council any more reasons to be scared of you. Please."

Justin swallowed and tried to seem nonchalant. "How about you stay out of trouble and I'll keep my powers to myself."

"Okay." Raven grinned, but Justin could see her look of concern as she climbed into the jeep.

Chapter 25

JUSTIN HAD BEEN looking forward to a long drive with Raven, but his backside was relieved to finally exit the jeep after bouncing around on a bunch of pot-holed back roads for almost an hour. He began to think they'd never reach Anya's place. The small, stone house they pulled up in front of looked to be as old as some of the nearby towering trees. He wasn't sure what he expected, but after Raven's comment about Anya's house, he definitely expected—more. When Mr. Hamilton and Raven ignored the front door and walked around behind the cabin, Justin thought it odd but he followed them.

"Where are we going?" Justin finally asked after walking for at least a minute along a dirt path in the forest.

"Anya's home," Mr. Hamilton said over his shoulder.

"Uh, didn't we just pass it?" Justin asked.

"No. That's her fake house."

"Fake house? Why would someone have a fake house?"

"You'll see," Mr. Hamilton said while continuing further into the forest.

"David!" Anya's voice called out as they reached deeper into the forest. Justin looked around, but couldn't see anyone other than Mr. Hamilton and Raven. "Come on up."

A rope ladder suddenly dropped out of the sky only 20 feet in front of them. Justin's neck snapped upwards and he peered into the tree canopy. As Justin surveyed the view above, he began to notice branches shaped in an unusual fashion. They seemed to curve and wrap around each other to form the floor, walls, and roof of the most amazing tree house he had ever seen. A huge grin spread across his face. "No way." He'd always dreamed of having a tree house, but he'd never dreamed of one this incredible.

"Justin. Come check out the view." Raven's voice broke through his thoughts causing him to notice that she was already half way up the ladder. He climbed up the ladder and poked his head through a large opening in the floor of the tree house.

A tall woman with long, wavy red hair offered her hand and pulled Justin up into the tree house. As she stood up, small braids plaited along each side of her hair swung back and forth. Bright turquoise beads at the end of each braid contrasted brightly with her vibrant red hair. Her fitted, black pants and shirt set off the radiance of her hair even further. She seemed to survey him up and down measuring him on the spot and then beamed with a smile that seemed to say something that was unreadable to him. "Hi, Justin. Welcome to my home."

"Thanks. Your home's awesome. How'd you build it?"

"I didn't build it. I grew it."

"What?" Up close, he could see large branches intertwined with one another to form the load bearing structure with smaller branches filling in to provide delicate shape and design to the home. But these weren't logs. Justin couldn't find a single cut end. He followed a few branches, but they curved and wrapped around until he lost track of them. "Wow. You've given new meaning to the term 'home grown'. How'd you do it?"

"Slowly. Even large trees like these can only be encouraged to grow so fast without causing long term damage. But Tree Elementers can help speed things along while still nurturing the tree. I love living up here and feeling free. Besides, the zip line down is a rush."

"Why do you have that old house at the road if you live in this amazing place?" Justin asked.

"This one doesn't exactly meet building codes and I'd gain more attention than I'd want if others saw it. We need to maintain our secret and that requires a low profile. So the stone house is for use when I have non-Elementers show up. But otherwise, I live here. It is a bit of a walk, but it's worth it."

"I'll say," Justin said.

"Lunch is ready." A girl with spiky, short blonde hair bounced down a set of stairs leading to an upper level. Justin guessed it was Katie. She looked to be a year or two older than him. She gave Raven a hug. "Hey, Raven."

Introductions were made and Anya suggested, "Let's head upstairs. The view is fantastic from there. The food should be great. Katie's good for something besides confusing new Tree Elementers into thinking they're talking to a tree." Anya gave Katie a parental look that clearly said that Katie still hadn't been entirely forgiven for confusing Justin.

After finishing most of his lunch, Justin finally got up the nerve to ask one of the questions he'd been wanting to ask for some time. "So, what's the deal with energy overloads when Elementers touch?"

"What do you mean?" Anya asked.

"Whenever Elementers touch. Energy seems to shoot into you and...other things happen."

"What are you talking about?" Mr. Hamilton said.

Justin looked at Raven, but she stared at her plate and her cheeks were flushed. "Raven, you explain it."

Raven raised her eyes to Justin. "You mean you felt it too?"

"Of course, I felt it. Don't Elementers always feel it when they touch?" Justin said.

"Uh, no. I've never felt it till you."

"Felt what?" Mr. Hamilton said.

"A surge of energy and—" Justin felt the heat rush into his face too.

"And what?" Mr. Hamilton repeated. When Justin hesitated to answer, Mr. Hamilton turned to Raven. "What is he talking about?"

Raven spoke in a quiet voice. "Each time we touch, a strange type of energy flows into me and I feel—" Raven slowly turned to look at Justin.

"What do you feel?" Anya asked, but Raven was suddenly mute. "Justin?" Anya asked.

"Uh, it feels like—" Justin looked at the others. "You mean none of you feel stuff when you touch?"

"You haven't really told us what happens. But no, touching another Elementer doesn't automatically cause energy to flow between us like you're describing," Anya said.

"Then why does it happen when Raven and I touch?"

"I don't know. Does it happen when you touch other Elementers?" Anya said.

"Uh, I don't think I've ever tried," Justin said.

"Now I'm curious," Katie spoke and reached out to touch Justin's hand.

Justin placed his hand in hers and waited for the energy surge.

"Um, nothing's happening. Do you feel anything?" Justin said.

"No energy and no *feelings*," Katie playfully emphasized the last word.

"Why don't you show us what you mean?" Anya said.

Justin wished he had never brought up the question. Admittedly, he really wanted to connect again with Raven and see if he felt those things another time. But in front of an audience? Oh well, he started this, so he laid his hand on the table with his palm up in invitation. Raven hesitantly placed her hand in his and the energy erupted. It reminded Justin of a volcano. The heat immediately shot into his body, energizing him. He noticed Raven's upper body jerk, probably from the shot of the energy. Justin felt Raven grip his hand tighter. It hurt a little because of the burns on his hand from the fire extinguisher, but the urge to be near her was stronger than the pain. He unconsciously shifted forward in his chair and was thrilled when she also moved closer and her leg brushed his. Justin's other hand found its way across the table and he began stroking the back of her hand with his fingers. He felt a crazy urge to touch Raven's face, but when he looked up at Raven he noticed she had a different look on her face. She looked alarmed and she seemed to be having trouble breathing. Seeing that the connection might be harming her, he forced himself to lift away his hand on top and released his grip with the other. Unfortunately, Raven had a vice grip on his hand.

"Justin, let go of her." Mr. Hamilton stood up.

"I'm trying to, but she won't let go." Justin grabbed his free hand and tried to pull Raven's hand away. "She has a death grip." Justin continued to try to pry off her fingers, but they felt like they were welded in place. "Raven. Let go of my hand. It's hurting you," Justin called out to no avail.

Perspiration began rolling down Raven's reddened face. Her eyes were wide open, but she seemed to be oblivious to everyone else. Her breathing became even more ragged. Justin looked up at Mr. Hamilton across the table. "Help me! I'm hurting her. Grab hold of her hand and I'll pull," Justin said.

Mr. Hamilton hurried to the other side of the table just in time to catch Raven as she passed out and collapsed on her chair. "Raven. Are you okay?" Mr. Hamilton gently lowered her onto the floor. "Raven, can you hear me?"

After a few moments, Raven's eyes fluttered open. "What happened?"

By this time, Anya had also circled around the table and knelt next to Raven. "When you and Justin touched, the energy flow between the two of you was too much for your body and you fainted."

Justin tried to hide his worry for Raven with a joke. "I tried to stop it, but you wouldn't release your grip. You're the first girl to ever refuse to let go of my hand."

Raven looked up at him. "I don't remember."

"David, help Raven over to the couch," Anya said.

"So what was that?" Katie asked Anya as they sat down in what seemed to be the living room of the tree house.

Anya shook her head. "I'm not sure, but I felt the energy flowing in both of them, and like Raven said, it felt strange. I think it was all four elements mixing together at once."

"Wait. How can that be? Justin may be able to access all four elements, but Raven can't," Katie said.

Anya reached out and touched Justin's arm, but nothing happened. "The connection seems to be unique to Justin and Raven. I'm guessing it's due to Raven's talent for connectedness. I think when she touches Justin she connects Justin up to his full potential to access all the energy. But when she does so, she's exposes herself to all four elements at the same time."

Anya looked at Justin. "Ever since I heard about you, I've been thinking about why you can access all the elements. A normal Elementer receives and sends their energy through what we often describe as a narrow tunnel or tube. We maintain the connection by focusing the energy within a narrow path. A path that is specific to a particular element. Even Wind Elementers manage the energy by focusing it. But it seems to be different for you. When you connected to the elements with Raven, you seemed to access the energies all around you. That's probably why you can access all four elements."

Anya continued, "Because we channel through tunnels, we can handle only so much energy at once. If we receive too much at a time, it can back up and cause an explosion within us. It has happened to Elementers before and they've lost their gift. The Council has sometimes destroyed the connection to those who broke the rules by simply overloading the Elementer with energy. But if I'm right, you have a much greater capacity to handle high loads of energy because the energy just flows around you. Raven can't handle the non-Earth elements, but on top of that, the amount of energy flowing through her was simply too much."

"Raven, until you can figure out how to limit your connection with Justin or Justin can learn to manage the amount and type of energy he accesses, the two of you need to maintain some personal space for the time being. Okay? Justin could burn your connection out." They both nodded from opposite sides of the room.

Chapter 26

"HOW CAN THE tree element help me fight against my attackers?" Justin asked while walking through the forest near the tree house with Anya and Katie.

"Justin, you've been told about the dangers of destructive energy. It's very hazardous, especially for you, due to your increased capacity. You need to learn how to use constructive energy," Anya said.

"Your tree house is great, but using my powers for construction isn't my top priority right now."

"I said constructive energy, not construction energy. We're talking about energy that builds and enhances nature versus destructive energy which destroys life. Destructive energy gets you out of balance and destroys your soul. But constructive energy repairs your soul and helps you return into balance. If you choose to use destructive energy to fight against your attackers, you'll damage, instead of protect, yourself."

"If I don't fight against them, they'll destroy me before I have the chance to do it to myself. It's not like I have much of a choice."

"There are always other choices. You just have to look hard enough and open your mind to the possibilities. You can use constructive energy against them."

"What? You think I'm going to stop a bunch of killers by overwhelming them with flowers?"

"You'd be surprised."

"Yeah, right. How can my Tree energy help me stop these guys?" Justin said.

"Use your imagination. That's your only real limit. How could you use a tree to take someone out?"

"A tree? Other than a person tripping on its root, a tree can't stop someone."

"Katie, Justin had a good idea. Why don't you show him how it's done?"

Justin felt a tickle on his ankle and glanced down. After all he'd seen over the last few weeks, he thought nothing could surprise him, but the sight of a tree root growing and wrapping around his ankles like an anaconda snake was a little creepy. "What the—?" He tried to move his feet, but the roots continued to slither up and around his legs. His bottom half might as well have been encased in cement.

"See. Just use your imagination. A tree root can be very effective," Anya said.

Justin watched as Katie caused the roots to pull back into the earth. Once he was free, he shook his legs to experience the feeling of mobility again. He looked at Katie. "How'd you do that?"

"I asked the tree nicely," Katie grinned.

"You can't actually talk to the trees, despite the fact that you made me think I had, at first," Justin said.

"Sorry about that. I would have explained things if you hadn't dropped the link," Katie said.

"You made me think I was going crazy. I still sometimes wonder if I've lost it when I see tree roots pop out of the ground and attack me," Justin said.

"So, tree roots are helpful. How else could you use plants to protect yourself?" Anya asked.

Justin scanned the overabundant greenery trying to imagine what the plants could do if they were animated. His eyes fell on a massive blackberry bush. "You could do some serious damage to someone with the thorny branches of a blackberry bush."

"Yes, I suppose it could become a painful whip or rope. But Justin, you don't want to use it as an offensive weapon. Remember, we don't want to hurt others unless absolutely necessary. The harm will reflect back onto us."

"How do you expect me to protect myself? Being a pacifist doesn't work when you're dealing with killers. I don't want to hurt anyone, but I'm not going to stand by and just let someone hurt me," Justin said.

"If an Elementer uses their powers to kill others, or even simply misuse their powers, the Elementer Council will overload the offending Elementer with so much energy that the Elementer's ability burns out and they can no longer connect. They call it the Wipe."

"But wouldn't they still be a danger to Elementers? If their powers were taken, they could still expose the secret."

"Long ago, Elementers discovered that if they applied the Wipe correctly, it had such a severe effect on the person that it wiped out their memory. A Wipe results in long term amnesia. It's still a destructive process since it does damage the person targeted, but it seems to be the least harmful option for everyone involved."

"You said I can handle more energy than other Elementers. So I should be able to do a Wipe on someone by myself."

"Justin, it isn't that simple. The equal amounts of all four energies at just the right amount must be used. If you use too much energy, you could cause them serious mental and physical damage or even kill them. You don't know the correct amount of energy to use and you're still learning to control your powers. Also, I'm not certain how your access to the elements really works. I could be wrong and the excess energy might not flow past you. It might encircle you and cause you to burn out. Besides, only Council members are permitted to Wipe another Elementer and it is even forbidden for them to do so without a two-thirds Council vote approving the Wipe."

"So I just sit and wait for another attack?" Justin asked.

"We'll find out who is threatening you and Raven, but do not, under any circumstances, try Wiping another Elementer. Promise me."

Justin stood there stubbornly for a while, but finally said, "Fine. But you need to show me other ways to protect myself."

Over the next couple hours, Raven and Mr. Hamilton watched Anya and Katie train Justin to use his Tree powers. Justin began to realize that the tree element unlocked far more power than he originally thought. He had a goose egg on the side of his forehead from losing control of a tree branch that ended up hitting him. The young branch was only half as thick as his wrist, but it easily knocked him to the ground as it swung at Justin almost as fast as a whip.

While trees carried a lot of physical strength, Anya taught Justin that even the smallest plants could be extremely effective. He just needed to learn how to take advantage of each plant's unique characteristics. Grasses weren't nearly as strong as a tree, but because they were numerous they could easily pull down, wrap up, and at least temporarily restrain even the strongest guy.

POWER REVEALED

Justin had traveled once to Africa with his Grandpa and the Acacia trees there had dangerous three inch spikes that were dangerous even when the branches didn't move. He could imagine the harm they could offer. He began to realize how vicious plants could be. Poison ivy, stinging nettle, and a long list of other poisonous plants were just some obvious examples. In addition, something as simple as pollen, if shot in concentrated form at someone, could stop them in their tracks with a sneezing fit. Anya also spent time teaching Justin how Tree energy could enhance the healing power of the plants. It all gave new meaning to the term "flower power".

After they wrapped up their training session, Anya brought him back up to the tree house and she ground up a few different leaves. As she applied the sticky glop to the bump on his head and held her hand over it, Justin felt energy tingle around the injury. The energy subsided after about a minute and Justin touched the spot. The bump had already shrunk substantially. Justin thanked Anya as she also helped speed up the healing from the burns on his hands too.

"Justin, I need to show you something." Anya motioned for him to follow her. He climbed the stairs behind her to the upper level of the tree house and stopped beside her as she knelt beside a wooden chest and pulled something out of it. She opened her hand to show it to him. "I want you to wear this."

Justin grunted and folded his arms across his chest. "You want me to wear a necklace?"

"It's not a necklace. It's an energy sphere. They are created by combining the elements using all four energies. It can measure how well balanced its wearer is. The sphere is clear if you are in balance, but if the destructive energy grows in you, the sphere will begin turning red. The deeper the color red, the more dangerous the destructive energy exists within an Elementer.

Because destructive energy distorts your perspective, energy spheres can act as an unbiased reminder to let you know that you need to get back in balance. It's never wrong."

"Do you wear one?" Justin asked.

"There was a time I needed one. During my college days I went a little off the deep end. Someone cared enough about me to intervene, put me in my place, and help me get back on track before the Council decided to step in. He gave this to me to help me see things clearer. At the time, I thought I should be able to do whatever I wanted and that the Council had no right to tell me what to do. But he told me that freedom is being who you really are, not doing what you want to do."

Justin's head snapped up to look at Anya. Something lodged in his throat. Justin had heard that saying more times than he could remember, but he'd only ever heard it from one person.

"Did Henry say the same thing to you?" Anya smiled. "Yes, it was your grandpa. He saved my life. I owe him more than I can say. Please, take the sphere and wear it. I think he would have wanted you to have it. He helped me when I really needed someone. I wish you had him to help you through this, but know that I'll do anything I can to help you." Justin could see Anya's eyes begin to tear up. It didn't really fit her tough exterior. She shook her head a few times as if to rid herself of the emotions. "Take it. It's not girly or I wouldn't have worn it either. Wear it under your shirt if it makes you happy, but put the thing on. I'm not going to let Henry down and neither are you."

Justin picked it up by the leather strap and put it on. He had to admit it wasn't so bad and he was glad to have something that represented Henry's Elementer life, something Justin had never been a part of. It made him feel like he reclaimed that portion of Grandpa's life.

"One more thing. David said you've met Alexei. Word of warning: I'd be careful around him. He can be fun. Trust me, I know. But Henry would have warned you to stay away from him," Anya said.

"What are you talking about? They were friends." Justin said.

"Henry and Alexei? Not a chance. Henry didn't support some of the more controlling aspects of the Council, but he absolutely stood up against the Elementer elitism of people like Alexei. Alexei and his buddies think that because Elementers have greater powers, we should be able to do whatever we want regardless of the consequences to non-Elementers. Henry always fought against such thinking. He believed we have these powers to serve others, not to lift ourselves above them. When I began hanging out with Alexei and his friends, your grandpa rather harshly yanked me back down to earth," Anya said and looked over at Raven and Mr. Hamilton grabbing their jackets in the other room. "Speaking of being brought down to earth, David looks like he's ready to go. I think it's time to show you the best way to be brought back down to earth. The zip line ends close to the cottage. Come on. It's a rush."

Chapter 27

THE WHISTLE BLEW and echoed through the high school gymnasium as the referee called the basketball foul. The crowd cheered.

"I'll be right back," Raven said.

"Want me to come with you?" Nikki asked.

"No, that's okay. The last time we went to the bathroom together the building almost burned down. I don't want to risk it again," Raven said. Nikki laughed, shook her head, and turned back to the basketball game.

Justin and Lewis moved their legs to the side to let Raven pass and she walked down the steps along the bleachers. Less than a minute later, Lewis spoke up. "Justin. Didn't you say you wanted to get a drink?"

"What?" Justin said.

"A drink. You said you wanted to buy a drink," Lewis repeated, but this time he motioned with his head repeatedly jerking it in the direction of Nikki who sat on the other side of Justin.

"Oh, yeah. That's right. The line-up for the snack shop has probably shortened." Justin turned to Nikki. "I'll be right back. Do you want anything?"

"Sure. Could you get me a Sprite? Thanks," Nikki said

As Justin stood up, he noticed Lewis use the opportunity to shift his position at least a foot or so closer to Nikki. Justin walked down the bleachers and toward the snack shop, but he figured Lewis wanted him to be gone for a while, so he decided to wander the halls for a few minutes. Heading down the empty main hall and turning left in the direction of his locker, he looked up to see Raven walking toward him.

"What are you doing here? Checking to make sure I'm not in the middle of some other disaster?" Raven asked as she came closer to Justin.

"I was just getting a drink."

"Over here?"

"I was stopping by my locker too."

"Oh," Raven said. "So, how are your hands?" Raven gently reached out to lift Justin's hands up from his sides, but stopped at the last moment. "Oops. I guess I'm not supposed to touch."

Justin definitely wanted to touch. He wanted it more than he would admit even to himself, but he wouldn't risk hurting her again. His feet took a step toward to her. He was close enough to notice she smelled like flowers, but he kept his hands at his sides. "Yeah, I guess I need to learn how to better control the amount and type of energy I access." He could feel his heart beat pumping faster in his chest. "So that we can touch without you refusing to let go of me." He gave her a lopsided grin.

"Very funny. You're not as irresistible as you think."

"I don't know. You were holding onto me pretty tight."

"Well, you need to work on your effect on women. You're not supposed to cause them pass out in order to make them fall for you."

"Yeah. I guess I need to tone down the charisma. But in the meantime, I hoped I could ask you for a favor."

"What favor?"

"I haven't been able to stop thinking about what Anya said to me about Alexei and my grandpa. She's got to be mistaken, but I can't ignore the feeling that I at least need to prove it. If Anya is right, then Alexei has been lying to me and I want to know why," Justin said.

"What does that have to do with me?"

"If he's been lying, I don't expect him to tell me the truth, so I want to look through his stuff. I thought the safest way to do so would be to keep him busy by having dinner with him at his hotel and have someone else go through his things in his hotel room."

Raven eyes opened wide. "You want me to break into his hotel room and rifle through his things? Are you crazy?"

"I already know you can unlock doors. You did so to steal my address. I'll keep Alexei downstairs so that there's no chance of him coming in on you. It'll be easy," Justin said.

"For you. You wouldn't be the one sent to jail or attacked by an Elementer."

"Raven, I wouldn't let him hurt you. He won't even know you're there. But we need to find out who our attackers are and if Alexei lied about Henry, there's a chance he's lying about other things too. Please. You don't want to just stand by and wait for someone to attack us again, do you?"

"Well, no. But can't I be the one enjoying the dinner?"

"Raven, it would seem less strange for me to ask him to meet me for dinner. We've already met. Besides, you're the trained criminal who knows how to pick locks. It'll only take a few minutes and you'll be out of there. No worries. Please. We need to find out who's trying to hurt us."

Raven started biting her lip causing Justin to smile. He liked her nervous habit and couldn't take his eyes off her lips. Finally Raven sighed. "Okay, but you have to make sure he stays away from his room."

"Absolutely. I'll keep Alexei busy and you slip in and search his things. A few minutes, tops. What could go wrong?"

Raven just scowled at him.

Chapter 28

RAVEN AND JUSTIN arrived at the hotel almost an hour before the Thursday meeting to make sure they had time to identify Alexei's room. It was easy. Raven's talent for connecting might be forcing them to maintain their distance, but it was good for finding Elementers. Most Elementers could sense another Elementer using their powers, but Raven could usually track one down to within a few feet even if they weren't using their energy.

Alexei was in his hotel room and she found him quickly. They snuck up to the third floor to determine his room number then slipped out through the back stairs and waited at a fast food joint down the street. Justin ordered some food for Raven to eat since she'd be playing the burglar while he ate dinner with Alexei, but she seemed too nervous to eat much. Ten minutes before the meeting, they returned to the hotel. Raven followed another guest in through one of the side doors to avoid any chance of being seen by Alexei. Justin walked around the building and waited in the lobby near the restaurant until Alexei came downstairs. They were given a table at the far corner of the restaurant upon Alexei's request.

As the waitress turned to take Alexei's order, Justin discreetly pulled out his phone under the table and sent a very brief text to Raven. He started the timer on his phone at 60 seconds. As the waitress walked away from their table, Justin picked up the salt shaker and started fiddling with it in his hands. After a short while he went to set it back down but purposely dropped it onto the floor. "Whoops," Justin said as he leaned over to pick up the shaker. Salt had spilled across the floor and Justin reached out with his energy to gather the salt together and drop it in the hand he had lowered to the floor. Alexei looked at Justin and looked around to double check that no one noticed. But no other guests were near them in the restaurant.

"Sorry," Justin said. "I can be a bit of a klutz." Justin laid the spilled salt on the edge of the table and replaced the salt shaker. "Thanks for coming so soon."

"It was good timing. I had to return to Seattle for business, so I simply came here a day early. But I was a little concerned about your cryptic words on the phone. Is everything okay?" Alexei said.

"Not really."

"What's wrong?"

"I don't want to sound paranoid. But I think someone is trying to hurt Raven and me," Justin said.

"Why do you say that?"

Justin proceeded to explain the attacks in the parking lot and the restaurant and the white car that followed him last Thursday night. He told Alexei about his suspicion of Rex. Justin was no longer certain that Rex was the attacker, but he didn't want Alexei to know that. Alexei seemed to want Justin to lay the blame on Rex, so Justin thought it best to play along to keep Alexei at ease.

"So you think Rex is behind the attacks?" Alexei asked.

"You said so yourself that he was working against Henry. If he killed a Council member like Henry, I doubt he would hesitate to kill Raven and me. But why would he want to hurt us?"

"I don't know," Alexei said. "He's a vengeful, determined man. I'm beginning to think there's nothing he wouldn't do."

"But why would he kill Henry? You said a vote was coming up. What was it about?"

"They were voting about the limits on Elementers and what we can and cannot do with our powers. Henry and some others on the Council believe that the Council is too restrictive and controlling. Henry wanted to give Elementers more freedom, but Rex is determined to restrict us all."

"What do you think should be done? Who do you agree with?"

"I come from a country that lacked freedom for too long. America is supposedly the land of the free, but even here people like Rex try to control everyone. We won't stand by and let him continue to oppress us. It looks like he's killing anyone who stands against him. He must be stopped."

"But why is he attacking Raven and I? We haven't done anything," Justin said.

"He probably sees the power you have and is concerned that once you gain better control of your powers, you'll be the one Elementer he can't control. He…" Alexei paused in response to his phone ringing. He pulled it out of his pocket and looked at the screen. "Just a moment. I need to take this call."

"This is Alexei," Alexei said and listened to the caller. "What? Just a minute." Alexei pulled the phone from his ear. "Justin, I need to talk to this person. I can't take it here with non-Elementers nearby. I'll be back in just a moment." With that, Alexei stood up and walked toward the exit of the restaurant by the lobby.

Justin's heart started pumping faster. He picked up his phone that he'd been hiding under his napkin and typed a swift text to

Raven. *Alexei may be coming back to room. Get out.* He hit the send button and wondered what he could do to help Raven. He didn't dare Earth Talk to her because Alexei would sense the energy they both used and might become suspicious. Alexei might hear her if she was talking on the phone. Justin couldn't sit there not knowing whether Alexei had returned to his room and Raven got out in time. Justin needed to be there to help her if Alexei found her. Justin could just say he was looking for the bathroom if Alexei saw him. As Justin neared the lobby, he passed his waitress and explained that he'd be right back.

Justin had a small hope Alexei would go outside to talk, but with the weather beginning to lightly mist, Justin wasn't surprised to see Alexei head toward the elevator. Justin crossed the lobby and peeked around the corner to see Alexei press the button to the elevator. Justin stood there trying to determine options while Alexei talked on the phone waiting for the doors to open. Alexei talked too quietly for Justin to hear him. Finally, Alexei lost patience for the elevator to arrive and walked further down the hall to the stairs. Justin checked his phone again. He hadn't received a return text from Raven. He had no way to get to Alexei's room before Alexei without being seen. What was happening with Raven?

Chapter 29

RAVEN HID AROUND the corner at the end of the hallway when her phone vibrated causing her to jump. She nervously laughed at herself and pulled out her phone. Justin's text message said, *1 min to go.* She hit the timer app on her phone to count down to sixty seconds and peeked around the corner relieved to find the hallway empty. She took a couple deep breaths and walked down the hallway toward Alexei's room.

At the door, she looked again at her phone and while she waited for the timer to reach zero, she tried to keep her hands from shaking. At least she wouldn't be using her hands to unlock the door. She had insisted to Justin that they come to the hotel the day before so she'd have time to practice on the hotel locks. Because the hotel doors used key cards, she wasn't sure she could unlock them without breaking the lock thus making Alexei suspicious. Thankfully, she discovered that the locks had a regular, metal manual override key so they proved to be easier to open than she expected.

The real trick was timing things precisely with Justin. Alexei would sense Raven using her energy to unlock the door just a few floors above him so Justin needed to mask her energy use. If he accessed the Earth energy downstairs at exactly the same time Raven used hers, Alexei probably wouldn't realize someone else was also using Earth energy. Raven looked again at her phone. *4-3-2-1-0*. Raven prayed that Justin was ready. She placed her hands on the door knob to make things look normal to anyone coming down the hallway and reached out with the energy. Despite having practiced at least ten times yesterday, her nervousness made it difficult to control the energy. After two failures, she finally succeeded in unlocking the door. She pushed it open and looked both ways down the hallway before walking into the room.

As the door closed, she leaned her back against it and looked at the room. She noticed a suitcase on the luggage rack, a laptop on the desk, and a computer bag hanging on the back of the desk chair. She hurried over to the desk and lifted the lid on the computer. It was off so she hit the power button. It might be password protected, but she figured it was worth a shot.

While the laptop booted, she laid the computer bag on the desk and began looking through it. The front pocket was filled with various business supplies and power cables. She tried to snap the flap closed but she struggled to maintain control over her fingers. She clenched her hands into fists for a moment to try to stop them from shaking and attacked the snap again with success. Next, she opened the main compartment. Behind the laptop section sat a few folder compartments. She pulled the papers out of the first section and flipped through the documents, but they were just travel papers including a few plane itineraries from NYC to Bellingham, Seattle to NYC, and one even from NYC to Paris. The other pages also seemed to be nothing of importance.

She placed the papers back in the bag and pulled out a blue folder from one of the other sections. Raven opened up the folder and noticed it contained various business documents. She laid the papers out on the bed in the same order as they existed in the folder so she could be sure to return things as she found them. After laying them out in two rows she began taking a closer look at them. They seemed to be a business analysis of some company named Lannix Chemical Company in Seattle. It was probably unimportant, but Raven figured she might as well take photos of the papers since she wasn't really sure what she was looking for. After pulling out her phone, she began snapping pictures of the documents. She was nearly done when her phone vibrated. It scared her so much that she dropped the phone on the bed. She quickly picked it up and looked at the text message: *Alexei may be coming back to room. Get out now.*

Raven's stomach felt like it suddenly changed places with her throat. She shoved the phone in her pocket and quickly began picking up the papers. But she realized she had placed them in reverse order. She rearranged the first few, picked up the rest of them, placed them in the folder, shoved them back in the computer bag, and hung the bag on the back of the chair. She almost darted out of the room, when she realized the computer was still on. She touched the mouse pad and began moving the cursor to make the laptop shut down, but the mouse pad was over sensitive and in her haste she moved it too quickly. She started whispering insults at the computer but then she realized she could just manually turn it off. She pressed down on the power button until she could hear the laptop shut down.

Running to the door, Raven grabbed hold of the handle and began to turn it when she heard through the door a Russian accent floating down the hallway. Alexei was already here. She couldn't get out without being seen. Raven spun around and scanned the room desperately for a place to hide. She considered the bathroom, but he might use it. She noticed the closet. Sliding open the door, she stepped into the closet and bumped the hangers. They clanged so loudly she suspected everyone in the entire hotel heard them. She grabbed hold of them to stop the noise and pushed them to the side against the wall to avoid bumping them again. She crouched down and pulled the closet door shut just moments before she heard Alexei stop in front of the door.

Raven wondered how many teenagers suffer heart attacks simply as a result of being suckered into doing stupid things for their friends. If she got out of this safely, Justin would owe her big time. She focused on bringing her breathing under control so Alexei wouldn't hear her.

"Dryden? Already?" Alexei said after entering the room. Raven realized he must still be talking on the phone. "No, I look forward to getting rid of him. I just planned on spending a few days skiing up in Whistler. But ridding the world of Dryden will be almost as much fun. After I'm done with the logistics for Lannix, I'll head to Texas to take care of Dryden. That will leave me plenty of time to finish preparations for the big bang. They'll never know what hit them."

While Alexei listened to the person on the other end of the line, Raven began worrying about Rex. She needed to warn him. She also wondered what Alexei meant by the big bang. The tone he used sounded ominous.

Alexei responded to the person on the phone. "Don't worry. When I get rid of Dryden, it will be clean. Everyone will think it was an accident just like when I removed our precious Zephyr. No one will suspect a thing." Upon hearing about the Zephyr, Raven unconsciously gasped. She covered her mouth with her hand waiting to see if Alexei heard her, but he was too focused on his phone call to notice the sound. Raven continued listening but she could barely believe what she heard.

"Yes, the restaurant fire got a little out of hand, but at least we were able to see what Justin is capable of. He'll be a great asset. I'll make sure he's on our side. Dryden and the Council are so controlling that it'll be easy to turn Justin against them. Between our staged attacks at the school and restaurant and Jake tailing Justin at night, Justin's a scared kid and wants my help. I've fed him plenty about Dryden so Justin is thoroughly convinced that Dryden is trying to kill him."

Alexei listened to the person on the phone for a while. "Do you need anything else? I should return to dinner. Justin will be wondering what happened to me." Alexei began walking for the door. "Okay. I'll call you once I've taken care of Dryden. Au revoir, Madame."

Raven waited at least a minute after Alexei left the room before she exited the closet. She desperately wanted to leave immediately, but after all she overheard, she decided it was important for her to search for any more possible clues about who Alexei was working with and what they are planning. Unfortunately, she couldn't find anything else interesting in the computer bag and Alexei's suitcase only contained clothes.

She took another look at the room to make sure it looked the same as she found it and remembered to move the closet hangars back to their original position. Not hearing anyone as she pressed her ear to the door, she slowly opened it, peeked into the hallway, and dashed down the hall to the stairs leading to the side exit. Once she sat safely in the fast food restaurant down the road, she sent Justin the text message, *I m done*, so he knew he could finish with Alexei at any time.

Justin would probably want her to wait before she spoke to anyone, but considering the threat to Rex's life and the other news she learned, she wanted Mr. Hamilton to be there when she spoke to Justin. She called her teacher and told him what she and

Justin had done and what she overhead. After being chewed out by Mr. Hamilton for at least five minutes, he told Raven to stay put and he'd come pick up both her and Justin. He also said he'd call Rex and warn him.

Justin walked into the restaurant and froze when he saw Mr. Hamilton sitting next to Raven. "You told him?"

"Both of you, out to the jeep." Mr. Hamilton marched toward the door.

Justin glared at Raven, but she walked toward him. "I'm sorry, but I had to call him. We need to talk. Please."

He wanted to refuse Mr. Hamilton's demands, but Justin needed to know what Raven found in Alexei's room, so he finally spun on his heels and followed Raven out to the jeep. Justin waited for Mr. Hamilton to chew them out for breaking into Alexei's room, but instead his teacher drove in silence. Justin began to ask Raven what she found, but Mr. Hamilton tersely told them to wait and something about his tone held Justin back. They finally pulled into a park with a covered shelter. It protected them from the rain and the weather deterred others from the outdoors providing them with sufficient privacy. Raven sat on the same side of the picnic table as Mr. Hamilton, so Justin sat down facing them impatient to hear answers.

"So what did you find in his room?" Justin asked.

"It wasn't so much what I found, but what I heard." Raven proceeded to give him a play-by-play on the events, describing everything she heard Alexei say, except for one thing.

"He said he'd get rid of Rex for us?" Justin smirked.

"Justin!"

"I'm kidding. It was a joke. Are you sure Alexei said he

planned to kill Rex?"

"Definitely. I know you thought Rex was the attacker, but that's what Alexei wanted you to believe. He said you'd be a great asset and they want you on their side. But I don't know whose side that is. The attacks were all about turning you against Rex and the Council so you'd join some club Alexei belongs to."

"It's a shame," Justin said.

"What is?"

"That Rex isn't the bad guy."

"Justin." Raven frowned at him.

"I'm just saying that I'd prefer Alexei to be the good guy. He's way more fun than Rex and he has a fabulous car." Raven shook her head at him. "Okay. Okay. I'm kidding," Justin said. "It's just going to take a moment to change gears. I suspected there was something wrong with Alexei after talking to Anya. I just didn't want it to be true. But we need to stop him from killing anyone – even if it is Rex."

Raven turned to Mr. Hamilton and began chewing on her lip.

"What's wrong?" Justin said, but Raven's forehead furrowed. She opened her mouth but nothing came out.

Mr. Hamilton spoke up. "Justin, Alexei said something else that Raven hasn't told you."

"What?"

"When he told the person on the phone he'd kill Rex, he said he'd do it as cleanly as he killed the Zephyr."

"Alexei has killed others? Who's this Zephyr?" Justin asked.

Now Mr. Hamilton became mute for a moment, but he took a deep breath in and continued. "There's a Head Elementer for each of the four elements on the Council. Each element has a different name for that position. The Head Wind Elementer is called the Zephyr after the Greek god of the west wind."

Justin's looked away shaking his head side to side, but Mr. Hamilton continued. "Your grandpa was the Head Wind Elementer. He was the Zephyr. Alexei killed him. I'm sorry Justin."

Raven reached out to comfort Justin, but he pulled away. "No. He died in a car accident," Justin said.

"On the phone, Alexei said that he'd make Rex's death look like an accident just as he had for your grandpa," Raven said.

Justin's emotions spun wildly inside of him mixing with the energy that the news had unleashed. He couldn't sit. Stumbling up from the picnic table, he backed away. He already suspected his grandpa had been murdered, so why was this news making his world spin? It wasn't because he found out Alexei was the killer. It must have been because it was real now. Henry really had been murdered and someone was to blame.

"He's gonna pay." Justin glared into the night.

Chapter 30

JUSTIN ALMOST DIDN'T come to school after learning last night that Alexei murdered Henry. But if he faked being sick, he would have gone crazy cooped up in his room all day. He wound his way down the hall through the press of bodies on his way to the cafeteria. Suddenly, a buzz of energy ran up Justin's arms giving him goose bumps. He stopped in his tracks and looked to find the source of energy. But halting in the middle of a packed hallway at lunch time is never a good idea. A mass of people ran into him causing him to ricochet between them like a ball inside a pinball machine. Pushing his way to the wall, he freed himself from the onslaught of bodies and looked around.

Behind him he saw Raven waving for him to come over to her. He wished it had been Alexei so Justin could catch the creep. Mr. Hamilton had called Rex, Anya, and a few other Elementers. They were all meeting here in Bellingham tonight to discuss what to do about Alexei and how to keep Rex safe. Justin wanted to act as soon as he heard the news from Raven, but Mr. Hamilton convinced Justin to wait and first talk to the others. He only agreed because he figured the others would increase his chances of catching Alexei. But waiting to act was killing him. The anger inside of him continued to grow like a cancer with each passing hour.

Raven pushed through the crowd in the hallway making her way toward him. "We need to talk," Raven said, "in private." She motioned to the left with her head and Justin followed her in that direction. Making their way down a few halls, they finally found an empty, small side hallway near the main gym. Raven turned to Justin. "How are you doing?"

"Fine."

"Is there anything I can do?"

"I'm fine, really. I just want to catch him as soon as possible," Justin said clenching his fists at his sides.

"Raven," a voice called out. Raven jumped in surprise, but Justin simply looked up in irritation. Eric walked up and put an arm around Raven's shoulders. "What are you doing here? I was on my way to meet you at lunch."

"I was just talking with Justin about our science project," Raven said.

"Justin?" Eric looked over at Justin with an air of superiority. "Oh, yeah. You're the guy from the restaurant fire and you were sitting beside Raven at the basketball game." His face hardened and added, "You seem to be spending a lot of time with Raven."

Justin was in no mood to be civil with this guy. Justin opened his mouth to make a rude remark, but Raven spoke up first. "Eric, I need to ace this project to get an A in Mr. Hamilton's class. Come on. Let's head to lunch. Justin, I'll talk to you later, okay?"

Justin nodded and watched with resentment as Raven placed her hand in Eric's grip and begin leading him away, something

Justin couldn't do with her without risking her life. Before turning the corner, Eric looked in Justin's direction and nodded to someone behind Justin. Eric's eyes then fell on Justin with a smug look. Justin knew that look. He'd seen it many times just before some brainless jerk decided to pick on him. He'd learned long ago to be aware of what went on around him as a matter of survival. Justin knew what must be waiting behind him without even turning around.

Any other day, he would have quickly walked away trying to avoid the situation, but not today. He was in the mood for a fight and if Alexei wasn't available yet, whoever stood behind him would have to do. He wasn't picking the fight and if he avoided them today, Justin was sure they'd just come find him later. He had power now and he wasn't going to be pushed around anymore. Slowly turning around, Justin saw Hank, the bully, standing just twenty feet away blocking the hallway. Justin smiled. He was glad it would be someone who deserved to be humbled.

"Hey, guys." Hank looked past Justin. "You were invited too? You'll have to wait until I'm done with him."

Justin turned around to find two more oversized guys walking toward him from the other end of the hallway. This would be a little more difficult, but Justin fumed when he thought about Eric sending three guys to rough him up rather than attempting to do it himself. Justin immediately began working out how to take on all three guys without making his special abilities obvious. First, he decided he needed a little more privacy so he opened the classroom door behind him, confirmed it was empty, and slid inside.

He quickly walked to the back of the classroom and turned to face his attackers as they entered the room. Justin decided the skills he would use. There were no water sources in the room, but it didn't really matter since it would have looked too suspicious for another water accident. Trees wouldn't be much use indoors. Justin figured he'd do some of what Rex did to him, but just make it look like the force came from him. If necessary, he could use some Earth energy in the same way.

Hank walked through the door and stopped at the front of the room glaring at Justin. "Eric doesn't appreciate you hanging out with his girlfriend. We wanted to make sure you got the message."

"And he's too scared to tell me himself?" Justin said.

"Scared of you? Funny. He's busy with his girl and we enjoy helping out in such ways," Hank said. The three goons fanned out walking down the center and sides of the room to box in their target. Justin connected to the energy and strode toward the guy on his left so he could deal with one person at a time. As he closed in on the guy, he cocked his arm back and shot a gust of wind at the guy as he swung his fist at the guy's stomach. The wind threw the guy back a few feet into a shelving unit and he lay on the floor stunned. The strength of the wind had been enough to pull Justin forward also. He stumbled a few steps trying to stay on his feet.

"Chris, get up! Stop being such a wimp!" Hank yelled at the guy on the floor.

Once Justin regained his balance, he turned to see Hank coming for him. Justin was furious at the guy, but some level of self-preservation still held sway making him want to maintain some distance between himself and the beast. Hank pushed a desk aside to hurry toward his prey. With only one desk between them, Justin placed his hands on the edge of the desk preparing to push it and propelled it at Hank with more wind force than was necessary.

Hank and the desk went flying back a couple rows. It wasn't clear whether the loud cracking sound came from Hank colliding with the desks or simply the desks themselves crashing into each other. Hank grimaced in pain and looked up at Justin. "You're going down!" Hank yelled.

"You're the one down on the ground. Not me," Justin said.

The third guy resumed walking toward Justin, but Hank sneered at him. "I told you, he's mine." As Hank stood up, he unconsciously held onto his side. "Come here loser. I'm going to teach you to respect your superiors."

"Be sure to point them out if you see any," Justin said as he stepped to the left to avoid tripping on any of the toppled desks. "Are you sure you're hungry for more punishment?"

"I'm gonna punish you." Hank rushed at Justin to tackle him into the ground. It took Justin a little by surprise, but he had time to shoot a narrow blast of wind and swing his fist just as Hank reached him. Justin's hand hit Hank's left cheekbone along with a great deal of wind force.

Hank's head snapped back and his body spun to the side and fell to the ground. Hank lay groaning on the floor while Justin shook his right hand. "Ow," Justin groaned. He'd never punched anyone with that much force before. His hand throbbed as if a brick had been thrown at it.

The first guy was back on his feet. With Hank incapacitated, the other two seemed to decide it was their turn. They were slowly closing in on Justin from opposite sides, when suddenly Guy Number Three rushed forward to tackle. Justin jumped to the right to avoid the hit, but his right foot tripped on a fallen chair sending him to the floor. The first guy lunged at Justin, punching him a couple times in the stomach before Justin had time to respond.

Connecting to the Earth energy, Justin yanked a desk from behind his attackers toward them until it smashed into his attacker in the side pushing the guy away from him. Justin started to sit up when he noticed the other guy's foot swinging toward his stomach. A moment later, a combination of fury and pain erupted. But Justin tossed the pain aside and focused on the anger. He no longer thought much about whether the fight looked suspicious. He grabbed the guy's foot when it came at him again. His hands screamed out in protest as they absorbed the force, but he couldn't let that slow him down. He shot a wind gust into his attacker's face knocking the guy to the ground. Justin scooted over, got up on his knees, and planted a solid wind punch at the guy's face. Spinning around, Justin found the other guy getting up so he planted a similar punch sending him again on his back.

Justin struggled to his feet. He almost doubled over from the pain that seared through his mid-section. Part of him was tempted to kick his attackers before leaving, but it hurt to make any sudden movements. Instead, he just threatened them with words. "And don't try that again or I'll do worse." He turned and slowly walked out the door. He had only made it about fifteen steps before he heard what sounded like two teachers coming down the far hallway. Justin jogged ahead, wrapping his arm around his waist to limit the pain, and scooted around the nearby corner before the teachers saw him. He kept that pace until he reached the closest bathroom to clean himself up and check his injuries.

He splashed water on his face when he heard Raven's voice. "Justin." He tried to ignore her. "Justin. I know you're in there." Justin was glad she couldn't come in the bathroom. He wasn't in any mood to be lectured. "Justin. I'm coming in if you don't come out."

Yeah, right, Justin thought.

The door slowly opened part way and long black hair and a pair of deep blue eyes peeked around the corner. "Justin, please come out." Justin had enough, so he walked over, pulled the door open further, and walked past Raven heading down the hallway.

He would have preferred to walk quickly, but it wasn't worth the pain it generated.

"What were you doing?" Raven asked once she caught up to him.

Justin reached a side door and shoved it open walking out into the rain. Unfortunately, it didn't deter Raven, but he hoped the water and temperature might help cool down his emotions. "What do you mean?"

"I know you were using your energy and pretty intensely. What happened?"

"You don't want to know."

"Of course I do," Raven said.

"Fine. Your boyfriend sent three of his buddies to try to beat me up. Is that what you wanted to hear?" Justin said.

"What are you talking about?"

"When you left me, Eric sent Hank and two other guys to remind me that you're his girlfriend and I'm supposed to stay away from you."

"You're kidding, aren't you?"

"Yeah, right. And I just imagined these bruises." Justin stopped and despite the cold rain he pulled up his shirt to show his stomach. The red bruises were already turning purple where he had been kicked.

Raven's mouth dropped open in shock. "Justin. Are you okay?"

"Let's just say they're worse off than me."

"You used your powers against them?"

"What else was I going to do? It was three against one, and if you count size, it was more like four or five against one. Don't worry, I made it look like it was me hitting back. I just used the wind to enhance the force when I hit them."

"Justin, I'm really sorry they bothered you. But, we can't use our powers that way."

"I tell you what. The next time you have a bunch of thugs

trying to beat you up, go ahead and stick your powers in your back pocket and take the beating. Then you can talk to me about not using your abilities. I've had enough of being told what to do, being pushed around by jerks, and sitting around waiting to avenge Henry. I've had enough, period. So stop telling me what to do. Besides, if you weren't dating such a jerk, I wouldn't have to defend myself. Why don't you just go back to him before he sees us together again and sends more of his goons after me?" With that, Justin stalked off leaving Raven standing there in the rain.

Chapter 31

"RAVEN, TELL THE group what you saw and heard at the hotel," Rex said.

Raven rose from the fallen log she sat on and stood in front of the others. Rex stood to the side with his arms folded in front of him. Three Elementers Raven had never met until today sat to the left on various large rocks. Mr. Hamilton and Anya sat in the middle on the log she had been on and Justin sat silent at the other end. She'd barely been able to get two words out of him on the drive here to Larabee State Park. Raven repeated the events that had replayed themselves in her mind dozens of times since last night. She knew that except for Rex, the others hadn't been told much before arriving, so she hesitated when she reached the part about the Zephyr. She was pretty sure none of them would take the news well and she felt terrible repeating the details in front of Justin. Glancing over at him, she hoped he'd look up at her so she could apologize with her eyes, but he stared at the ground.

Raven bit her bottom lip, took a deep breath, and continued. "When he told the person on the phone he'd kill Rex, he said he'd do it as cleanly as he killed —the Zephyr."

"What?!" Anya yelled. "Alexei said he killed Henry?" A hard mask fell over her face. "No more. He has to be stopped."

Rex interrupted the exclamations by the others. "Anya, he will. I guarantee that," he said with conviction. "But we need more proof if we going to convince the Council to Wipe him."

Steven Collier, the Tree Elementer to the left of Raven, spoke up. He wore a red golf shirt, khaki pants, and had perfectly combed blonde hair. Raven figured he was in his forties. "Our top priorities are keeping Rex safe and looking over the documents Raven found to see if we know what Alexei is planning."

"I agree we need to protect Rex." Grant Williams was an Earth Elementer, so Raven had heard his name before. His royal blue dress shirt and matching blue and gray tie were striking against his chocolate brown skin. He had one of those smiles that made you feel at ease. But after hearing the news his smile disappeared. "It's clear from the call Raven overhead that he's working with someone else. We need to find out who it is and how many other Elementers are involved. If they are up to something, even if we stop Alexei, someone else may just fill his place. How do we get Alexei to tell or show us who he's working with?"

Rex stepped forward. "We need to find out what Alexei is up to, but if any of you think I'm going to hide from him while he's out causing problems, you don't know me very well."

"Rex—" Steven said.

Rex interrupted. "Don't argue with me, Steven."

"I don't mean to doubt Raven, but I still find this hard to believe," Selena, a Water Elementer, said with her heavy Latina accent. She had long black hair and a tiny frame that rose only a couple inches over five feet. "Alexei may break the Elementer rules. But murder? Aren't we jumping to conclusions?"

Justin finally spoke up. "Jumping to conclusions? Raven heard him say he killed my grandpa and plans to kill Rex. What more proof do you need?"

"We do need more evidence if we going to convince the Council to Wipe him," Rex said.

"More proof?!" Justin jumped up out of his seat. "Raven heard him admit his guilt. What are you waiting for?"

"No one has the right to Wipe another Elementer without approval from the Elementer Council. Approval requires a two-thirds vote by the Council. While I believe what Raven heard, they are going to demand further evidence. So we need to find it," Rex said.

"How are we going to get sufficient proof?" Grant asked. "I've looked through the papers you emailed me. They're just some business documents. Alexei is an investment broker. They won't help convince the Council to vote on approving a Wipe. We need to find out more about what he is up to."

"I'll do it. I'll get him to tell me what he's doing." Justin stood up in front of the log with his fists clenched beside him. "What do I need to do?"

Raven turned to face her teacher. "Mr. Hamilton, tell him he can't do this." But Mr. Hamilton remained quiet. Raven turned to Justin. "Alexei may want you on his side, but if he finds out your working against him, he'll kill you."

"That's why it has to be me. He wants me on his side. I'm the only one who can get the truth from him," Justin said with a black stare.

"Mr. Hamilton? Anya?" Raven pleaded for support.

Finally, Rex spoke up. "Justin is right. He's our best bet. But only if he can keep his cool and not behave like a ten year old and blow up like he did when he created that microburst."

Raven expected Justin to argue back at Rex, but instead he responded with an emotionless voice, "I'll be fine."

"You think you can keep your cool and make friends with the man who murdered your grandpa? You can't let him suspect you know anything," Rex said.

Grant spoke up. "I don't know about this. If Alexei learns that we know about him, he'll make it even harder to prove his guilt in the future."

"It's too dangerous to send a boy. There must be an alternative," Selena said.

"I'm open to other options. What ideas do you have?" Rex stood there with his thick, muscular arms folded across his chest. Raven glanced at all the other adults, but they all remained mute. "That's what I thought. Justin isn't much of an option, but he's the best solution we have right now."

"Thanks," Justin said. Raven figured he was too angry about Alexei to bother letting Rex get under his skin.

They spent the rest of the meeting formulating their plan. Justin would contact Alexei asking him to come out and train him. He'd say that he had an argument with Mr. Hamilton and he wanted a new guide. Justin needed to convince Alexei he was fed up with the Council and wanted to know how to get out from under their thumb. Raven figured it wouldn't be hard for Justin to act the part about the Council since it was basically true, but she wondered if he could pretend he didn't know that he was talking to his grandpa's murderer. She worried Justin couldn't restrain himself from lashing out against the monster.

After the meeting ended, Raven waited till Anya finished talking with the others and then approached her. Raven hadn't told Mr. Hamilton about Justin's fight earlier that day. Mr. Hamilton would have noticed the energy, but he wasn't sensitive enough to be able to tell whether Justin was just Talking or using his powers in other ways. Raven pulled Anya aside because she knew Anya's healing skills. If Justin was going to face Alexei, she wanted him to be healthy to keep him as safe as possible. She made Anya promise not to say anything to the other Elementers before she told Anya about Justin's need for healing. Anya insisted Raven tell her how he got hurt. Once Anya learned about the fight, she picked up her bag and told Mr. Hamilton she was taking Raven and Justin for a short walk before they left.

After stopping by Anya's car to pick up a few things, they found a secluded spot in the forest. Raven sat down on a fallen log while Anya spread a special ointment on Justin's midsection. Justin was irritated with Raven for telling Anya, so she kept her distance from him to avoid another argument. Justin sat there holding his shirt up near his shoulders, wincing in pain, and glaring at Raven. Well, he could be mad, but she wasn't going to be quiet if it meant endangering his life.

"Look at the color of the sphere, Justin," Anya said.

Raven looked closer and noticed a pinkish-red glass ball hanging from a leather strap tied around Justin's neck. She had never seen it before. She guessed that Justin must always wear it under his shirt. But with his shirt pulled up, she could see it hanging against his tan, bare chest. The thought distracted her for a moment until she looked up and realized that Justin saw that she had been staring at him. Raven struggled to keep her face from turning the same color as the sphere.

"We talked about this, Justin. You can't let yourself fall out of balance. Red means you're filling with destructive energy," Anya said.

"The thing doesn't work. It was red long before I fought those guys. It's been getting darker since Friday night, but I didn't do anything destructive until yesterday," Justin said.

186

"Justin, we're not just harmed by destructive actions. Dwelling on destructive thoughts has the same effect. Thoughts may be slower, but they can weaken us just the same. I know you're mad at Alexei for killing Henry. I am too. But if you focus on thoughts and feelings of anger and revenge, it can do significant damage to your soul, even if you never act on them," Anya said.

"That's ridiculous."

"Is it? How were you feeling prior to those kids bothering you?"

"Of course, I was angry. I just found out someone I know murdered my grandpa. How do you think I'd feel?"

"I suspect it was more than that. How many times have you been in a fight before?" Anya asked.

"What does that matter?"

"How many times?"

"Plenty of times. I used to get picked on as a kid," Justin said.

"Did you want to fight?"

Justin clamped his mouth shut and didn't say anything.

"You wanted to fight, didn't you?" Anya asked.

Justin pulled back and lowered his shirt. Raven could tell from the look on Justin's face that Anya was correct.

"How…?" Justin didn't finish the sentence.

"How did I know? Because I've been there before. I told you, I had gone off the deep end and Henry pulled me back. Kicking and screaming, at first. When you let the destructive energy become a part of you, it messes up your perspective and you can't see what it's doing to you. But I guess I neglected to tell you one thing. It isn't just doing destructive actions that can fill you with that destructive energy. Thinking destructive thoughts, especially if they are the main focus of your thoughts, have almost as much effect on you. You need to give up those destructive thoughts and trust the sphere."

"What? I'm suddenly supposed to not care that Alexei murdered my grandpa?"

"No. You care, but you can't focus on feelings of anger or revenge. If you can't get back in balance, Justin, you're too unreliable for us to allow you to meet with Alexei. Either you need to get back in balance or I'll tell the others we need another plan," Anya said.

"You can't do that to me!"

Anya leaned toward Justin her red hair swinging forward. Her piercing green eyes locked on Justin. "You want to make a bet? I can and I will. For our sake and yours. You don't have any idea how dangerous destructive energy is for Elementers. I do, from experience. And I won't stand by and let it happen to you. So either you can try to test what I'm willing to do or you can let me help you. But don't think just because you're a Multi-Elementer that you can stop me. You're still learning and I owe it to Henry to protect you from your own foolishness until you know better."

Raven sat on the log watching the two of them stare each other down guessing that Anya would win this battle. Justin was stubborn, but Raven also knew how much Justin wanted to be the one to stop Alexei and he needed their help to do so. Justin finally glanced down, kicked a rock, and grunted, "Fine."

Raven watched as Justin unwillingly followed Anya in a combination of meditation and energy training. After about twenty minutes, the sphere hanging from Justin's neck was definitely lighter in color, but nowhere near clear yet. Anya wrapped up the exercises. "Better. Promise me you'll do it for thirty minutes before bed and when you wake up each day. Agreed?"

"Fine." Justin clearly wasn't thrilled about doing so, but Raven was relieved that he definitely seemed to be in a better mood than he had been the rest of the day. "Can we go now?" Justin asked.

Anya nodded her head and Raven stood up to follow the two of them. Raven was thankful that they were at least planning the event in detail, but Alexei was a dangerous man and Raven's stomach tightened up at the thought of what could go wrong when Justin would meet Alexei.

Chapter 32

MIST WEAVED AMONG the trees as Justin followed Alexei through the forest. The narrow path made it impractical to maintain a conversation. Justin was grateful because he needed a break from talking with Alexei in order to reestablish his calm. Making small talk with Henry's killer didn't simply make Justin's stomach turn, it made him want to use his powers in every way Anya warned him against. He seriously wanted to hurt Alexei and it took all the self-control he could muster to pretend to be civil with the creep. He began to question whether he could really pretend to be friends with this monster to get information from him and just walk away risking the chance that Alexei might get away with murdering his grandpa. What if the Elementer Council didn't vote to wipe Alexei clean? And even if they did, Justin didn't think being wiped clean was penalty enough for taking Henry away from him.

Alexei needed to pay for his crime. Anya had clearly suspected Justin's thoughts and warned him this morning that it wasn't his right to make Alexei pay. She cautioned Justin that if he tried to take justice in his own hands, the Council would wipe him clean even if they voted that Alexei's punishment was just. The Council dispensed justice, not individuals, and to ensure order, they wouldn't hesitate to punish anyone for going rogue. But even with the warning echoing through his head, another part of him argued that he needed to make sure Henry's death was avenged.

Justin's mind was so buried in these thoughts that he didn't notice someone approaching him on the path from the other direction. He didn't have time to move out of the way before the hiker bumped into him. "Sorry," the guy apologized as he rearranged his day pack and continued down the path.

Justin refocused his eyes on the path ahead of him. "How much farther?"

Alexei turned his head back toward Justin without stopping. "Not far. If I remember correctly, it's just past this last hill."

When Justin had asked Alexei to help him train, he had suggested going to Larrabee State Park, but as Justin got in the car, Alexei said that a friend of his had suggested a better place and drove east toward Mt. Baker. Once they parked and started on the path, Justin had sent a text message to Raven to inform the others where he was. Justin planned to get the information from Alexei on his own, but the others had insisted that they remain close just in case something went wrong. With the text message and Raven's Elementer tracking ability, Justin knew they could find him, but it would take them a while to catch up since none of them drove as fast as Alexei.

After reaching the top of the hill and heading downward, Alexei stepped off the path and headed into the brush. Justin followed him and after pushing aside a few low handing branches, Justin walked into a grassy meadow. "Finally. We thought you'd never arrive." Justin glanced up to see two men and a woman standing in the middle of the meadow. None of them looked like hikers, but for different reasons. The speaker wore surf shorts and a t-shirt with a large tattoo of a surfboard on a wave covering his fore arm. The woman was dressed more for Wall Street than a nature trail and the second guy looked like he belonged on a Harley motorcycle. His blond buzz cut towered a head above the others and his biceps were probably bigger than the woman's thighs. He wore all black and the look on his face was equally dark. Justin instinctively backed up a couple steps.

It didn't take a mastermind to figure out that something wasn't right. He needed to let the others know. Justin reached into his pocket to grab his phone, but it wasn't there. He dug his hand into his other front pocket, but it too was empty. Quickly, he shoved both his hands into his back pockets, but his phone was gone.

"Looking for this?" the voice had a heavy southern accent. Justin turned toward the voice behind him. The hiker that bumped into him earlier on the path held up what looked like Justin's phone. The guy wore a grungy University of Oklahoma baseball cap and looked at Justin with a mocking grin. Justin stepped forward to grab his phone, but the guy tossed it to Alexei.

Alexei caught the phone. "Thanks, Patrick. I'll remember to be more careful with my wallet around you."

Justin scanned and looked at all five people in the meadow. They all had the same confident grin like cats that had cornered a mouse. Justin's stomach tightened and his heart quickened. "Can I have my phone?"

Alexei ignored the question. "Justin. I really wish you hadn't found out about Henry." Justin told himself that Alexei couldn't be aware that they knew about him, but the tightening around his chest suggested otherwise. "We could really use you on our side. You know that the Council is only going to try to control you. That's no way to live. Especially for someone as special as you are. You could still join us. You don't have to be Rex's little pet."

"What are you talking about?" Justin said.

"We know that Raven overheard my conversation. I realize that you think I'm the bad guy, but I didn't have a choice. Henry found out what we were up to. We tried to explain it was necessary, but he wouldn't listen to reason. It's really all Henry's fault. If it wasn't for his stubbornness, this all could have been avoided."

"Don't you dare say his name!" A ball of anger ignited in Justin's chest replacing any fear. Rex's reminder that they needed information from Alexei voiced itself in Justin's head, but he no longer cared. Justin reached out to the energy and hurled a nearby boulder at Alexei. Unfortunately, a wind gust intercepted the rock and sent it careening into a tree.

Alexei stood there shaking his head at Justin as if her were a seven-year-old kid. "If we hadn't found it necessary to remove Henry, or you had never found out, things would have been much simpler." Justin wondered how Alexei could have found out that Justin and Raven learned his secret. But he pushed the thought aside since it didn't matter much right now. Alexei took a couple steps closer toward Justin. "The Council is either going to remove you, Wipe you, or control you. We're alike Justin, so I know you'll hate the Council."

"I'm nothing like you!"

"We both need our freedom."

"But I won't kill people to get it."

"If you stay around, you'll find that it's sometimes forced upon you. Just like Henry forced it on me. But I don't want to kill you either. We aren't the bad guys. The Council has been robbing Elementers of their freedoms for centuries and it is time we help liberate all Elementers. Are you sure you won't join us?"

"I'm going to take you down."

"Too bad. It's truly a waste to have to kill you, but we can't have you working against us. Consider it a favor. We'll be saving you from a life of being controlled by the Council." Alexei tossed Justin's phone to him. "Here you go. I hope you don't mind that Patrick used your phone to send a message to your friends."

Justin reached out to catch the phone and scrolled to his last message. It only contained one word: "HELP!" Justin figured he couldn't wait any longer. He needed to get out of here and fast. He opened himself to the energy to send a blast of wind at Alexei and the others when a slicing pain shot into the back of his head causing his legs to buckle and a sheet of darkness to fall over him.

Chapter 33

"LET'S GO TO Pier 57 on Friday."

"Boris, we have the job on Friday."

"Not until two thirty. We can go earlier and then be back to the factory to do the job in the afternoon."

The voices seemed distant as if they were coming from the other end of a tunnel. But a familiar voice broke through with more clarity.

"Quiet, you two," Alexei said.

"What? The kid's knocked out cold. Besides, even if he was awake, he'll be dead as soon as the others show up."

Justin opened his eyes only just enough to catch a view of his surroundings, but everything was blurry. He struggled to force his eyes to focus and tried to recall where he was. He remembered the anger and disgust as he rode next to Alexei in his car. They hiked into the forest, someone pick pocketed his phone, and Alexei had others waiting for them in the meadow. The meadow. His eyes began to focus better and he recognized the small meadow and the creek running along the edge. Alexei and the others were standing in groups with their backs turned to him about ten feet away

He tried to move, but his ankles were bound together with rope and his wrists were tied together behind his back. A dirty tasting cloth pulled between his teeth was bound tightly behind his head. He tried to call for help, but the only sound he could make was a muffled groan. How did this happen? Justin remembered Alexei admitting that he had killed grandpa. He remembered connecting to the energy and then feeling a searing pain in his head. A throbbing ache became uncomfortably evident at the back of his head.

He tried to sit up to look around, but dizziness flowed over him and he dropped his head back down bumping the spot where he must have been hit. A quiet grunt escaped through the gag. As he lay there trying to overcome the dizziness and pain, he tried to figure out how he could escape. Anya had built an intricate house with trees. She had begun to show him how to manipulate branches and roots. Maybe he could manipulate the roots of a nearby bush to serve as extra fingers to untie the ropes around his ankles. He connected to the energy, but before he could begin to move the branches, a powerful gust of wind picked him up and threw him at least six or seven feet. The gust dropped him abruptly onto a small rock outcropping. Justin's back immediately arched up trying to protect itself from a sharp rock jutting into his lower back.

"None of that." Alexei's mocking voice carried across the meadow. "No connecting to any energy. Patrick isn't only good at pick pocketing. He's also great at felling trees and he'll drop that one on you if you even begin to connect to the energy again. The tree is big enough to crush a house. So, right now, you just need to sit still and wait for your friends to arrive. You've been asleep for a while, so they'll be here soon. We just received a message that they're almost here. The fun is about to begin."

The text message they sent to Raven from his phone came to Justin's mind. Raven and the others would be hurrying here to help him, unaware they were entering a trap. Justin needed to warn them, but after already murdering his grandpa, Justin didn't doubt for a second that Alexei would hesitate to kill him. Justin figured the only reason they kept him alive was to use him as bait, but if they thought the bait was getting in the way, dead bait would be almost as effective.

"Just stay put. The party will begin shortly," Alexei said as he motioned for the others to move out of the meadow and into the cover of the trees.

Justin struggled to wiggle his hands free, but moving caused the rock to further dig into his back. An idea came to him. He pulled himself into sitting position, doing so slowly enough to not seem threatening to Alexei. He wiggled a little to the left to place his wrists next to the sharp stone. Moving slowly, to hopefully avoid detection, he rubbed the rope that bound his wrists hard against the sharp edge of the rock. Twice he slipped and cut his hands on the rock, but did his best to hide the pain and continued rubbing the rope against the sharp edge to break free. He couldn't see the rope, but after a few minutes, it definitely had more give when he pulled against it. He figured he needed only another minute or two to break free.

The sound of people walking up the path caused him to rub hard and fast against the rock. He had to warn Raven and the others of the danger. Rex came into view walking cautiously into the meadow. Justin tried to yell a warning at Rex, but the cloth just transformed his voice into a garbled mess. After looking around the meadow and seeing no one, Rex motioned with his hand toward someone behind him. Anya slowly came into view. Justin urgently shook his head left and right trying to warn them away, but they weren't paying much attention to him focusing instead on looking out for Alexei. Everyone except Raven emerged into the meadow. Rex, Anya, and Mr. Hamilton began walking toward Justin while the others spread out looking for Alexei. Justin continued to shake his head, but they ignored the warning, so he raised his wrists and shoved them hard against the rock successfully breaking through the rope, but also cutting into his left wrist. Clenching through the pain, Justin wiggled and pulled his hands free, yanked off the gag, and called out, "It's a trap!"

A loud cracking sound tore through the meadow and Justin turned his head to see a tree as wide as a bus and many times longer falling directly for him. With his feet tied, he doubted he could move out of the way in time, so instead he connected to the energy and shot a gust of wind at the tree. He must have underestimated the mass and moving force of the tree, because the wind seemed to only move the path of the tree a few feet. Another powerful gust blew across the meadow shoving the massive tree further to the left causing it to crash a few feet to the left of Justin. The ground shook as it hit the earth and chunks of wood shattered in every direction. Justin curled into a ball and wrapped his arms around his head trying to protect himself.

Once the onslaught of tree fragments diminished, Justin felt the earth begin to shake again. But this time it wasn't from the tree. It was an earthquake. Justin looked up to see Rex, Anya, and Mr. Hamilton struggling to maintain their balance as the ground shook beneath them and a crack opened wide between Anya and Mr. Hamilton The crevice split further and the ground swallowed Anya whole. Forgetting about the rope around his ankles, Justin leapt up to run toward her but only succeeded in falling on his face. He rolled closer to the fallen tree to hoping to remain unseen, pulled his knees toward him, and worked on the knots to untie his feet as quickly as possible. He could hear the chaos swirling around him as he struggled to undo the last stubborn knot and wondered where Raven must be.

Finally free, Justin jumped to his feet, still hidden partially by a boulder sized piece of the fallen tree. He scanned across the meadow searching for Anya, but did a double take when he saw what looked like massive snakes writhing in the air. On second glance he realized they were powerful jets of water being shot by Mr. Hamilton and Selena toward the surfer guy and the well-dressed woman who deflected them. Grant shot and dodged rocks with the huge guy and Rex sent a mini tornado toward Alexei.

Justin was relieved to see Anya back up on solid ground, even if a little battered up, but he noticed she was fighting Patrick, the pickpocket, and Steven. Justin was certain Steven caused the branches of the bush near Anya to whip at her. Why was he attacking her? She created a wall of blackberry bushes to block the thrashing limbs, but she was busy with what looked like the strangest sword fight Justin had ever seen. Anya and Patrick were clearing manipulating multiple branches of two nearby trees as the branches tried to attack the other Elementer and at the same time protect their puppet master.

Hurrying forward, Justin reached out to the wind energy to shove Steven away, but just before Steven fell to the side, one of Steven's branches broke through the barrier Anya had created and pulled on her left foot. She fell forward and the distraction caused her to lose sight of the attacking tree. One of the branches hit her across the shoulder and head as she fell to the ground. Justin immediately connected to and shot a burst of tree energy directly at Patrick hijacking his connection just like Justin had done to Rex during their training session a little over a month ago. Next, Justin took control of the tree and swung two branches at Patrick sending him flying almost ten feet and smashing into the trunk of a large Douglas fir. His body crumpled to the ground and lay there motionless.

Movement came into the edge of Justin's vision. He turned to see Steven rising to his knees and look up at Justin. Branches from a nearby blackberry bush swung at Justin from the side and hit him before he had time to stop them. The thorns tore at Justin's clothes and skin. Justin gritted his teeth, linked up to the earth energy, and pulled the ground apart below Steven. The earth heaved under Steven causing him to fall into the newly created chasm. Justin opened another rift swallowing up the bush that attacked him. He turned to see Steven using roots to lift himself out of the crevasse in the ground. Justin connected to more of the roots near Steven and wrapped them around the man.

Justin could feel Steven trying to gain control of the roots to free himself. Physically binding an Elementer, had limited effectiveness. As long as Elementers were conscious, they could access their energy to fight back. Alexei's comment of being forced to kill crossed Justin's mind, but he wouldn't be forced into it. Instead, Justin figured he needed to knock the guy unconscious. Not knowing how much force to use, but having limited time to think about it, Justin reached out to a tree near Steve, extended a new branch, and swung it at Steven's head. Justin cringed when he heard the branch thud against Steven's skull. He was relieved that Steven's energy connection dropped because he didn't want to have hit the guy in the head again.

With the two Tree Elementers taken care of, Justin rushed back to Anya. He confirmed that she had a pulse and was breathing, but she was out cold. He looked around for help and noticed that Grant must have taken care of the other Earth Elementer because he was helping Rex gang up on Alexei at the far side of the meadow. Alexei struggled and fell back. He had a gash on his forehead and favored his left arm. Justin smiled in satisfaction until a blast of wind threw Rex and Grant into the creek wiping the grin off of Justin's face. Alexei turned and bolted in the direction of the path. Justin jumped to his feet and raced across the meadow to prevent Alexei's escape.

Alexei had a head start, but running was Justin's thing. Ignoring the branches that clawed at his face, Justin sprinted down the path oblivious to everything except catching Alexei. While running, Justin connected to the energy and tried to open a chasm just in front of Alexei to catch him, but the running messed with his aim and the rift opened many feet to the right of Alexei. He tried three more times, once just in front of Alexei but his opponent leapt over the hole and continued running.

Alexei rounded another bend in the path hiding him from Justin's view. As Justin came around the corner, he skidded to a stop as he took in the sight before him. Justin had never felt so much anger and fear at once. His blood seemed to pulse hot with energy, but it was coated with a thick, cold chill. Alexei stood thirty feet in front of Justin holding a knife at Raven's neck. Raven's eyes were wide with fear. Alexei stepped back, pulling Raven with him. "It seems that Raven wanted to be part of the action. She's going to come with me for protection."

Justin balled his fists so tightly that his short fingernails dug into his hands. He began walking toward Alexei. "She's not going anywhere with you."

"If you take another step forward she won't be going anywhere – ever again." Alexei yanked Raven, pulling the knife tighter against her throat. Justin's breath caught and he froze. But his mind raced trying to figure out how to free Raven and take out Alexei at the same time. Justin knew Alexei would react immediately if he sensed Justin connecting to the energy. Maybe cooperating would cause Alexei to let down his guard.

"Okay. Go." Justin slowly started stepping back. "Just don't hurt her." Raven's eyes pleaded for help. Justin wanted to assure her he wasn't abandoning her, but he didn't want to do anything to suggest to Alexei that he wasn't being completely compliant. Instead, he just looked into Raven's eyes and hoped she knew he was there for her.

Alexei continued backing up down the path and around a corner out of sight. Justin wished some of the others would arrive, but he wasn't going to wait for help. Since Alexei could sense his connections nearby, Justin needed to use one of his other advantages: speed. Waiting a few more seconds to make sure Alexei wouldn't hear him, he hurried off the path to the left trying to avoid stepping on any large fallen branches to keep his progress as silent as possible. After running at least a few hundred feet perpendicular to the path, Justin swung right and burst forward to reach the parking lot ahead of Alexei. There was no time to go around all the obstacles, so vicious blackberry bushes ripped up his arms and pants trying to slow him down to no avail.

Breathless, Justin finally saw the parking lot through the trees. He slowed down to remain quiet and peeked through the dense plant life looking for Alexei. The Ferrari was still there and Alexei and Raven were nowhere to be seen so he stepped out into the opening and looked around trying to construct a plan Raven would approve. The cover on Mr. Hamilton's blue jeep was pulled back due to the unusually sunny weather and Justin noticed his teacher's emergency backpack sitting in the back of the vehicle. Justin had gone rifling through it during the long drive to Anya's house. He had been surprised to find a can of bear spray among the items. Mr. Hamilton had explained he took it for protection while hiking. Alexei wasn't a bear, he was more like a snake, but the spray might be just what Justin needed. He hurried over, opened the backpack, grabbed the bear spray, and hid behind the far side of Alexei's car.

The next few minutes seemed like an hour, but he crouched lower behind the vehicle when he heard footsteps and Alexei's voice yelling at Raven to move faster. The crunch of rocks signaled their approach through the gravel parking lot. As Raven emerged first around the side of the car she jerked back in surprise upon seeing Justin. By this time, Alexei only held onto one of her arms to speed up their pace and with Raven jerking back in surprise, Alexei's face was partially exposed. Justin leapt up and sprayed the can on the side of Alexei's face farthest from Raven. Alexei immediately hollered out in agony letting go of Raven and clutching at his eyes. "Run!" Justin yelled to Raven. But he looked at Raven and saw her stumbling away rubbing at her eyes and coughing. Justin grabbed her sleeve, careful not to touch her skin to avoiding connecting with her energy. "This way!" He pulled her back into the forest away from the parking lot and the path in case any of Alexei's friends returned. Once they were a good fifty feet into the thick forest, Justin stopped and sat Raven down on a fallen log. "Don't rub your eyes. It'll make it worse. Are you going to be okay?"

Raven looked up at Justin through the tears caused by the pepper spray and forced a smile. "Yes. Thanks."

"Okay. I need to go back and stop Alexei from getting away."

"I'm coming to help you."

"Yeah, right. I attacked you with bear spray. You can't fight if you can't see. I'll be fine." Justin stood up and looked one last time at Raven. "Please, just stay put." He sped back toward the parking lot slowing as he approached the opening. Alexei opened his car door. Justin reached out to the energy and blew a gust of wind at Alexei pushing him away from his car. Alexei stumbled, but he regained his balance.

"Is that you, Justin?"

In answer, Justin stalked out of the trees toward Alexei. "You're going to pay for what you've done."

"Funny, Henry said the same thing and now he's dead. It's time for you to follow him."

A searing ball of anger ignited in Justin's gut and swelled throughout his chest. He could feel the elemental energy fueling his anger making it expand beyond his body. Anya's warning voiced somewhere in the back of his mind, but he didn't care and pushed the caution aside. The energy fueling his anger intensified causing sparks to crackle along his skin and clothes. Justin stepped toward Alexei without an ounce of fear. All he could feel was anger and power.

Alexei backed up sensing the energy and threw a blast of air at Justin. There was no need to connect to the elements, Justin was already a part of them. He simply swung his arm as if swatting a fly away and the wind redirected to the right. Justin could taste the anger and energy in his mouth. It reminded him of a combination of burned toast and popping candy. The ground shook violently beneath both their feet. At the same time, the wind picked up howling between the trees. Justin could feel the environment around him begin to reflect the anger and chaos inside of him.

"You may have power, Justin, but you can't control it and there's no way we, or the Council, are going to let you stick around long enough to control it." Alexei had to lean into the wind to avoid being pushed over. Alexei's hair flew wildly around his face and Justin could see fear enter Alexei's eyes as another vehicle blocked his backward. Alexei swung his arm and a massive dust devil sprung up heading directly for his opponent. Justin attempted to swat it away, but as his energy touched the swirling wind, it just fueled the dust devil instead of redirecting it. The mini tornado grew in speed and size heading directly for Justin. With it only a car's distance away, Justin tried redirecting it again, but again it just intensified the wind more. The storm picked him up and tossed him violently against one of the cars.

Justin wasn't sure if the cracking sound he heard came from the car or his bones. The throbbing in his head had returned with more force. His whole body seemed to ache. He also noticed he had lost connection to the energy. Looking up he saw Alexei climbing into his car. Justin reached up with his arm in an effort to drop a tree across the road to block the car, but to his surprise, he couldn't access the energy at all. Alexei's Ferrari kicked up a large dust cloud as it sped around the corner and out of view. Justin wanted to run after the car but he knew that Alexei was out of his reach.

"Justin!" He looked up in response to multiple voices calling his name. Both Mr. Hamilton and Raven were hurrying toward him from separate directions. His whole body felt completely drained of energy, so he just laid there against the car as they both chastised him for risking his life to go after Alexei. He didn't really hear what they had to say, his mind focused on trying to figure out how he would beat Alexei the next time he found him. But how would he find him?

Chapter 34

JUSTIN PICKED UP his backpack from his bed and swung it at his bedroom wall, but halted mid-swing when the pain in his shoulder rudely reminded him that he had been thrown at a car only a couple hours earlier. Grimacing, Justin walked over to his bedroom window. Mr. Hamilton's jeep sat parked a few houses down the street. Justin had told them he didn't need a babysitter, but because two of the Elementers escaped, in addition to Alexei, they insisted Justin needed extra protection if he insisted on staying at his house.

He didn't want to be sitting at home, but his parents wouldn't agree to let him spend the night at a friend's house on a school night. As a result, Mr. Hamilton and Grant were taking turns staking out his house to make sure neither Alexei nor his friends showed up. Justin argued he could take them out on his own, but after losing control against Alexei, even he doubted his usefulness if he couldn't control his powers. He didn't tell anyone, not even Raven, that he lost control of the energy. Rex might use that information against Justin with the Council. Alexei was a liar, but Justin suspected that there was some truth to Alexei's comment that the Council wouldn't let Justin stick around long enough to control his powers.

A voice in Justin's head began thinking Rex might be right. Maybe he couldn't control four powers at once. Maybe they should just wipe his powers away. What good were they anyway if he couldn't control them? He had already hurt Raven with them, sent a tornado at himself, and allowed Alexei to escape. Besides, a lot of good having powers were to Henry. If he had been normal, he'd still be alive. Being an Elementer got him killed. Justin thought that maybe he should just volunteer for the Wipe. Nobody wanted him to have the powers anyway.

Besides, the Wipe didn't look painful. When he returned with Raven and Mr. Hamilton to the meadow after Alexei got away, Justin watched Rex, Grant, Selena, and Anya, do a partial overload on their three prisoners. Mr. Hamilton explained that they were just overloading them enough to temporarily inhibit their ability to connect to the energy until they could get permission from the Council to do it permanently. It usually only obstructed their powers for a few days and had no effect on their memory. Doing so was technically allowed, but only if absolutely necessary. As the group needed to keep their prisoners from escaping, it was the only practical option. A partial overload was the same as a Wipe, but done at a lower magnitude. Four Elementers, one from each element, sent their energy at equal levels toward the target during the entire process. Mr. Hamilton explained that if the levels weren't equal, the overload would become imbalanced and dangerous to everyone involved.

They took Anya to the hospital and Raven was staying at a hotel with Selena near the hospital. With her Mom out of town, Raven just told Marcela, her housekeeper, that she was staying at a friend's house. Rex was staying at a cabin near town owned by a friend of Mr. Hamilton's. Alexei could easily find out where Mr. Hamilton lived and they couldn't exactly drag three people tied up and gagged into a hotel.

Rex already contacted the Council Chairperson and a virtual Council meeting was to be held. But a couple of the Council members were traveling and were still unreachable so the meeting wouldn't be held until tomorrow or Friday. Even if they approved Wiping the three Elementers clean, the Wipe wouldn't happen until Saturday or Sunday because only Council Members were authorized to do Wipes and Rex and Grant were the only Council members from their group. A Tree and a Water Elementer Council Member would need to fly out to Bellingham to complete the Wipes.

Justin had sat beside Alexei for all that time when he could have overloaded the creep, but he had played Rex's game and now Henry's murderer was free and nowhere to be found. Henry was dead. Anya was seriously injured. Raven had almost been hurt or killed. So what if they had a few prisoners. Alexei needed to be stopped and instead, Rex and the others were hiding out waiting for instructions from the Council.

Justin couldn't sit still any longer. Even though he had expended a lot of energy during the fight, all the frustration from Alexei and the others escaping was balling up inside of him and needed a release. Pushups and sit ups weren't enough. He needed to run. After pulling on his running shoes, Justin walked down the hall to his parent's room where his mom was folding laundry.

"I'm going for a run."

"Did you eat yet? We saved you some dinner in the fridge," his mother said.

"I'm not hungry right now. But I can't sit still to do the rest of my homework."

"Okay, but don't take too long. I haven't seen much of you

lately."

Justin wanted to remove the shroud of sadness wrapped around his mom, but her smile seemed to be buried in the coffin next to Henry. He couldn't bring grandpa back, but at least he could make grandpa's killer pay.

Justin nodded goodbye and leapt down the stairs ignoring the discomfort in his shoulder. He went out the rear door and through the backyard gate into the alley to prevent Mr. Hamilton from seeing him. He knew his teacher would tell him it was too dangerous to go running, but Justin wasn't going to hide.

It wasn't raining, but the moisture hung in the air and settled on Justin's skin and clothes. He looked up as he walked down the alley, but he couldn't see a single star as the clouds blocked any visibility. Everything had been clear back in Texas. Not just the skies, but his life. Things were far from perfect, but at least he knew where he stood. But now he felt like the truth about so many parts of his life was clouded behind layers of lies. Who could he trust? He was told that being an Elementer required hiding the truth. So how could he decide who he could rely on? Rex and the others had been wrong about Steven Collier. Who else wasn't what they seemed?

The questions were spinning around in his head, refusing to be answered, when an arm suddenly wrapped around Justin's neck and a hand clamped over his mouth pulling Justin back into the shadows of the alley.

Chapter 35

JUSTIN YANKED ON the arm of his attacker, but that caused the assailant to squeeze tighter against Justin's wind pipe. Justin tried to reach out to the energy, but it seemed to sputter much like an old car refusing to start. Figuring he didn't have much time before Alexei's goon ended his life, Justin stomped down on his attacker's foot and then elbowed him sharply in the stomach. His foe still held on as he bent over, causing both of them to fall to the ground. Justin rolled away and jumped to his feet, but before he took his first stride to run away, the assailant spoke and his voice caused Justin to stumble back in shock.

"What were you doing with that man who picked you up in the red car today?" the man demanded of Justin.

The world seemed to tilt on its side and Justin struggled to find his balance. He stared at the man, but the shadows clouded Justin's view of the man's features.

Not receiving an answer, the man queried further. "Who are you?"

Justin couldn't speak, but the man's voice couldn't be real so answering didn't seem important since he figured he must be in some twisted dream. Justin stood glued in place, waiting to wake up, but unable to take his eyes off the figure. The man stood up and took a step forward allowing the distant street lamp to illuminate a portion of his face. The sight of the man's hazel eyes peering back at Justin caused Justin to step back in fear. He couldn't handle having his heart ripped out again. "You're not real," Justin said more to himself than to the ghost in front of him.

"You know me, don't you?" the man said.

The face was the same. The voice was identical. But the man seemed to be a stranger. Proof that none of this was real. Justin had discovered that trees hadn't been talking to him, but he figured he really had to be hallucinating this time. "Of course I know you. You're my grandpa. But you died last month, so you can't be real."

"Your grandpa? That would make sense. Who was that man you rode with in the red car earlier today?"

"Alexei?" Justin continued with the conversation, hoping to end it quickly and wake up. "He's the creep that killed you."

"Killed me? Kid, do I look dead to you?"

"No, but I went to your funeral," Justin said.

"Did you see my body there?"

Justin paused for a moment. "Uh, no. It was a closed casket because the car accident resulted in an explosion."

"I don't know whose funeral you attended, but it wasn't mine."

Justin wanted to believe his grandpa was alive, but could it really be so? "How can you be my grandpa if you don't even know me? Besides, if you don't know me, how did you know to come find me?"

This man in his dream seemed way more tired than Justin ever remembered seeing his grandpa. Henry always seemed full of energy. Always ready for another adventure. But this man sighed and allowed his shoulders to droop. "I don't remember anything until four weeks ago. I woke up in a warehouse with no memory, my hands tied behind my back, and five or six guys standing around talking about how they were going to stage my death with a car accident. I pretended to be asleep, they carried me out to a car, and everyone left but the guy I saw you with earlier today. As they discussed, he untied me and waited for me to wake up. I pretended to wake up once I was confident he was the only one nearby. He acted like a friend, tried to convince me that I had simply bumped my head, and told me the GPS would direct me home. But I suspected he had tampered with the brakes or something so I wasn't about to drive the vehicle. When he leaned in close to start the GPS, I pushed him hard and his head bumped against the metal of the car door frame. I guess I was lucky because it knocked him out and he fell to the ground. I stood up to run away when I noticed a small camera fall out of his coat pocket. I didn't recognize it, but I just had this feeling that it was mine and important, so I grabbed it and ran. Since then, I've been trying to find out who I am."

"Why didn't you go to the police?"

"From all the things I overheard the men saying in the warehouse about how dangerous I was, I thought I might be a criminal. And besides, I didn't know how much harm I had done to that guy. I hadn't stayed around to make sure he woke up. I have to admit I was a little relieved to see him today. Even though he tried to murder me, I worried I might have killed him."

Justin looked at him closer. Could this really be true? "So you don't remember anything?"

"Not before waking up in the warehouse."

"They must have Wiped you. Do you still have any of your powers?"

"Powers?"

"Uh, don't worry about that right now. If you don't remember anything or anyone, then how did you find me?"

"The camera I picked up must have been mine. It had photos of you and I at Moody Gardens and other tourist spots in Galveston, Texas. I made my way there hoping to find you. I showed your picture to just about everyone in town, but no one knew either of us. All I had left were some images on the camera of newspaper articles and financial reports about an oil company and a chemical company. Those documents also made me wonder if I had been mixed up in some illegal activities sabotaging companies. I researched online at the public library day after day trying to find anything about myself, you, and information that might link my attackers to the companies on the camera, but I wasn't finding anything. Then, one day, I got lucky. I was searching online when I noticed one of those lists of little news lines below the story I read. The link was about a teen who rescued two girls from a fire. I wasn't finding anything useful so I guess the article seemed like a good distraction. But when I clicked on the link, there in front of me, was a photo of you. It took a few days to hitch hike all the way up to Bellingham and then a couple more to track you down."

"Is it really you?" Justin asked.

"I hoped you could tell me that."

Justin stepped within a couple feet of the man and peered into his eyes trying to catch a glimpse of his soul. The man smiled for the first time and some dead part of Justin's heart re-ignited. "Henry!" Justin bear hugged his grandpa. "It is you!"

After almost a minute, Justin released his hold on his grandpa and stepped back. He was glad it was dark while he blinked away a couple tears. "Come on, we need to tell Mom." Justin pulled on his arm.

"Just a minute. Before we go anywhere, I need some answers first."

"Okay. Shoot."

"So what's my full name?"

"Henry O'Malley."

"Who is this Alexei and why were you hanging out with him if you thought he killed me?"

"We didn't think he knew that we knew that he killed you—or tried to kill you. Anyway, I tried to get information to implicate him, but one of the other Elementers was a traitor and told Alexei what we knew. They planned an ambush and tried to kill us all. We fought back and caught three of them, but Alexei and two others got away."

"What is a teenager doing being involved with such dangerous people?"

"I'm an Elementer like you, except that I can access all four elements."

"What are you talking about?"

"Oh, that's right, you don't remember. You were an Elementer for years, so I'm not about to hide the truth from you. Basically, there's a small number of people who have special—abilities. You have them too. I mean, you had them. I think you lost your memory because those people overloaded you with their powers. When a person is fully overloaded, they also lose their memory. But why would they do a Wipe if they were just going to kill you?"

"I don't know what you mean by powers, but from what I heard them talking about, it sounded like they were supposed to get some information from me, I fought back, things got out of hand, and I couldn't remember anything so I was of no use to them. What did they want from me?" Henry asked.

"I think you found out about what they were up to and they probably wanted to know what you knew and who you told the information to," Justin said.

"So you don't think I was involved in it?"

"Definitely not. You were trying to stop them."

Henry stood up straighter. "Good. So who's parked outside of your house?"

"Oh, that's just my science teacher, Mr. Hamilton. He's one of us and is worried that the others might return and attack me at home. I can handle myself, but I am kind of concerned about my parents. They can't protect themselves from –" Justin eyes grew wide and his heart beat sped up. "You can't protect yourself either. You've got to get yourself out of here, Henry. If Alexei or any of his goons see you, they'll try to kill you immediately. Alexei must not have wanted to admit that you got away so he just pretended that he killed you. I'm guessing he figured you had lost your memory and he hoped you'd stay lost. Who knows? He may even have people searching for you right now. Your safest option is to remain dead as far as everyone else is concerned."

Justin looked back down the alley at his house and then turned backed to Henry. "Mom and Grandma would love to know you're alive. Even Dad would be thrilled. But right now I think it's best that no one knows. If anyone even suspects you're alive, it could mean your death. I couldn't protect you last time, but now I know what's going on – kind of – and I have the power to protect you. I'm not going to let you get hurt. Until we understand what's really going on and stop Alexei and the others, I need you to stay dead. Will you do that – for me?"

"How am I supposed to figure out the truth if I'm hiding under a rock?" Henry asked.

"I want to know the truth just as much as you do. I promise to help you find it, but you need to stay hidden. Deal?"

Justin held out his hand and Henry hesitated and then grasped Justin's hand and shook it. "Okay, but only if we—" The ring of Justin's phone interrupted Henry.

Justin pulled his phone out of the exercise case strapped to his bicep. "Hello."

"Justin. They're here. I need your help!" Raven said between breaths.

"Who's there? Where are you?"

"I'm at the hospital with Anya and Selena, but Boris and the other Water Elementer that escaped are both here and are trying to kill us. Anya is barely able to move and Selena split up from us and I can barely feel her energy. I can't do this on my own. We need your and Mr. Hamilton's help. Please hurry."

"Find somewhere to hide. We'll be there quick." Justin hung up and grabbed the arm of his grandpa. "Henry, some of us are in trouble and I need to go help them."

"I can come," Henry offered.

"Maybe later. But right now I need you to stay out of sight of our family and all of the Elementers. Where can you stay tonight?"

"I'm sleeping at the Lighthouse Mission near downtown."

"Please go back there and stay put. Take my phone." Justin shoved the black, metal phone into Henry's hand. "I'll call you as soon as I can. Just stay dead. Okay?" Justin squeezed Henry's arm and then rushed out of the darkness into the lighted street running around the corner to the front of his house. As he ran, a hand seemed to squeeze Justin's heart, but the tightness wasn't from the exertion of the run. He now had Henry back and there was no way he would let anyone take Raven away.

Chapter 36

RAVEN HAD TRIED doing her homework in the hotel room, but she couldn't concentrate. Selena had gone over to the hospital to watch over Anya, so Raven turned on the television to stop thinking about the events of the day. She could still feel the knife pressed against her throat and the smell of Alexei's cologne. It was a scent she had always liked, which she found extra disturbing. She swore she could still smell it now. The phone rang causing her to stop unconsciously rubbing her throat and reach for the phone. "Hello?"

"Hi Raven. It's me, Selena. I want to stay with Anya a little longer. Would you mind bringing over my laptop? I need to get some work done and I could use the distraction."

"Sure, I'll be over in a few." Raven collected Selena's things and slipped on her coat. As she stepped outside, a misty rain quickly left no part of her face dry. The mist looked mild, but it could leave you drenched in minutes. Sure, it was a little on the cool side and the rain could make a mess of your hair and clothes, but Raven didn't understand why more people didn't like walking in the rain. Being in it made Raven feel even more connected to nature. You were immersed in it, whether you liked it or not. She lifted up her face to the sky to feel the rain fall on her face. The corners of her mouth turned up in satisfaction. The rain made her feel more alive.

But that last thought flooded her mind with the noise from the day again. She likely would be dead if it wasn't for Justin. She wasn't sure she'd ever be able to forget the choking fear she had felt, especially after Justin backed off and let Alexei pull her away. But he had come to help her – again. Raven felt for the first time, that there was someone who was really there for her, no matter what. It seemed silly. They barely knew each other, but her parents had never really been there for her. Nikki was a good friend, but a little flakey. Marcela was super sweet, but it was her job to take care of Raven. And Mr. Hamilton was her guide, but it was his job too. But Justin – he had risked his life for her twice already. He said they were just friends, but Raven couldn't help but begin to feel more than that.

Her thoughts were wrapped up in Justin as she walked through the sliding glass doors and into the main lobby of the hospital. She heard a familiar voice that yanked her sharply back to the present. Her heart lurched and began racing in place. She searched in the direction of the voice. Even from the back, Raven recognized Boris, the Earth Elementer that had been part of Alexei's trap. Raven had seen him before when she had met a group of Earth Elementers. His heavy Polish accent was unmistakable and his massive size made it easy to recognize him, even from the back. She could sense that the guy in surf shorts, t-shirt, and sandals standing beside Boris was an Elementer too. He must be Diederik, the Water Elementer that also escaped. Raven hurried down a side hall out of view and leaned against the wall. The painted cement bricks were cold and hard against her back and hands. She strained to hear Boris' voice over the murmur of other voices and activity in the lobby.

"Yes, I'm here to visit my sister, Anya. I forgot her room number."

"Just one moment, please." A voice interrupted him over the sound of a ringing phone.

Raven peaked around the wall into the lobby. Boris was impatiently strumming his fingers on the desk making it obvious to the receptionist that he didn't appreciate the wait. But the look on the woman's face made it equally clear she didn't like his pushiness and she rotated her chair away from him. Raven scanned the lobby. The elevators were on the far side of the lobby. She'd never get across unnoticed. A sign identifying the stairs gave Raven hope. The stairwell door was in the lobby, but only about ten feet from where Raven stood. She could possibly slip past them undetected. Trying to come up with a plan of action, Raven's attention was pulled away by the sound of a screaming toddler being carried by her mom down the far hallway. Raven's eyes passed over Boris and the other guy and realized that they were equally distracted by the scene. Figuring this was her chance, she pulled her raincoat hood over her hair and hurried into the lobby and toward the stairs as quickly and quietly as possible. She pressed on the large metal door handle and slid into the stairwell.

Leaping the steps two at a time, Raven tried to come up with a plan. Anya was in no condition to fight with a broken leg and ribs and they certainly didn't want a confrontation in a hospital of all places. Raven reached the fourth floor breathlessly and rushed down the hall into Anya's room.

"Raven?" Anya looked up from her bed noticing the girl's anxiousness.

"Where's Selena?" Raven scanned the small, bare room quickly.

"The bathroom. What's wrong?"

Raven banged on the bathroom door. "Selena, we've gotta

go. Boris and the other Elementer are here."

Selena opened the door. "Here? At the hospital?"

"Yes, they're on their way up. I saw them in the lobby. We have to get out of here."

"Let's get Anya in the wheelchair." Selena pushed the chair next to the bed. "Help her sit up."

Raven hurried to the bed, slid her arm under Anya's back, and paused to look at Anya's face. "Ready?" Anya gritted her teeth and nodded. "One, two, three." Anya gasped in pain as she used muscles near her broken ribs. But she pushed through the agony and together they helped her into the wheelchair.

Selena peeked out into the hallway while Raven pushed Anya right behind her. "It's clear. Let's go." They hurried down the hallway as fast as they could without drawing too much attention to themselves.

"Wait!" Raven called to Selena. "They'll likely be coming up the elevator any second. Let's hide in a room and let them pass first."

Selena stood for a moment, trying to decide the best course of action, but finally conceded. "Okay, over here."

Raven followed her to a door with a window facing the hallway that opened to the elevators. They'd be able to see Boris and Diederik pass. Selena pushed open the door and Raven pushed Anya into the room.

"Well, hello." A man's voice made Raven jump. She turned to see an old man with gray hair and a mischievous grin. "The workers here get prettier every day. I wasn't looking forward to my physical therapy, but if you're going to be doing it, maybe I won't mind." Raven's cheeks heated up a deep shade of red and she stood there not knowing what to say.

"She's just a volunteer," Anya spoke up. "She's returning me to my room, but I can't seem to remember where it is. All the rooms and hallways look the same. Sorry."

The man's smile dropped a little. "Could you help me with my pillows?"

Anya and Raven looked toward Selena who hid around the corner out of view of the man. Selena nodded an affirmative to Raven without turning away from the window.

"Sure. I can help." Raven released her hold on the wheelchair handles and stretched out her fingers to release some of the tension in them from holding on too hard. She walked over to the man's bed and arranged the pillows as quickly as possible. "Is that good?"

The man patted her hand. "Much better. Thanks, Honey." He had a southern drawl. It made Raven think of Justin. His Texan accent was light, but right now she really wanted him here. Raven was backing up toward the end of the bed when she noticed Selena jump to the side against the wall. Raven's eyes opened wide and she held in her breath. Selena turned to Anya and nodded.

"Sorry for intruding," Anya said to the man, "but I should get back to my room before they wonder what happened to me. Raven?"

Raven exhaled and grabbed onto the wheelchair with another vice grip as if it were her life line. "Goodbye," Raven said to the man.

"Thanks for the help. You're welcome back anytime."

Selena slowly opened the door, peeked down the hallway, and after a few moments, frantically waved them forward. Raven didn't bother to look down the corridor, she simply darted across it and into the elevator alcove before Boris and Diederik had a chance to see them. She pressed the elevator's down button multiple times. "Come on." Raven urged the elevator to come, but the two elevators had the first or second floor numbers lit. She thought of using her Earth powers to raise the elevator, but that would only alert their attackers of their location, so instead Raven continued to press the button multiple times every couple seconds.

"That won't make it come any faster," Anya said quietly.

"But it makes me feel better. How can you be so calm?" Raven asked as she watched Selena standing near the edge of the hallway keeping an eye out for the return of Boris.

"Freaking out doesn't help. We can't access the elements if we're too out of balance."

Raven knew Anya was right, but knowing something and doing it were two very different things. The number above one of the elevators changed from one, to two, to three. Raven gripped onto the wheelchair handles getting ready to go, but the light halted at three. "Hurry up," Raven wanted to yell, but she certainly didn't want to attract Boris' attention. She was definitely out of balance, but she simply wasn't used to this kind of stress. Weather could be incredibly unpredictable when flying, but she always had a back-up plan and a back-up, back-up plan for every possible scenario. This was not a scenario she had prepared for so she had no plan and that seriously rattled her nerves.

"It's here," Anya said.

The number four lit up above the elevator. "Selena," Raven loudly whispered. The heavy metal doors slowly slid open. Once they were open half-way Raven wheeled Anya into the elevator. Selena hurried in behind them as Raven pressed the ground floor button and then held down the close-door button. The doors began sliding closed causing Raven to breathe a sigh of relief. But her breath caught in her throat as she saw Boris rush into her view from across the far hallway. Raven held still hoping to go unnoticed, but as the doors closed the last six inches, Boris's scanning eyes locked with Raven's. The cold look in his stare gave Raven the same feeling as the time she jumped off the dock into Lake Whatcom early last spring. The sudden cold had locked up her chest making it impossible to take in a breath until she swam over and pulled herself out of the water. This time, it took a few attempts to successfully suck in some air. The heavy steel doors closed, but they didn't give Raven any sense of protection. Instead, the elevator now reminded her of a cage.

"He saw us, didn't he?" Anya tried to turn to face Raven, but winced in pain from trying to rotate.

Raven's throat gummed up so she simply nodded and focused on the numbers above the elevator door. The number lit changed from four to three. It was possibly the slowest elevator on the planet. Finally, the number two illuminated, but then Raven felt a buzz of Earth energy and the elevator jerked to a halt.

Selena turned to Raven. "Get it started again."

Raven reached out to the element and tried to move the elevator cable, but it wouldn't budge. If she pulled any harder, it might snap. "It's stuck. I think he welded the cable to the gears somewhere."

"We don't have time to find the cause. Boris could cut the line if he wanted. Raven, open the doors," Anya said.

The heavy metal doors resisted, but Raven forced them open half way and stopped. Her heart sunk. The floor of the elevator stopped at least four feet below the second floor.

"Help me out of this chair," Anya said.

Selena put her hand on Anya's shoulder. "You can't climb up there with broken ribs and legs."

"Do you have a better idea?" Anya said.

Raven looked at Selena, but both of them were mute.

"Me neither. Besides, one of my legs is only a sprained ankle. So help me up. They'll be here any moment once Boris finds Diederick." Selena and Raven bent over, placed one of Anya's arms over their shoulders, and wrapped one of their arms around her back and helped her up. Anya gasped in pain and sucked in pockets of air as she stood up. "Raven, you first. Then both of you can help me from each end. Go!"

Selena bent down on a knee and Raven used it as a foot stool. Raven was thankful for her days in gymnastics making it easy to swing up her leg over the side and pull herself over. As she pushed herself up on her knees, she could feel the energy pulsing near her. An ominous feeling crept up from behind her. She turned and noticed the door to the stairwell across the other hallway. Raven could sense their attackers running down the stairs.

"Raven, give me your hands," Anya called.

Raven turned to Anya and then back at the stairwell. She had to slow Boris down to give her time to help Anya and Selena. Raven reached out with the energy to the door and melted the lock and then reached down with her arms to grab Anya's wrists.

Anya's eyes locked with Raven's. "Don't pull, please. My ribs won't like that. Just help steady and direct me." Anya took a deep breath. "Now."

Selena helped Anya step onto the seat of the wheelchair. Anya's legs started to buckle. Raven held tight to Anya's wrists, but the extra tension wrenched against Anya's ribs. "Ughh!" Anya gasped. Selena wrapped her arms around Anya's thighs preventing her from collapsing.

"Anya—" Raven began suggesting something else, but Earth energy erupted toward the stairwell door behind Raven. Before Boris could finish opening the door, Raven enveloped herself in the energy and melted the entire circumference of the door to its neighboring floor and door frame. It would definitely look suspicious, but she needed to earn them some time to get away.

Raven turned back to Anya. Pain etched deeper into the woman's face, but determination stood out even more prominent. "Are they stopped?" Anya asked. Raven nodded. "Okay, let's get me out of here." Selena crouched down and guided Anya's left foot that was in a cast onto her shoulder and held it in place. Anya gave a Herculean push and Raven helped her over the ledge. Selena began lifting up the wheelchair.

"Forget the chair," Anya said. "We're going to have to take the other stairs, so the chair won't help us. Besides, you can use it to help climb out. Come on."

Raven helped Anya stand while Selena climbed out of the elevator. Anya shifted back and forth deciding to favor the leg in the cast. She leaned heavily on Raven, the exertion clearly taking its toll on Anya.

"Take Anya and get out of here," Selena said.

Anya looked up. "What? You can't stay and fight both of them alone."

"I'm not going to fight. I'm just going to slow them down. Head to the hotel, but just don't let them follow you there. I'll meet you there. Now go!" Selena said.

Raven hesitated, but then Anya's legs buckled and Raven had to grab around Anya's waist to keep her upright. Anya was in no condition to be moving around, never mind fighting. Raven needed to get her out of here. "Okay. But please be careful."

Chapter 37

JUSTIN RAN UP behind Mr. Hamilton's jeep and banged on the metal frame of the passenger door. Mr. Hamilton jumped in his seat, saw Justin, and unlocked the door.

"You surprised me. What are you doing out here. I didn't see you leave the house."

"It doesn't matter. Start the car. Raven, Anya, and Selena are in trouble at the hospital." Justin climbed in the car and closed the door. "Please. We need to hurry!"

The drive to the hospital wasn't far, but it felt like forever. Mr. Hamilton wanted details, but Justin didn't have many to give. He wanted to Earth Talk or call Raven on her phone, but right now the most important thing was to keep her hidden till they arrived and he didn't want to do anything that would draw attention to her.

Knowledge that Henry was alive spun around in Justin's head, but it didn't entirely seem real. The fact that Justin hadn't been able to connect to any elements when Henry surprised him also stood at the forefront of his thoughts. How was he supposed to help Raven if he couldn't even use the energy? He needed his powers now more than ever. Justin tried to think of the meditation exercises Anya taught him. This wasn't the time or place for quiet time, but he put aside his aversion to meditation, closed his eyes, and tried to calm the storm swirling around inside. To help Raven he needed to center himself enough to access the energy again.

As they approached the hospital entrance, Justin said, "Drop me off before you park the jeep."

"Justin, we need to work together."

"We will. But Raven could be hurt in the time it takes to park, so drop me off and then you can catch up." Without waiting for an answer, Justin opened his door, forcing Mr. Hamilton to slow down. Justin jumped out. "Hurry in," he yelled as he ran toward the entrance.

Justin nearly ran into the automatic glass doors because they slid open too slowly. He scanned the lobby, didn't see anyone he recognized, and found both the elevators and the stairs. He wasn't going to stand around and wait for an elevator, so he shot toward the stairs, shoved the door aside, and raced up the stairwell for the fourth floor. He halted at the second floor landing. The door stood askew and the metal edging reminded him of a candle when the wax melts and leaves hardened drip lines down the sides. Raven or Boris must have been here.

The door screeched as Justin pulled hard on the handle forcing the door to rotate on the now warped hinges. He heard voices down the hallway and quietly, but quickly, walked toward them. In an alcove off of the main hallway stood a couple of nurses and a man in a dark suit standing in front of a partially opened elevator that had stopped between the first and second floor.

One of the nurses tried explaining things to the man in the suit. "Shirley thought she had heard someone, but by the time she got off the phone and came over to the elevator, it was empty."

Justin hurried down the far hallway and began peeking into the rooms. He received a couple surprised or irritated looks from the occupants, but he only cared about his friends' safety. The fourth door stood closed and wouldn't budge when he pushed on the handle. This was taking too long. He began to continue moving down the hall when he noticed through the narrow window in the door what looked like a woman's foot sticking out on the floor past the hospital bed. His stomach tightened up. Justin pushed on the door handle again, but it wouldn't budge. He didn't figure they locked hospital rooms. Boris might sense his use of the energy, but he figured the brute couldn't pinpoint its use as closely as Raven. If he could, then Justin would deal with him.

Justin took two deep breaths and tried to connect to the earth energy. His fingers seemed to crackle with static electricity for a few seconds and then the faucet turned on and the energy flowed. Relief also flooded through him. He had no time for elegant lock picking. Instead, he used brute force to rotate the inner lock clockwise. He looked around, but nobody was in the hall to hear the clank and screeching of scraping metal. He slipped into the room, closed the door behind him, and hurried toward the body. Selena lay prostrate on the floor between the two hospital beds with a broken chair over her. Justin lifted the two main pieces of chair off of her and gently shook her shoulder. "Selena? Selena, can you hear me?"

Selena let out a small moan and moved imperceptibly. Then she rotated her head to look at Justin. "What happened?"

"I think someone hit you over the head with a chair," Justin said nodding toward the chair fragments.

Selena touched the back of her head and winced. "I think

your right. But what happened to Diederick?"

"The Water Elementer that dresses like a surfer?"

"Yes. The last thing I remember was sneaking up on him and encasing him in ice."

"Then where—" Justin noticed a puddle of water on the floor under the bed closest to the window. He ducked his head down and looked under the bed. "Oh!" He jumped to his feet and hurried around the bed. On the floor in front of him lay Diederick with his feet encased in ice. "He's over here. He must have fallen over and banged his head against the metal table because he's out cold, in more ways than one."

"It must have been Boris who hit me with the chair. But where is he?" Selena said.

"He must be looking for Raven and Anya. Where are they?"

"They were heading toward the stairs to get out of the hospital."

Justin reached in his pocket for his phone, but Henry had it. "I need your phone." Selena pulled out hers and handed it to Justin who dialed Mr. Hamilton's number. "Selena and I are on the second floor. Take the stairs to the right, go past the nurse desk, and down the left hallway a few rooms. You'll need to help Selena get Diederick out of here. I'm going to look for Raven and Anya."

Mr. Hamilton tried to argue but Justin hung up. He turned to Selena. "He'll be here in a moment." Then he hurried out into the hallway and saw a sign at the far end identifying another set of stairs. Justin ran down the hallway, but slowed down as he typed in Raven's phone number. The first two unanswered rings made Justin speed up, but then he thought he heard a voice. He stopped on the stairwell to hear better.

"Raven, is that you?"

"Yes, I can sense you up on the second floor. Take the stairs. The elevators aren't safe. We're hiding out in the women's bathroom on the first floor near the cafeteria. They haven't looked in here yet."

"Hold still. I'm on my way." Justin jumped down the stairs two at a time and slowed his pace only slightly after receiving a grimace from a passing nurse. There were no signs for the cafeteria down the first hallway, so he headed toward the center of the hospital and then down the one to the right where the signs pointed him. Not thinking about anything but Raven's safety, he pushed open the door to the women's bathroom just as a cute, blond teenager came out.

"Oh, sorry." Justin couldn't help but turn a little red. "Uh, wrong bathroom. Sorry." Justin went into the men's bathroom next door to make it look like he wasn't trying to sneak into the women's bathroom, even though that was exactly what he tried to do. He waited less than ten seconds and then entered the hall again, saw the girl walking toward the lobby, and entered the women's bathroom hoping Raven and Anya were now in there alone.

"Justin," Raven called as he entered. She was helping prop up Anya against the far wall.

Justin rushed over to them. "Are you okay?"

Anya raised her eyebrows at him. "Do I look okay?"

"Well, no." In fact, he had never seen her look so pale. Anya was normally vibrant, but the pain and exertion had drained it all away. "Come on. We need to get the two of you out of here."

"But what about Selena?" Raven asked.

"Don't worry. I already found her and Mr. Hamilton is helping her remove an incapacitated Diederick out of here. The jeep is in the parking lot. Let's go." Justin slid his arm behind Anya's back and Raven did likewise as they helped her into the hall.

Justin could hear Anya's ragged breaths, but speed was more important than comfort right now. Suddenly Anya's legs gave out entirely causing the muscles around her broken ribs to pull even harder. "Aagh!" Anya yelped.

This wasn't going to work. He couldn't hold her tighter to support more of her weight because it just placed more pressure

on her broken ribs. Justin guided them to a wall. "Wait here."
Justin raced down the hall before Raven could object, looking
in rooms for a wheelchair. After the fifth or sixth room he saw
one parked just inside the door. He peeked in and saw an old
man sleeping. Justin quickly wheeled the chair out of the room
and back to Anya helping her sit down in it. "Is that better?"

Anya forced a grateful smile at Justin through the pain.
"Yes. Now let's get out of here."

Justin wheeled Anya down the hallway toward a sign
identifying an exit to the right. As they were turning the corner,
Justin glanced down the hallway toward the lobby and saw
Boris's large frame entering into view and looking their way.
"Let's move it. I just saw Boris."

"Did he see us?" Raven asked while running for the exit.

"I think so."

After passing through the sliding doors, Justin halted.
"Here, you push her. I'll take care of Mr. Beefy."

"Justin," Raven began to argue, but Justin knew it was their
only chance.

"Go! Call Mr. Hamilton, find his jeep, and go back to the
hotel. I can take care of myself. Tell Mr. Hamilton to come
back once you're safe."

Raven hesitated for a moment, but then seemed to accept this
as the best option. "Just be careful." Then she hurried behind a van
pushing Anya in the wheelchair with one hand while using her
other hand to hold the phone as she called her teacher.

Justin scanned the area and noticed a grove of trees beyond
the parking lot. That would be the best place to face Boris.
Justin could use the trees against the Earth Elementer and
hopefully keep the fight hidden from others. But the grove lay
on the other side of the main entrance where Boris would likely
be exiting at any moment. Skirting between cars, Justin raced

across the parking lot trying to remain hidden by moving behind as many large vehicles as possible. He only crossed half of the parking lot when he noticed Boris standing outside of the main entrance scanning the area.

Justin hid behind a van and peaked around it to view his opponent. A woman walked past Boris and Justin couldn't help but notice that she looked half the size of the man. The little bit of light that broke through the clouds shone on the brute making him look even more intimidating. Justin tried to remind himself that physical size had nothing to do with their ability to wield the elements. But if he lost the ability to connect to the elements again, he'd become a punching bag for the brute. Justin pushed the thought away. He only lost control before because he let the anger take over. He'd keep his cool this time.

Justin needed to keep Boris distracted so the others could get away. He waited for Boris to look in another direction and then bolted out from behind the van heading straight for the grove. It wasn't till he was halfway there that he felt he could spare the time to turn his head and look in Boris' direction. The guy had noticed Justin, but thankfully hadn't attempted to stop him with the elements. Instead, he chased after Justin a good hundred feet behind.

Once well inside the grove, Justin weaved through the trees to lose his pursuer and then hid behind one of the larger trunks. Trying to quiet his breathing, Justin listened carefully for the loud footsteps that soon came. Sticks easily snapped under each heavy step that continued to move closer to his hiding spot. Options of attack rolled across Justin's mind as he waited for Boris to be well out of view of those in the parking lot and not too close to be able to easily lay his paws on Justin. When the steps sounded like they were within twenty feet, Justin peeked his head around the trunk just enough to view his attacker. Boris caught sight of him and immediately opened up a hole in the ground right where Justin stood. Justin had faced this before and leaped to the side just before the crack split open, but he lost his footing due to the shaking of the earth and fell to the ground. Again, the ground below him began to stir encouraging Justin to get back on his feet and move. He felt his back leg lose its footing as the ground dropped out from underneath him, but he had enough momentum to keep moving forward.

Before Boris had a chance to do anything more, Justin reached out and blew a gust of wind at his opponent. Despite his massive size, the wind was powerful enough to throw Boris like a doll against a tree. The tree wasn't big enough to withstand the force and it cracked on impact leaving it bent at a thirty degree angle. Unfortunately, Boris could handle the force. He shook his head and pushed himself back onto his feet. "Vere are you, you little punk?" he roared in his heavy Polish accent, scanning the trees for signs of Justin. "Come out and face me!"

Justin had stood up to enough bullies in the past, but he wasn't crazy enough to face this guy hand to hand. He wanted to give the others more time to get away, so he stayed hidden listening to the guy's ongoing threats. The splatter of rain began falling against the leaves, but only a few rain drops made it through the canopy to fall on Justin's face. He thought about how he could use it.

As Boris's voice circled and began nearing, Justin peeked out again but this time Boris didn't see him. Reaching out to the water and wind, Justin combined and froze much of the approaching rain drops and then targeted the ice balls at Boris. Justin could hear the ammunition hit their target. "Aargh!" Boris howled. "You're dead kid!"

Before the brute finished his sentence, Justin reached out to the trees and urged the branches above Boris to silently slither down above his head. By the time Boris noticed them, they were wrapping around him. Boris tried to punch them away, but he only broke two before the rest had firmly encased him like a boa constrictor. Justin's opponent reached out with the earth element opening up chasms to bring the trees down. But as two trees fell, more branches took their place. With each breath he exhaled, the branches tightened further constricting his access to oxygen. His connection to the Earth element weakened. In little over a minute his head dropped to the side.

Justin only wanted Boris out of commission, so he guided the branches to loosen their grip on the guy slightly and laid him on to the ground still encased in the living cords. Justin kept his distance for almost a minute to make sure the brute didn't suddenly recover. It seemed to take a lot to knock this guy out. Once he was confident the guy was knocked out for good, Justin walked close enough to kick the brute's massive feet and received no response. Justin leaned closer and just barely sensed some breathing. Boris's large frame lay on the ground while Justin tried to figure out how to get the guy out of here unnoticed. He was far too big to carry.

Justin walked to the edge of the grove looking for any signs of Mr. Hamilton returning, but his jeep was nowhere in sight. Justin connected to the water element and reached out to his teacher. "I've got Boris. Can you come and help me carry him out of here? Park close to the grove of trees. The guy is going to be heavy to carry."

Thoughts of Henry occupied Justin's thoughts as he waited for his teacher to arrive. But an explosion of earth energy and loud booms yanked him out of his reverie. Justin spun and ran back in the direction of Boris, but a crater sat at least ten feet wide and a few feet deep in the place of Boris' prior spot. Four trees had been uprooted and had fallen to the ground. Justin scanned the grove, but he couldn't see Boris anywhere in sight. He ran to the far edge of the grove and scoured the view, but his opponent had seemingly vanished. Justin kicked a small boulder the size of a volleyball to let out his frustration. It hurt his foot far more than the rock, but he didn't care. He needed to catch these guys before they found out that Henry was still alive.

Chapter 38

"WHY DID YOU let him get away?" Rex demanded of Justin as the others stood nearby in the cabin while Rex and Justin stood facing off. The fury of the storm outside had picked up and rattled the windows in the old cabin.

Justin balled up his fists. "Why did I let him get away? You guys already let him escape once before. I stopped him by myself and even fully tied him up in branches. By the time I looked for Mr. Hamilton and returned, Boris was gone. I couldn't carry him out by myself and you're the one who said I can't do a Wipe, or even a partial overload."

Grant leaned forward in his chair. "Rex, it's done. Let's figure out what we're going to do now. At least they were able to capture Diederick. Now there's only two left: Alexei and Boris."

Rex finally took his glare off of Justin. "Fine. I recommend we all stay here tonight."

Justin lifted up his arms in exasperation. "I told you. My parents are not going to let me stay at a friend's house on a school night. They're going to be upset as it is that I won't be returning home until almost ten o'clock on a Thursday night." That wasn't Justin's only concern though. He needed to return home soon so he could call Henry in private. "Besides, my mom knows I haven't finished my homework yet."

"Hmm. What a surprise," Rex said.

"Stop it, you too!" Anya said with more force than matched her body. "Grant and David can take turns watching at Justin's house. Stay put until it's time to go to school. At least at school David can watch out for you and Raven. With only two of them left. I don't think they'll try attacking again."

"They did today," Justin said.

"Only because they thought I'd be injured and alone in the hospital," Anya said.

"Fine." Justin sat back on the couch.

"It looks like the earliest the Council will be meeting is tomorrow evening. Now that we've also temporarily overloaded Diederick too, they should be able to vote on him also and fly someone out here by Saturday morning. Until then, we try to stay out of trouble," Rex said looking directly at Justin.

"What?" Justin raised his eyebrows and shoulders.

"Um." Raven's voice spoke up quietly but Rex didn't seem to notice. "But what about the things Alexei said about a big bang?"

"What about it?" Rex said.

"What if he's planning something soon?" Raven said.

"Our priority is taking care of our prisoners until the Council votes and others arrive. Besides, all we have are a few bits of information. It doesn't mean anything," Rex said.

"Well, maybe it does mean something. I needed a distraction while stuck in the hotel room so I began looking again at the

237

photos I took from Alexei's hotel room. I can't get his voice out of my head when he spoke about a big bang and how they won't know what hit them. You didn't hear his voice. I may not have proof, but I just know he intends to do something horrible. I can feel it. We need to stop him," Raven said.

"Raven, how can we stop him when we don't even know what he plans to do?" Mr. Hamilton said.

"That's why I went through the photos. We need to figure out what he's up to before it's too late. Alexei said he was preparing for a 'big bang'. At first, I thought he meant that figuratively. But what if he was being literal? Lannix is a chemical company. What if he intends to blow up the factory?"

The comment Henry made about researching a chemical company crossed Justin's mind. "What if Alexei's sabotaging companies?" Justin said.

"Why would he do that?" Grant asked.

"Raven, once we take care of the others, then we can worry about Alexei. One step at a time. We don't want anyone else hurt like Anya," Rex said.

The discussion was over. Grant offered to drive Justin home and take the first shift at his house. Justin walked over and sat on the arm of the couch beside Raven. He wanted to reach out and comfort her, but he knew he couldn't touch her. "I'll see you in class tomorrow?" Justin said.

Raven raised her furrowed forehead. "Yeah. Be careful."

Chapter 39

THE NEXT MORNING, Justin pumped the pedals of his bike as fast as he could up the hill. He only had two class periods to get to the Lighthouse Mission, visit with Henry, and return to school before English class. He didn't want Mr. Hamilton, Raven, or even Lewis and his other friends to know he had skipped classes. Justin was concerned that Henry's safety depended upon no one else knowing he was alive.

As he sped down the street, Justin came to a stop in front of a park near the shelter Henry stayed at. An elderly couple sat together on a bench near the entrance to the park. Justin climbed off his bike, locked it to a nearby pole, and walked past a young mother pushing her son in a stroller down the path. Justin tried to shake off his nervousness by rolling his head and shaking his arms. He told himself it was ridiculous to be nervous about meeting his best friend, but after returning home last night and calling Henry, Justin realized that while Henry was still Justin's best friend, Justin was a stranger to Henry. That left a pain in

Justin's chest, but he hoped they could find a way for Henry to regain his memory.

Henry sat on a bench farther down the path. Butterflies scattered in Justin's stomach and he took a deep breath to calm himself. "Hi, Henry," Justin said as he sat down on the bench next to his grandpa.

"If I'm your grandpa, why do you call me by my first name?"

"When I was seven, you told me that best friends call each other by their first names, so I should call you Henry."

"What kind of teenager is 'best friends' with an old man?"

"You're not old. Okay, well maybe technically you are. But you're more fun than anyone I know. Even my friends back in Houston thought you were cool. You and I go white water rafting, surfing, rock climbing, and do all sorts of great things together. You never let my blankouts stop us from doing things. You even somehow convinced Mom and Dad last year to let me go with you on your research trip to Africa. That was incredible. We go to sports games. You even took me to a rock concert once. I know you didn't really like the music, but you came with me and my friends and had fun with us. You always said that age was a state of mind and you were staying twenty-seven."

"Hmm. Sounds fun."

"It was. It is. Now that you're back, we can continue to do so. Well, once we take care of Alexei and his friends."

"Yes, speaking of that, I brought the camera like you asked."

Justin reached out and accepted the small, red camera. He hoped that it might hold some clues to help them move forward. Scanning past the photos of their trip to Galveston made Justin look up at Henry and smile. "When we went to the waterslide park in Galveston, you were easily the oldest person riding the slides by at least twenty years. All the other adults were too wimpy to have any fun. That was a great weekend."

Henry smiled briefly, but then his mouth closed in a tight

line and the wrinkles on his forehead magnified. "I don't remember any of it."

"That's okay. We'll find a way to help you remember."

"What if we can't?"

The thought jarred Justin, but he hid his concern. "Then we'll just have to make new memories for you. But don't worry about that right now. First, we'll take care of Alexei and then we'll get your memory back."

Time passed too quickly as Justin answered questions about Henry's life and then they reviewed the images on the camera. Henry told Justin what his research had uncovered about the two companies recorded on the camera. Justin felt bad leaving Henry alone, but he was anxious to talk to Raven about what he learned. Besides, if he wasn't back to the school before English class, Raven would call the others and they'd start searching for him. A hug felt awkward right now, so Justin simply squeezed Henry's shoulder, said he'd call tonight, jumped on his bike, and pedaled like mad to try to return to school before his next class.

Chapter 40

JUSTIN COULD BARELY wait for English class to end. It seemed ridiculous to be wasting his time sitting in class listening to Ms. Chalmers drone on about Romeo and Juliet. He had way bigger problems than those two ever had and his were real. Thankfully, the bell rang at last. Justin grabbed his backpack and walked up to Raven's desk. She looked like she hadn't slept well last night. He wished he had something to ease her worry, but what he had to say would probably only heighten it and after looking at the images on Henry's camera, he couldn't wait. "Can we go somewhere and talk? Privately?" She looked up and nodded. Justin told Lewis he'd meet them later at their table in the cafeteria and followed Raven down the hallway and into a deserted classroom.

Raven sat on top of a desk next to Justin waiting for him to speak. Justin took a breath before starting. He hated to not be entirely truthful with Raven, but he didn't want to tell anyone about Henry yet, not even Raven. He knew she'd never do anything purposely to hurt him or Henry, but what if her knowledge even somehow suggested to someone else that Henry was alive. Justin felt he couldn't risk that right now. "My grandma just sent me Henry's old camera and I looked through the photos. Most of them were of Henry and me on the last trip we took together, but the last images were of some documents and news articles. I almost deleted them until I recognized the Lannix logo in one of them."

"Your grandpa researched the same company that Alexei is investing in?"

"Yeah and the images were taken only three days prior to Henry's – death." Justin almost said something else, further proof that he shouldn't tell anyone yet about Henry. It would be too easy to let the truth slip out.

"What are the pictures of?" Raven asked.

"The first few are about some oil company that suffered a major explosion at one of their refineries due to a natural disaster and how their stock price plummeted. But there are some shots about Lannix. The first image is just a news article about Lannix expanding its operations. The next one is a report about the projected growth of the company stock."

"Growth?" Raven asked.

"Yeah, why?"

"The documents I photographed showed that Alexei shorted the stock."

"What? English, please," Justin said.

"He kind of did the opposite of buying stock shares in the company. But you only buy short if you think the stock price is going to drop. Why would he short a stock if the company is doing well?"

"How do you know so much about the stock market?" Justin asked.

"Mom has lots of boring cocktail parties at the house and she

243

always expects me to attend. There's nothing to do but listen. It's surprising what you learn when you listen." Raven paused for a moment. "Justin, what is the date of the article about the company's stock?"

"Last month. Why?"

"Let me Google the company." Raven pulled out her phone, typed quickly, scanned the contents, and then held out her phone for Justin to view. "Look at this. The price has risen quite a bit over the last month. I'm not seeing anything that would suggest the company's stock will drop and those articles don't seem to suggest a drop. If Alexei is an investor, he would know better than to short a strong company."

As Raven spoke, Justin scanned through the remaining documents Henry had taken photos of. "After the article about the oil company whose refinery exploded, Henry's next photo is of a chart showing the drop in stock price for the oil company."

"No, he wouldn't," Raven said.

"Wouldn't what?"

"What if Alexei could do something to make the company's stock fall? He could make a lot of money. You said that the company suffered a natural disaster, right?" Raven said.

"You think he wants to blow up the factory to make the stock price drop and make some money?" Justin asked.

"Not some money. A lot of money. It's a large international company and if the notes on his documents truly reflect all of the short buys he's placed under different names, he could make millions if the stock price plummets."

"Even if you're right, after what happened today and the fact that Steven must have told him we saw his documents, he'll probably cancel the sabotage," Justin said.

"I don't think so. Steven knew we just thought they were business documents. Besides, Alexei bought a huge amount of short buys. Unless he has millions in the bank, which I doubt, he probably bought them on margin."

"Margin?"

"Basically, he borrowed part of the money to short that many stocks. It's a common practice. But the risk of going on margin is that if the stock price rises, you're required to put more money in your account to maintain a certain minimum percentage of the growing stock price." Raven held her phone out for Justin to see the screen. "It shows here that the company's stock price has been rising significantly for the past few weeks. If he's on margin, he can't afford to let it climb much higher. He'll have to do something and soon. But how do we find out when and where?"

Justin was determined to catch Alexei. It was the only way he could help ensure Henry's safety. But what did he have to go on? All he knew—all he suspected—was that Alexei planned to blow up Lannix. The documents showed that the headquarters were in Seattle, but the company was international so the sabotage could happen anywhere. But Alexei had once said that he had been coming up to Seattle for business. Maybe Lannix was the business. Unfortunately, that was only a guess, and they needed more evidence than that. Justin tried to remember if Alexei had unintentionally dropped any other clues.

He shook his head in frustration. "I don't have any idea." Justin slammed his hand on the desk he was sitting on. "We need to find him now." None of them would be safe until they stopped Alexei. Memories of the fight in the meadow surfaced. He remembered the fear he had felt when he woke up after being knocked out and overheard them talking about killing him. He had to admit that the words had sent a chill through him. The words insisted on replaying in his mind again and again, but by the third or fourth time, he recalled the first part of the conversation. Boris had been asking one of the others about going somewhere on Friday.

Wait! He must have meant this Friday. That was tomorrow. But where had he said he wanted to go? Justin tried replaying that part of the conversation over and over in his head. The words seemed to be just beyond the grasp of his memory. He reached out mentally trying to grab the words each time he replayed it in his mind. An image of a boat or dock came to mind, but he couldn't recall the words. "The water? A dock?" he said out loud. Irritated, he pushed himself off of the desk and paced back and forth.

"A dock? What are you talking about?" Raven asked.

Justin barely noticed Raven. He was absorbed in his thoughts trying to mentally return to the meadow and what he heard that day. A picture of a dock continued to be stuck in his mind. The recording playing in his head was barely recognizable as if it came through a thick layer of fog and static. "A Pier? Pier…pier…pier twenty-seven?" He stopped and looked up at Raven. "Have you even heard of a pier twenty-seven?"

Raven bit her lip and shook her head slowly. "No. But Seattle's Pier fifty-seven is fun to go to."

"Pier fifty-seven? That's it!"

"What's it?" Raven asked.

Justin explained what he had heard Boris say. "Alexei said he is doing business in Seattle and Boris said he could go to Pier Fifty-seven before two thirty PM on Friday, they must be planning to attack the Lannix factory in Seattle tomorrow." Justin stopped and grinned triumphantly at Raven.

"We've got to go tell Mr. Hamilton right away," Raven said starting to get up from the desk.

"Wait." Justin halted Raven. Last night's discussion replayed in his head. "There's no way they're going to approve going down to Seattle tomorrow." After some convincing, Raven finally had to admit that Justin's was probably right about the adults not condoning the trip to Seattle. Anya was in no condition to do much of anything. Rex and Grant were obligated to the Council to keep a close eye on their prisoners. And there was no way they'd approve Mr. Hamilton and Selena going to Seattle with two teenagers to confront Alexei and who knows who else. Besides, they'd continue to say the evidence was insufficient, but Raven agreed that she felt the information made it pretty clear that Alexei planned something bad at Lannix's factory in Seattle tomorrow. She didn't like the idea of just the two of them going alone, but she couldn't just stand by and let who knows how many people be hurt or killed at the Lannix factory. After a long discussion she finally agreed that telling the adults about the plan was too much of a risk since they would most likely refuse the plan and do all they could to stop Raven and Justin from going.

She raised the question about transportation to Seattle, but Justin explained his plan for that. When she said she was impressed with the plan, Justin pointed out that he could strategize when necessary. It could work, but both of them would have to do some convincing to make the plan have a chance of success.

Justin hurried to the cafeteria anxious to catch Lewis before lunch period ended. He'd persuaded Raven. Now he needed to convince Lewis to help with his plan. He waited until the group finished lunch and then he walked with Lewis back to his locker. Justin tried to sound casual as he brought the subject up. "So remember when your Mom drove us to the restaurant and was talking about wanting to visit Seattle?"

Lewis turned to Justin and looked at him strange. "Yeah. Why?"

"My science project with Raven isn't working out like we planned and it's due next week. So we need to start over, but we don't have much time. Raven had a good idea, but it requires us to go to the Museum of Flight in Seattle tomorrow afternoon. Her mom's out of town and my parents are busy. Do you think we could get your Mom to take the three of us? It could be fun." Justin tried to sound upbeat.

"Doesn't it close around five?" Lewis asked.

"Yeah, we'd need to leave after fourth period to get there by two o'clock to have enough time to do our research. Would your mom mind us missing a couple of classes?"

"Probably not. She believes my education should happen just as much outside the classroom." Lewis suddenly stopped talking and raised his eyebrows. "Wait. Raven Ashley asked you to go to Seattle with her?"

"Yeah. It's for our science project."

"Raven Ashley asked you to go with her to another city? She has a boyfriend. A rather large one," Lewis said.

The reminder of Eric and his goons made Justin clench his teeth, but he didn't care what Eric or his buddies thought about him spending time with Raven. He beat them up before and he'd do so again, if necessary. But he didn't need to get into that with Lewis. "It's not like that. Raven and I are just friends."

"Right. I've seen how you look at her. I'd be a total outsider."

"I don't look at her different than anyone else."

"Whatever." Lewis smirked.

"We could do something fun after going to the museum," Justin said. Lewis just looked at him skeptically, but Justin saved the best carrot for last. "What if Raven invited Nikki to come with us?"

Lewis' eyes opened wide and a huge grin spread across his face. "What time do you want my mom to pick us up?"

Raven stood along the sidewalk waiting for Nikki's mom to pick her up. "Nikki, I need you to come so that Eric isn't jealous about me going with Justin," Raven said.

"Should he be jealous?" Nikki asked.

"No. Of course not. Justin and I are just friends."

"So you haven't noticed that Justin qualifies under the tall, dark, and handsome category?"

"What? No."

"You don't think Justin's cute?"

"Well, maybe. But we're just friends."

"And on top of cute, he risked his life to rescue you from a burning building. You've never thought about why he did that?"

"He did it because we're friends."

"Raven, you've only known him for a couple weeks. A guy doesn't run into a burning building to rescue someone unless he's a fireman or he really likes you."

"Some guys do. Justin's just that kind of person."

"Okay. If you say so."

"So, you'll come with us?" Raven asked.

"Sure. What fun will it be around here with you gone?" Nikki said.

Raven gave Nikki a big hug. "Thanks!"

"Besides, since the two of you are just friends, I could have some fun getting to know our cute hero."

The smile disappeared from Raven's face and her forehead crinkled. Nikki laughed. "I'm just kidding. Say what you want, but I can tell he's interested in you and I think you're more interested in him than you want to admit." A black SUV pulled up in front of them. "What time on Friday?" Nikki asked.

"After fourth period."

Nikki opened the passenger door and climbed into the vehicle. "Okay. See you tomorrow."

Raven waved goodbye and looked down the road for the gray rental car Selena would be driving to pick her up.

"Raven!"

Raven turned around to see Justin coming down the front steps of the school. Once he reached her, he asked, "So what did Nikki say?"

The words, "tall, dark, and handsome" came to mind, but she certainly wasn't going to repeat those to Justin. Raven looked at Justin and tried to find a reason he didn't match Nikki's description, but she couldn't. Instead, she noticed how his biceps flexed as he ran his hand through his hair.

"Raven?"

She shook her head to clear her mind. "Oh. She's coming. Now we just need to plan what to tell Mr. Hamilton and the others."

"He's going to know something is up by last period since we won't show up for science class. We'll send him a text message while we're on the road letting him know that we're okay so that he doesn't worry. They'll be upset with us, but there will be nothing they can do to stop us as that point. We'll get chewed out by them. I hope you don't mind."

"So will you."

Justin chuckled. "Yeah, but I'm used to it."

"Well, then I guess at least you won't be alone when you get in trouble this time."

"Are you okay with all of this?" Justin said as he rubbed his neck.

Raven noticed the cute curls that formed at Justin's neck because he'd allowed his hair to grow a little long. She wanted to touch them, but she forced herself to refocus. "We have a plan for getting down there, but we don't know what to expect when we arrive."

"We'll improvise – together. That's what friends are for right? Helping each other stop evil madmen from blowing up factories?"

Raven shook her head and smiled. "Only friends like you,

Justin."

Chapter 41

DESPITE NIKKI'S ATTEMPTS at match making, Raven succeeded in placing Nikki between herself and Justin in the back seat of Mrs. Johnson's car. While Raven wanted to sit next to Justin, she definitely did not want to accidentally make a connection with him and have the kind of reaction she had experienced before, but this time in front of Nikki, Lewis, and his mom. Besides, she couldn't risk draining much of her energy before facing the dangers she expected at the factory in Seattle. Lewis would definitely have loved switching spots with Raven, but Mrs. Johnson expected Lewis to sit up front so she could ask him about his day.

Mrs. Johnson then moved on to interrogating everyone and telling stories about all the crazy adventures she and Lewis's dad had before Lewis was born. Raven was so nervous about the upcoming confrontation, she wasn't fit for small talk, so she was relieved that Mrs. Johnson and the others carried the conversation during the two hour drive to the museum.

Raven tried not to think about what they were approaching, but she couldn't help it. She hoped they would encounter only Alexei and Boris, but Alexei had been on the phone with a woman that Raven was quite sure wasn't Lanae, the Water Elementer they caught. Therefore, if there was one more person involved, who's to say there wasn't ten or fifty more? The tension continued to build inside her stomach, so she tried to focus on the few things that were planned. It gave her a feeling of control and surety. Raven had already called a Seattle taxi company yesterday to schedule a pick up from the museum at 3:00 PM. The taxi company agreed to have the taxi driver send them a text message five minutes before he'd reach the museum. They picked the museum because it was only a couple miles from the Lannix factory. Other than the location and a general layout of the buildings visible via Google Earth maps, they didn't know what to expect when they arrived. Justin seemed to thrive on the unpredictability of it all, but it just made Raven's stomach queasy.

Mrs. Johnson pulled into the museum parking lot and Raven took a couple deep breaths to calm herself. Thankfully, Nikki had been preoccupied with the conversation with Mrs. Johnson and Justin, that she didn't notice Raven's one or two word replies. Raven slowly climbed out of the green Subaru and followed the others toward the museum. As they stepped up to pay their entrance fees, Raven reached for her purse and realized she must have left it in the car. Mrs. Johnson handed Lewis her car keys. "You kids aren't going to want me tailing along, so I'll head off to explore. Lewis, would you be a gentleman and run out to the car and get Raven's purse for her? Just don't lose my keys, okay? I'll meet you all back here at five PM when the museum closes, okay?"

"Yes, Mom," Lewis said while the others nodded.

"Thanks, Mrs. Johnson," Raven said as Lewis' mom waved and headed further into the museum.

"I'll be right back." Lewis said and headed out the exit and jogged toward the car.

Raven felt ridiculous for forgetting her purse. She was so nervous she wasn't thinking straight. But a frazzled brain would lead to a frazzled body when confronting the others. She needed to focus fast.

While waiting in line to pay for their admission, Raven needed a distraction so she began giving the others a mini tour of the entrance of the museum. Raven pointed out to her friends a wood and fabric flying machine hanging from the ceiling. She explained that it was based on Leonardo DaVinci's drawings. Once they were through the line, Raven led them to the left into the massive glass-walled portion of the museum. Planes sat on the floor. They hung from the ceilings. From afar, they looked almost like model airplanes, but as you approached each full-size plane, you discovered the history and lives of the pilots who had flown the skies with each beautiful, elegant machine. The taxi wouldn't be arriving for almost fifteen minutes, so she took the opportunity to calm her nerves by surrounding herself with something she loved: flying.

After describing the history of one of the planes, she quoted, "When once you have tested flight, you will forever walk the earth with your eyes turned skyward."

Justin turned to her. "Who said that?"

"Leonardo DaVinci, but it's just as true today."

Justin tilted his head to the side, kept his eyes on her, and grinned.

"What?" Raven asked.

Justin shrugged his shoulders. "Nothing. You really love flying, don't you?"

"I told you, I do."

"Yeah, but I didn't realize how much. It's just fun to see."

Raven didn't know how to take that comment so she paused

her tour commentary and let the others look around on their own. A minute later, her phone buzzed in her pocket. She nearly dropped it on the floor in her rush to pull it out. The text message popped the peaceful aviation bubble she had been in and now she was exposed again to thoughts about Alexei and the danger ahead. Raven walked near Justin and discreetly lifted her hand with all fingers extended to give him the five minute warning. Justin nodded and he looked to see where Nikki and Lewis were located.

Not surprisingly, Lewis was following near Nikki, but sensibly leaving enough space between them so he didn't seem like a stalker. Justin waited a couple minutes and then walked over to them. "Raven and I need to go do some of our research. It'll be boring, so the two of you can go check out the other parts of the museum and we can find you later."

Raven noticed that Lewis's face lit up in response to the idea, but Nikki spoke up. "Oh, that's okay. We don't mind hanging out with you guys." Raven knew this was a possibility, so they moved to plan B. It wasn't a great plan, but it was better than nothing.

Justin stepped back. "Okay. But I need to go to the bathroom. Keep looking around and I'll come find all of you," Justin said and then headed toward the front of the museum.

After about a minute, Raven said she needed to go to the bathroom also. Nikki offered to go with her, but Raven said she'd be fine on her own and promptly started walking away to deter Nikki from deciding to come with her. Once she rounded the corner into the main entrance, she saw Justin motioning to her near the front doors. Nervousness propelled her forward as she followed Justin outside into the stormy, cool air sending shivers down her back. Justin leaned down to talk through the passenger window to the taxi driver. "Are you here for Raven Ashley?" A female taxi driver with short, messy, brown hair and more than a handful of wrinkles that life had generously given her nodded tiredly. Raven grabbed hold of the cold, metal handle, pulled the door open, and scooted over to give Justin room to sit. Raven stared ahead and focused on steeling her courage while Justin gave directions to the driver.

"Raven?" She turned in response to his voice. Justin leaned his head toward her. "It's all good. Everything is going smoothly—accordingly to plan. Just how you like it, right?" He gave her a smile for encouragement, but she could see something else in his eyes. An unstoppable determination. Another shiver ran through her, but it wasn't from the cold. While she was scared for herself, the look in his eyes made her more scared for Justin. She worried he'd risk anything to stop and catch Alexei. But she was sure there wasn't anything she could say or do to convince Justin to turn back and she wasn't about to abandon him to face Alexei, and any others, all alone.

"Just promise me you'll be careful." Raven lifted her hand to touch his, but held back at the last inch. "Please."

Chapter 42

AS THEY DROVE past the factory, both Justin and Raven unconsciously lowered themselves in their seats keeping an eye out for Alexei and any other Elementers. Peeking over the back window, Justin scanned for any signs of Alexei or Boris, but the only movement they saw was the swirling storm that became more intense by the minute.

"Here is good," Justin said to the taxi driver.

The driver pulled over along the sidewalk and glanced at the two of them through the mirror. "That'll be ten fifty."

Raven pulled out a twenty dollar bill from her purse and handed it to the woman. "Keep the change."

The woman's tired face lifted just a bit. "Thanks. Do you need me to wait for you?"

"Oh, no. Our—friends—are nearby. Thanks," Justin said pushing hard on the door against the wind and quickly climbing out of the taxi.

Once the taxi drove away, Raven turned to Justin. "I don't see them anywhere."

"Let's take a closer look," Justin said as they crossed the street and headed in the direction of the factory. They walked quickly past the factory to view the other side and then passed by again looking for any sign of Alexei. "Can you sense them?" Justin asked Raven.

Raven stopped and seemed to zone out. Justin watched her hair swirl around in the blustering wind. After about twenty seconds Raven looked at Justin again and shook her head. "No, nothing. Maybe we were wrong."

"They may not have arrived yet. We're early. I want to take a closer look. The property next door is abandoned, or at least no one seems to be around right now. Let's go in. We can view the side of the Lannix property from there." Justin walked along the wire link fence and pushed on the gate. A locked chain held the gate in place. Justin held up the lock. "Time for the master criminal."

"Very funny." Raven reached for the lock and in a few moments it popped open.

"You're pretty handy to have around," Justin teased as he loosened the chain from around the fence to create enough space for them to squeeze between the gates and then he locked it back up. He didn't want anything to look suspicious.

Justin caught up to Raven and they walked toward the far end of the property along the bay. The weeds were overgrown here and were buffeted about by the storm. The two of them kept their distance from the fence abutting the Lannix factory because they didn't want to draw attention to themselves. As they passed, they searched for Alexei, but to no avail. Once they reached the water's edge, they turned around and started heading back, passing again an old abandoned building on the property. As they passed, a few birds scattered away from the building in surprise.

As they neared the street again, Raven halted. "What is it?" Justin asked.

"I can feel someone coming."

Seconds later, Justin saw a fire red Ferrari drive past the factory. Justin ducked down behind a bunch of overgrown blackberry bushes and pulled down on Raven's jacket. "That's Alexei's car."

"You're sure it's his?"

Justin nodded. "Oh, yeah. Alexei has a red Ferrari. There's no way a car that hot and expensive just happens to be owned by someone else right where we expected to find Alexei. That's him. You were right. Now we just need to find out what he's up to, stop him, and catch him."

The two of them peered through the bushes expecting to see Alexei pass by them at any moment. But Justin was surprised when he saw Alexei and Boris stop in front of the gate to the empty property. Boris blew the lock and pulled the chain from the gate. The guy seriously lacked any finesse. Justin and Raven tiptoed around the massive blackberry bush as Alexei and Boris passed to use the bush as cover between themselves and Alexei.

The men stopped half way down the property along the fence and Boris used his earth energy to bend back part of the chain link along a seam in the fence and then walk through the opening.

"That's so weird," Raven whispered. "I'm sensing the same thing like when we were attacked in the park. He's using his energy, but he's somehow masking most of it so that I can't sense it well. Before, I thought the energy was something else, but I just saw him use his energy and he is definitely masking it somehow. I've never heard of such a thing."

"Well then, let's stay close enough to keep an eye on Alexei and

Boris," Justin said as they quietly made their way toward the opening, trying to move behind as much overgrown vegetation as possible.

Justin and Raven carefully followed at a distance behind Alexei and Boris into the Lannix property. They watched Boris stop underneath a security camera. In a few seconds, smoke poured out from the camera before being blown away from the wind. Alexei and Boris entered into the nearest building through an open loading dock door.

Justin and Raven hurried behind to follow them, but suddenly two Lannix employees in orange jumpers walked out onto the loading dock, and the youths had to hide behind a recycling bin.

"How are we supposed to get in now?" Raven asked.

Justin thought of options and then a grin spread across his face. "Follow my lead." Justin pulled out two large, uncrushed cardboard boxes from the recycling bin, stacked them on top of one another, and picked them up. Raven looked at him strangely. "Just keep the boxes in front of your face and they'll think we're employees," Justin said. Raven gave him a skeptical look but she picked up a couple boxes. He looked behind himself once, nodded to Raven, and then walked up the concrete steps to the loading dock and through the open door at the farthest point away from the workers. Once he was inside and around the corner out of view of the workers, he sat down the boxes and made sure Raven was behind him. "Let's find Alexei."

They moved between storage tanks and aisles of tall shelves, making a point to avoid any other employees. Thankfully, this area of the factory didn't have much activity right now. As they rounded a tall storage tank, Justin saw Alexei standing outside a door. Boris was inside a small room and had his hands on a bunch of electrical equipment. Soon Justin saw smoke drifting up from the console. Boris exited the room and closed the door behind him. Justin noticed the sign on the door, "Fire Safety".

"What are they doing?" Raven asked from behind Justin.

"I think they just destroyed the fire alarm and fire protection system. With that damaged, the employees won't be able to contain whatever Alexei has planned."

"They're clearly trying to do something bad. We need to stop them."

Justin was irritated with himself. They should have stopped these two before they ever entered the Lannix property. He had been waiting for the optimal moment, but clearly it had passed. Justin halted when he peeked around an aisle and saw the two men stopped behind a large metal storage container about thirty feet away. Boris was crouched down and had his hand on the pipe leading into the tank.

"Justin. He's heating up the metal. These are dangerous chemicals. This is not good. We need to stop them and warn everyone to get out of the building," Raven said.

"You're right, but they just destroyed the fire alarm system."

"Then I'll call 911."

"Raven, how will you explain you know someone is sabotaging the factory? You can't draw that attention to yourself."

"I'll come up with some excuse and leave it as an anonymous tip."

"They'll be able to trace it back to your cell phone. It's too dangerous. They'll think you might have had something to do with it, especially after they find out you had also just been in another fire only a week ago."

"Well, we have to warn them somehow."

"You're right. You need to run back to the museum and use a phone there. So many people pass through the museum that they won't be able to know it was you who made the call."

"Justin, it's just over a mile away. That'll take too long. We need to warn them now."

"I'll keep Alexei and Boris distracted long enough for you to get the message out. I promise. Just run fast."

"We don't know how easy it is to create an explosion. I'm not leaving you here if it could go off at any moment," Raven said.

"They won't set it off while they're here. Alexei is not about to sacrifice himself. He's far too selfish for that."

"It's two against one. You need my help. I'm not leaving you to fight them both on your own."

"I'll pick them off one by one. No worries."

"No worries? Of course, I'm worried."

Justin paused and took a step closer to Raven. She sucked in a breath. They weren't touching, so it wouldn't hurt Raven. But Justin could feel the electricity, a different kind of energy, swirling between them. "You said you believed in me. Did you mean it?"

"Yes," Raven whispered. "Of course I did."

"Then believe me when I say I can do this." Justin stood up taller but still looked into Raven's eyes. "I need to do this." Justin paused for a few seconds and then took a step back. Not only did he need to prove to himself that he could do this, he also needed to be sure Raven was safe and the best way to do that was to get her as far away from these goons as possible. "And you need to warn everyone. I'll make sure there are no big explosions, but we should get everyone out of the factory as soon as possible if only to make sure they don't see or aren't hurt by any objects flying around during a fight. Okay?"

Raven hesitated and then finally nodded slowly. "Fine. But don't get dead, Justin Wilder. Promise me."

"Promise. Now go!" Justin nodded in the direction of the loading dock doors.

Raven turned, took a couple steps, glanced back at Justin,

looked like she was about to say something, but then looked away and ran around the corner out of Justin's sight.

Chapter 43

JUSTIN TURNED TO look back on Alexei and Boris, but neither of them were in sight. Moving toward the far end of the building, he found Boris tampering with another storage tank. Justin scanned the area, but couldn't see Alexei. Boris wasn't his priority for personal reasons, but it seemed pretty clear that Boris was the muscle and means behind the sabotage. Justin needed to stop him before anyone got hurt. Fighting Boris here in the factory would definitely gather too much attention and might even trigger the explosion he was trying to prevent. Besides, even if he succeeded in knocking Boris out without a fight, the beast was too big for Justin to carry or drag out of here without being noticed. He needed to draw Boris out of the factory and then take him on.

A cart full of metal pipes sat less than six feet behind Boris. Justin connected to the wind and sent it barreling into Boris. Because he was crouched down, the cart shoved him into the storage tank banging his head solidly against the metal. It didn't knock him out, Justin didn't expect it to. The guy had a seriously thick skull. All Justin aimed to do was grab Boris' attention and make him mad enough to chase after Justin.

After taking a second or two to unscramble his puny brain, Boris looked up to see Justin who had stepped out into view. "Wow, and I thought that this skull of yours might have cracked the storage tank. You really should be more careful."

Boris growled like a bear. "You little punk. I'm going to finish you off." He stood up and stepped toward Justin who spun around and began running for the loading dock doors. Boris had strength, but Justin knew he could easily outrun the guy. Justin dodged between tanks and other equipment to avoid being an easy target for Boris to fling something at. He didn't want the guy to start a fight here in the factory. Once he cleared the loading doors, Justin didn't waste time with the stairs and instead jumped off the ledge. The jar sent a shot of pain through his shoulder, but instead, he focused on making it to the opening in the fence. Pushing himself full speed, he neared the fence before Boris exited the building. As Justin started to step through the opening, the pulled back fence section flapped back in place. Justin connected and pushed on it with his earth energy, but Boris held it in place with his energy. Boris was closing the distance, so Justin focused on another section of fence a few feet down and ripped a seam in the fence and pushed back a flap with such force that the whole fence shook.

Justin darted through the hole and sprinted seventy feet to the abandoned building. Boris ripped out large chunks of earth and sent them hurling toward Justin who shot gusts of wind to redirect the projectiles. The second projectile grazed Justin's bad shoulder, but not enough to knock him down. As Justin approached the building, he blasted the door open and ran in.

Taking quick stock of the area, he ran down a nearby hallway, slipped into a room that must have once been an office. Slowing down his breathing, Justin listened for Boris' arrival.

Heavy steps inside the entrance announced Boris' presence. "Vere are you, you little punk? Come out and face me." Boris headed in the opposite direction, so once he was far enough away, Justin slipped out of the room he hid in and snuck down the hallway toward his opponent. Upon reaching the main entrance, Justin took a left away from Boris, hoping to find a better spot to attack from. The building must have been some kind of fabrication factory. Whatever they produced was gone, but lots of metal working machines were scattered throughout the large rooms Justin passed along. Near the west side of the building, Justin finally found what he was looking for. A large room empty of metal machinery with no windows. With Boris being an Earth Elementer, Justin preferred to face him in a spot where there was limited earth and metal for Boris to use against him. Sure, Justin wouldn't have them either, but he had alternatives.

Now he just needed to draw Boris in. Justin headed back down the hall and listened. Boris' heavy feet clomped along the crossing hallway. Justin braced himself and then stepped into the hall pretending to sneak across it. "Punk!" Boris yelled out and barreled down the hallway. Justin spun on his heels and ran back to his selected room, but slow enough that Boris would reach that hallway and see Justin before he entered the room. As Justin passed one of the manufacturing rooms, a large metal cutting machine that was nearly as tall as Justin came sliding out of the door and broadsided Justin into the wall. Justin tried to get up, but his arm was pinned between the machine and the wall. He directed earth energy to push the machine but Boris used equal force against it. It budged a little, but not enough to pull out his arm. Boris closed the distance so Justin quickly connected to the wind and shot a gust tipping the machine. Justin had to twist to the side to avoid it from crushing his legs, but he was finally free.

As Justin looked up, Boris was above him and lifted Justin up by his shirt and threw him at the wall. His back and head cracked against the wall. Justin lifted his head and shot a wind gust at Boris. It didn't hold much power since Justin was disoriented from colliding with the wall, but it was enough to slow Boris down and give Justin enough time to get up and stumble into the empty room.

Justin placed his back against the same wall as the door so Boris wouldn't see him immediately upon entering. But he stood far from the door to stay out of Boris' reach and struggled to maintain his focus despite the dizziness. As soon as Boris rushed into the room, Justin shot a burst of wind from the sky causing the roof and surrounding walls to come crashing down in the hallway in front of the door. The force knocked Boris down, but more importantly, it blockaded the door. There was no way out of the room.

As Boris lifted his head and started to push himself to his feet, Justin moved to the center of the room, planted his feet firmly, and began spinning the air in a large circle around him. Similar to a hurricane, the center where he stood was perfectly calm. But he could hear the roaring of the wind spinning furiously around him. Boris stood up and stalked toward Justin, but as he reached the edge of the wind it pushed him over and threw him to the side. He got back up on his feet and this time ran toward Justin. His speed allowed him to get closer to Justin, but doing so exposed him to the faster winds at the center of the circle. The wind picked him up and shot him against the wall. The drywall caved in leaving a huge dent where Boris' body collided.

Boris struggled to get up, but before he had time to stand,

Justin decided to finish this fight. He needed to get back to the factory and find Alexei. Closing his eyes, Justin dropped any imagined barriers between him and the energy. Feeling it flow around and through him, the lines between the two became blurred. He joined with the wind as if it was the breath in his lungs and then he exhaled. The wind roared around him, but the hum resonated deep inside Justin. It felt like a natural extension of himself. For a few moments, he forgot about Boris until Justin opened up his eyes. Something tightened in his chest and a stab of fear caused him to stagger back. The walls of the room were nearly shredded to pieces and Boris was being flung about in the current with the wind and all the debris.

Justin immediately released the connection and the wind slowed, dropping Boris to the floor. For a moment, Justin stood frozen afraid he might have killed the guy. Boris wasn't moving. Justin crept up to him and leaned over pressing his fingers against the guy's neck desperately hoping he'd feel a pulse. When he felt a rhythmic beat against his fingertips, Justin breathed a sigh of relief.

Justin thought about Alexei, but he knew he couldn't just leave Boris here, even if he molded make shift metal restraints. The brute was resilient and had proved twice already that he could wake up and escape easily. There was only one option Justin could think of. He knew it was risky, but the only way he knew to incapacitate Boris for a while was to do a partial overload. True, he'd never done one, but he had watched and sensed the others do it. He stepped back, opened himself to all four elements, let them flow through him until he could manage them in equal amounts. Justin had to reign in the wind energy, but once he had them in balance, he directed the flow toward Boris. Justin tried to mimic the levels he had sensed when the others did the partial overloads in the meadow, keeping it just below what he thought appropriate just to be on the safe side.

POWER REVEALED

Suddenly, a ring buzzed from Justin's pocket taking him by surprise. His connections jumped around and he quickly dropped them all to avoid creating an imbalance. Justin pulled out the phone he borrowed from his Mom and looked at the text message: *Help—alexei found me in the museum—raven.* A stone plummeted to the bottom of Justin's stomach. He may have got his grandpa back, but there was no way Justin would allow Alexei to take Raven from him. Justin blasted a massive hole in the wall leading to the hallway and shot forward running to the museum as fast as possible hoping desperately that he would reach Raven in time.

Chapter 44

RAVEN BELIEVED NO one noticed her run out of the building, through the opening in the fence, and back up to the street. When she passed through the gates, she noticed Alexei's red Ferrari parked a little ways down the road. She quickly pulled out her phone and took a photo of it as further proof that Alexei was behind all of this. Then she turned and began running toward the museum.

She hadn't even reached the end of the block before a gust of wind hurled her against a chain link fence. Raven scanned the street and saw Alexei running toward her. Not good. Before even standing up, she connected to her element and shot a large pile of rubble at Alexei. He blew away the projectile heading toward his stomach, but he didn't notice a discarded tire rim that she hurled from behind. It knocked him on his face and Raven got up and sprinted toward the main road hoping it might have knocked him out long enough to reach her destination.

Half way to the museum, her lungs were already beginning

to burn. She wasn't used to such a fast pace, but she knew she had to reach the museum and make that call before Alexei found her or a lot of people might be killed. A loud horn blaring and screech of tires caused Raven to turn around and see Alexei's car run a red light and rocket down the road toward her. Despite being unable to outrun the car, impulse caused her to turn and run while trying to think of a way to stop Alexei. Pulling another car into Alexei might do the job and would seem normal, but Raven didn't want to risk a stranger's life. Throwing some large object at his car could never be explained, unless it was natural.

Raven reached out deep into the earth and just when she was ready to do it she spun around, braced her footing, and faced Alexei's car quickly closing the fifty feet between them. Then she set off an earthquake and promptly ripped a gap in the road right in front of Alexei's car and pulled up a massive pile of asphalt and dirt. Alexei braked and yanked his car to the right, but his momentum smashed the front driver's side of his car directly into the solid obstacle. The earth works were certainly out of proportion to the magnitude of the earthquake, but Raven figured they would just think it was a weakness in the rock or some other explainable reason.

Not waiting to see if Alexei was trapped in his car, Raven spun around and ran to the museum. Once she neared the main entrance, she slowed to a fast walk to look behind and to catch her breath somewhat before entering. Showing the stamp on her hand, Raven entered the museum and headed in the direction of the administrative offices. Last year, a pilot friend of her dad's had given Raven a full behind the scenes tour of the museum. Raven had loved it all, but she never thought at the time it would have helped her in this way. Reaching the employee only door, Raven looked behind her to make sure no one was watching and then used the energy to unlock the door and slip into the hallway.

She heard employees on the phone and at work, but she walked past a few of them acting like she belonged there. The threat of being caught kept her heart rate pumping as fast as it had been during the run. Finally, she reached a small, empty meeting room with a speaker phone sitting on the center of the table. Looking up and down the hallway to make sure she wasn't noticed, Raven then slipped into the room and locked the door. She picked up the speakerphone and tried to pull it over behind the door, but the cord was too short, so instead she sat down on the ground below the window and dialed 911.

"Seattle 911. What's the exact location of your emergency?"

"It's at Lannix Chemical Company on Othello Street near the King Country Airport." Raven tried to talk in a different voice, but the nervousness made her voice crack and she tried to keep her voice down so no one would hear her in the hallway.

"What's the nature of your emergency?"

"Someone is trying to blow up the factory. They've already damaged the fire system. Please hurry, a lot of people are in danger."

"Ma'am, what makes you think someone is trying to blow up the factory?"

"Because I saw them. Just hurry. Please." Then Raven hung up. She wasn't prepared to answer any more questions. Clearly, the woman didn't entirely believe her, but they'd have to send police and the fire department just in case it wasn't a crank call. She set the phone back on the table, unlocked the door, and listened to make sure the hallway was clear. Forcing herself to not run down the hall, she swiftly exited the employee area and began walking ahead through the museum with no direction in mind trying to decide what to do next.

At least she knew that Justin would only have to deal with Boris since Alexei had come chasing after her. Raven was

272

confident that Justin could handle Boris, which meant that he would be safe and the explosion should be avoided. But where should she go with Alexei possibly still on the loose? She doubted the car accident would have stopped Alexei for long. He was a snake and had a way of getting out of things. Should she return to the factory to help Justin or had he already taken care of Boris and was on his way to the museum? It wouldn't be good to be seen near the factory with the police and firemen showing up.

As she refocused on her surroundings and rounded a corner, she gasped and jumped back pressing herself against the wall. After taking a deep breath, she carefully peeked around the corner to see Alexei standing in the crowd searching for her. He was less than ten feet away. She shimmied along the wall a few steps and then pulled herself away from its protection and hurried away in the opposite direction.

She hadn't covered more than ten feet when she heard her name called out. Looking up in the direction of the voice, Raven saw Nikki waving at her standing on the far side of Alexei. Raven couldn't resist glancing directly at Alexei to see if he had heard her name. As she glanced in his direction, her eyes locked with Alexei who stared coldly at her less than twenty feet away. That moment of recognition seemed to freeze time. She could feel the deadly message Alexei held in his glare and the memory of his knife pressed against her throat immediately returned. Then just as abruptly as time seemed to stop, it promptly released its grip on her and sped up faster than Raven felt she could keep up with.

Raven bolted for the other section of the museum hoping to lose Alexei. At least she had the advantage of knowing the layout of the museum. People stared at her as she sprinted across the room, but she just dodged her way around them. Nearing a hallway, she sacrificed part of a second to look behind her. A tour group passed through and Alexei had to push his way through them. But Raven thought she also saw Nikki following in their direction. She wanted to yell at Nikki to stay away, but she didn't have time and she didn't want to draw Alexei's attention to Nikki.

Rushing down the hallway, Raven pushed open the door to the stairs. She hurried up the steps, but as she rounded the corner on the stairwell, she nearly ran into a man busy reading a file while heading down the stairs. Raven stepped back, lost her footing, and had to grab hold of the rail to avoid losing her balance and falling down the stairs. She called out a sorry out of habit and rushed up the stairs and down the hallway. After passing a few exhibits, a small hallway cut to the right for the purpose of bathrooms. She spun right, quickly pushed open the door, hurried into the farthest bathroom stall, and locked the stall door. A small level of relief flooded over her as she realized that she had escaped Alexei. Quick, shallow breaths caused her chest to heave as she tried to force her nerves to calm down.

The bathroom door opened and Raven shifted to the left to make it look like she was in front of the toilet in case some woman checked for empty stalls. Her breathing stopped when she heard a man's voice. "Raven. I know you're in here. A woman outside told me you just came in. Come on out."

The door opened again and Raven's forehead furrowed as she heard Nikki's voice. "Uh, you have the wrong bathroom. This is the ladies' room."

Alexei didn't even respond to Nikki. "Raven. You can't get past me. You might as well cooperate." Alexei hissed the words, reminding Raven of a snake.

"Wait. How do you know Raven?" Nikki said.

"You're friends with Raven," Alexei said it as more as a statement than a question. Raven wanted to scream that she had never seen Nikki before in her life. If only Nikki would say no. She had no idea how dangerous Alexei was.

"What's it to you?" Nikki said. Something banged against the wall. "Ow! Get your hands off of me you freak!"

"Raven, unless you want me to show your friend what real pain means, you better come out now. You know what I'm capable of, so don't try my patience."

"Okay." Raven pulled out her phone and typed a text message to Justin as fast as possible. *Help. Alexei found me in the museum. -Raven.*

"Now!" Alexei barked.

"I'm coming out." She quickly stuffed her phone back in her jacket and turned the handle to open the stall door hoping Justin had stopped Boris and would find her soon.

Alexei had Nikki pushed up against the wall with his hand pressing against her neck. Nikki kicked at Alexei and tried with both arms to pull his hand from her neck, but he was much stronger than her. Alexei leaned toward Nikki. "Stand still and shut up or I'll cut off your air supply."

"Nikki. Please don't fight. He'll hurt you," Raven said.

"Listen to the girl. She knows what she's talking about." Alexei pushed hard against Nikki's throat.

"Stop it!" Raven took a step toward them. "What do you want?"

Alexei released the pressure on Nikki's neck a little allowing her to breath. "I want to know who's here with you."

"It's just me and Nikki."

Alexei shoved hard against Nikki's throat and then finally released causing her to cough. "Don't make me ask a second time."

"Okay. Okay. It's only Justin and I." Alexei pushed hard again cutting off Nikki's air supply. "Honest! The others were too busy with—" Raven hesitated to say too much in front of Nikki. "—and they also didn't think you'd be here."

"Where's Justin?" The bathroom door opened but Alexei

kicked backward with his foot slamming the door shut again. "Seal the door closed. Now!"

"Okay. Okay." Raven stared at the handle on the door. It took her a moment to connect to the energy with her nerves frazzled. Someone tried to push the door open again, but Alexei kicked it closed holding it in place.

"Do it!" Alexei hissed.

"Give me a second. I'm trying to focus." Raven felt the energy flow into her and she directed it toward the door melting a portion of the lock like she had in the school office. "It won't open."

Alexei stretched his free arm behind him and pulled on the door handle but it wouldn't budge. Raven glanced over at Nikki who looked questioningly at her. Averting her eyes she avoided Nikki's questions, Raven focused again on Alexei who spoke up again. "Good. Now tell me where Justin is."

Raven had to say something for Nikki's sake. "He's somewhere here in the museum."

Alexei glared at Raven. "You are going to pay for wrecking my car, but first, I want to talk to Justin, and the two of you are coming with me." Alexei nodded toward Raven. "Over here."

Raven hesitantly took a couple steps forward. As she neared Alexei, he grabbed her arm and pulled her near him, spinning her around. Before Raven could pull away, he grabbed her in a head lock. He was stronger than she expected. "The two of you are going to listen carefully. We are all going to walk downstairs and both of you are going to behave. No running off. No calling for help. If you act normal, you might even live to see tomorrow. Understand?"

Nikki nodded slowly but Raven could only mumble in agreement due to Alexei's tight grasp. Alexei released his hold on Nikki's throat and grabbed tightly to each side of her cheeks from under her chin. "You and Raven seem to be good friends. I'm going to let you go, but if you do anything I don't like, anything, including just looking at people the wrong way, I will snap Raven's neck. Understand?" Nikki nodded. "Raven, don't even think of using your powers. I'll sense it if you even begin to connect to the energy, and I'll make sure that is last time you connect or do anything else. Got it?"

Nikki glanced at Raven questioningly but Raven looked away knowing the questions Nikki must have for her. Alexei loosened his hold around Raven's neck and placed his hand around the back of her neck. She could feel his fingers digging into her flesh. "Are you both ready?" They nodded. "What's your name?"

"Nikki."

"Okay, Nikki, open the door - slowly." Nikki reached for the handle, but the door wouldn't budge.

"Raven, use the energy, just this once, and unlock the door." Nikki stepped aside waiting for Raven to reach for the door, but Raven stood still, connected to the energy, and focused on reforming the metal inside the lock.

"It's ready," Raven said. Nikki turned and looked at Raven like she was crazy.

"Open the door," Alexei said.

"The door's locked."

"Not anymore. Open the door. Do it now. I don't like repeating myself."

Nikki shook her head like she thought it was a waste of time, but she pulled on the door handle and froze in surprise when the door opened this time. Nikki turned and looked at the two of them in confusion, but Alexei nodded at her to move forward. Raven followed Nikki out into the hallway wincing as Alexei dug his fingers harder into her neck. Scanning the empty hallway, Raven searched for Justin, hoping he had received her message.

Chapter 45

THE WIND CAUGHT the door as Justin hurried into the museum out of the wind. He had covered the mile plus distance to the museum in less than six minutes, but Justin was worried it wasn't fast enough. His biggest hope was that Alexei wouldn't hurt Raven right away because he needed to use her as bait to get to Justin.

A mass of people milled through the area ahead of him. The museum was huge and if he ran around aimlessly looking for her, Alexei may lose patience and hurt Raven before Justin found her. If only he could sense other Elementers like she could. But he stopped. He might not have Raven's talent, but he was an Elementer. Besides, he and Raven had a special connection. Maybe he could sense her energy. He closed his eyes to concentrate. He'd never tried to find someone by their energy before, but he had cut off Mr. Hamilton's and Patrick's energy, so he knew how to recognize it. Once he focused on looking for the energy concentrations, he was able to sense an Earth Elementer. It was fuzzy and he couldn't pin point the spot, but she seemed to be in the direction of the main display with all the hanging planes.

Justin headed in her direction, but he stopped when he heard someone call out his name. "Justin! There you are." Lewis waved at Justin as he approached from across the room. "Where have you guys been? We've looked all over for you and now I've even lost Nikki."

"Lewis, I need your help. We need to find Raven right away. I think she's in trouble."

"Why? What's going on?" Lewis asked.

"I don't have time to explain it all. Will you help me find her?"

"Sure. Where do you want me to look?"

"My guess is that they're in the main room with the hanging planes. I'll start looking on the right side along the windows. You look on the left side. But if you see her, don't go up to her. Just call me on my phone. Okay?"

"Why?"

"Lewis, I don't have time to explain. Please, just call and wait for me." They had reached the room and Justin split off to the right side of the room. Justin scanned the room, but the mob of people jumbled amongst the mix of planes and other flying contraptions parked on the floor and hanging from the ceiling made it difficult to spot Raven. As Justin searched through the crowd, he thought about how to take care of Alexei with so many people nearby. Justin neared the end of the end of the room when his phone buzzed. He pulled it out of his pocket and read Lewis' message. "Found them under the red and blue hanging plane." Justin shoved his phone back in his pocket, looked up to spot the plane, and hurried in that direction.

Justin skidded to a halt when he heard Nikki's name called out. He saw Alexei grabbing onto Raven's arm. Nikki stood next to them and Lewis was walking toward them. "Lewis." Justin hissed under his breath. What was he doing? Justin watched as the scene unfolded across the room. Lewis confronted Alexei, probably telling Alexei to let go of his friends. Alexei pushed Nikki to the side, stepped forward, and punched Lewis in the stomach with what must have been extra wind energy. Lewis shot back with great force and collided against the wall. Struggling to his feet, Lewis cradled an injured arm as he resumed his approach.

Justin had to do something quickly, but he needed to stop Alexei solidly so that his friends could get away and to prevent a fight near bystanders. He didn't want anyone to get caught in the cross fire or see anything strange. But whatever he did it also needed to look 'normal'. Especially since Lewis' confrontation had already gathered the attention of a nearby family standing close to the large helicopter.

Looking from Lewis back to Raven, Justin noticed that she had spotted him. Alexei was still focused on Lewis. Justin couldn't Earth Talk to Raven since Alexei would notice, so instead Justin held up his hand with his fingers extended and lowered one finger at a time counting down from five to zero. At zero, Raven yanked her arm away from Alexei's grasp and Justin shot a burst of air directed at Alexei's legs. The force flipped Alexei backwards causing the back of his head to solidly smack against the floor.

Raven grabbed Nikki's hand and pulled her toward Lewis. Then she let go of Nikki's hand urging her to run up the stairs. Raven grabbed hold of Lewis' arm and yanked him up the stairs to the next level. Nikki ran along the next level and headed up another set up stairs to the third level. Raven seemed to be calling her to stop, but Justin stopped watching them and turned his attention back to Alexei.

The Russian sat up and looked in the direction where Justin's energy came from, but Justin was hidden behind the landing gear of a plane. "Where are you Justin?" Alexei called out. Justin felt a spike of wind energy erupt and he heard a door crash open. Justin turned to see three more doors bang open along the far end of the glass wall as a violent and sustained gust of wind rushed into the building. Justin wondered what Alexei was up to, when suddenly one of the cables snapped that suspended a cherry red plane to the ceiling at the far end of the room. Justin looked back at Alexei, but Justin couldn't spot him. Justin linked up, felt Alexei's energy, and tried to cut off his connection, but Alexei's hold was too strong.

The wind and the drama with the plane had either grabbed the attention of everyone in the entire exhibit hall or had driven them out of the area. The wind continued to roar through the massive hall ripping out a second cable from the ceiling. Justin glanced up in the direction of Raven and saw her running alongside the third floor railing back toward the stairs. But he watched in horror as a gust of wind lifted Raven off her feet and over the railing.

She succeeded in grabbing onto two of the posts hanging dangerously over the edge. Justin heard over the noise of the wind Raven scream out his name. He knew she couldn't hold on long so he darted in her direction forgetting all about Alexei. But Justin only covered half the distance to Raven when a gust picked him up and threw him against a plane. He looked up in horror to see another gust hit Raven causing her to lose her grip and fall toward the floor two stories below. There was no time to reach her so Justin sent out a solid blast of wind that blew Raven sideways softening the impact of the fall. She hit the floor and rolled to the side.

Scanning the area, Justin caught sight again of Alexei and

LEAH M. BERRY

launched a blast of wind at Alexei smashing him hard against the wall. Justin ran past an unconscious Alexei toward Raven and knelt down to help her up, but she shrank away from him. He knew why she pulled away, but it still pained him. "Sorry for trying to touch you. I'm an idiot."

"You're not an idiot. You just saved me from splatting. The Lannix factory?"

"It's fine and Boris won't be causing any problems. But Alexei can so let's get out of here. We need to find a more private place to fight him."

"Raven!" Nikki rushed up beside Justin. "Are you okay?"

"Yeah, just some bruises I think. Help me up?"

Nikki reached out and helped Raven up and then looked over at Alexei. "Let's get out of here before that psychopath gets up," Nikki said.

The four of them hurried toward the space section of the museum. It was located across the street and was best reached by crossing the tubular overpass above the street. Half way across the overpass, Nikki must have felt far enough away from danger because she slowed down. "Who was that guy and how do you know him?" Nikki demanded.

"We don't know him," Raven said.

"Then how did he know your and Justin's names? He accused you of wrecking his car."

Justin wasn't sure what to say, but Raven spoke up. "We met him only half an hour ago here at the museum. We were working on our science project and he introduced himself. He seemed harmless enough at first. We shared our names, but then he started getting real weird. We left the area and went to work elsewhere. When Justin left to check out one of the other exhibits, the guy approached again and started creeping me out. I tried to hide from him when you called my name and he caught sight of me."

"Sorry," Nikki said.

"It's not your fault."

"We need to get security and report him," Lewis said.

Justin stepped in on the conversation. "I agree, but all of the security guards are super busy right now because of the fallen plane and possible injuries. How about we stay away from the guy for a while until security has things under control and then we can report him."

"Good point, Justin," Raven said.

As they neared the end of the overpass Nikki stopped walking. The others halted to look at her, but she hesitated seeming to have trouble figuring out what to say. "Raven, what happened when you fell?"

Justin looked at Raven nervously. Raven smiled and shrugged. "What do you mean?"

"Don't get me wrong. I'm super glad you're okay. But something—cushioned your fall."

"Cushioned my fall? My body doesn't feel like it was cushioned."

"Raven, you fell two stories and only have bruises."

"I guess I'm just lucky."

"Yes, but—" Nikki hesitated.

"Nikki, I saw her blown to the side too," Justin said. "The wind in there was crazy. It's no wonder it pulled one of the planes from the ceiling."

Lewis shook his head. "I tell you. The weather has been insane lately. First, that crazy wind in Bellingham that helped put out the fire and now another one down here in Seattle that knocked down the plane. Weird."

"Yeah, real weird," Justin said.

Chapter 46

THEY WERE ENTERING the space section of the museum when Raven paused. "Alexei is coming." Raven glanced behind her to make sure only Justin heard. "I can sense him."

"The best place to confront him is outside on the tarmac. I didn't see anyone out there, but I'll head out right now and try to encourage them to come inside."

"How?"

"I'll stir up the storm a little. They won't want to be sitting in a metal plane or out on the tarmac and risk being tasered by Mother Nature. Besides, it'll help draw Alexei out there when he feels the energy. Take Nikki and Lewis and hide in the Space Shuttle Trainer while Alexei passes through."

"You don't have to fight him by yourself. I can help."

"I know you can. If it wasn't for you, the power pole that nearly fell on us in the school parking lot would have fried me like well-cooked bacon. But you're hurt and someone needs to keep Nikki and Lewis safe. If we both disappear again, you know they'll come looking for us and Alexei wouldn't hesitate to take them out if he thought they were in the way."

Raven sighed and grimaced. "Fine. But that not dead requirement is still in force. Promise?"

"Promise." Justin wanted to say – and do – much more. Instead, he just said, "Be careful," and headed for the doors.

As Justin exited the building leading to the Air Park, the wind grabbed the door and blew it wide open. Justin reached for the handle just in time to prevent the door from banging against its hinges. Justin shivered as the rain and cold wind blew at him. He zipped up his jacket, peered across the tarmac. He was fed up with the cold weather, but at least the storm had hopefully sent everyone indoors already.

Seven airplanes, including the original Air Force One and an old Concorde, were parked out on the tarmac in front of him. The area seemed devoid of people until he approached the planes and noticed small sheds near a couple of the planes and museum employees huddled inside each.

Justin moved to the side to stay out of direct sight of either employee. He thought of locking them in their sheds so they wouldn't see anything, but if they had radios, they might call for help and draw more people out here. Justin needed to drive them into the museum quickly, so he went for the dramatic, sending a burst of wind at both sheds. The door to the shed next to Air Force One was nearly ripped its hinges and the door to the other shed banged violently against its frame repeatedly. Both employees quickly exited their sheds. In her rush to get out of the shed, the middle-aged woman tripped over a toppled traffic cone and fell down. Justin started to move to help her, but stopped himself since he knew they'd insist he go inside with them. So instead, he whispered an apology and waited for her to stand back up and hurry into the building with the college age guy from the other shed.

Justin figured they wouldn't have left if any guests were in the planes, but he wanted to be sure. A car honked behind Justin. The Air Park was right next to the street in full view of too many people. Justin needed to check the planes without being seen from the museum employees inside and he needed to keep his confrontation with Alexei hidden from bystanders, but how? Something from one of Mr. Hamilton's training sessions came to mind. Justin reached out to the water element. Within moments, a layer of fog descended upon the Air Park. It didn't take long before the cars passing by looked more like phantoms floating through an airplane graveyard.

The fog had barely settled when Justin left his hiding spot and hurried to the nearest airplane and up the metal staircase. The interiors of the planes were sealed off with plexiglass walls except for the center aisles to allow visitors to walk through them. It reminded Justin of some strange mummification process for planes. That combined with the howling wind outside gave Justin an eerie feeling that he had to shake off.

Justin walked down the stairwell from the last plane when he felt someone's wind energy and Alexei's voice sounded in his head. "It's still not too late to join us." Justin scanned the tarmac for Alexei, but the thick, grey fog obstructed his view. "The Council fears you. They're going to do everything in their power to control you." Justin was disgusted by Alexei's voice and wanted to brush away Alexei's lies, but deep down Justin knew there was some truth in his statement. The Council did fear what Justin could do and they would try to control him. But he wasn't going to resort to joining Alexei to maintain his independence.

"Justin, this is your last chance to enjoy real freedom," Alexei said.

"Freedom?" Justin spat out the word. "Freedom to commit

mass murder?"

"I didn't want to do it, but sometimes you have to do what is necessary to maintain your freedom."

"How would killing those people help you keep your freedom?" Justin responded while searching for Alexei through the fog.

"It requires money to live my lifestyle."

"So it's true. You were going to kill all those innocent people just because you wanted more money!"

"Without money, I don't have the freedom to do what I want."

Henry's saying returned to Justin's mind. "Freedom is being who you really are, not doing what you want to do." For the first time, the words finally seemed to make some sense to Justin. No one could take his freedom away. Not his dad. Not his teachers. Not the Council. Not Alexei. They might be able to affect what he can do sometimes, but no one, not anyone or anything, could tell him who he had to be. That was up to him. He wasn't even going to let his powers define him.

"Becoming a murderer like you isn't going to free me. No one can take my freedom away."

"If you can't be reasoned with, then there's only one thing left to do," Alexei said.

Justin felt the wind energy intensify in the air around him. He spun around still scanning for Alexei in the mist, but a powerful burst of wind knocked Justin off his feet and up into the air. His stomach lurched from the sudden elevation change and his heart raced as he rose higher and higher. The ground disappeared below him in the fog. Justin shot a wind gust to send him back down to the ground, but his feet hit the tarmac so fast that his legs couldn't keep up with the speed causing him to stumble forward. His arms instinctively reached out to break his fall. His hands hit first and then he rolled to the side. His wrist stung and a shooting pain in his ankle suggested a strain, but it could have been much worse.

Rather than try to catch sight of Alexei, Justin sent a wide, powerful gust in the general area where Alexei's energy originated. Justin heard a crash, groan, and some cursing in Russian coming from the direction of the Concorde. Justin limped in that direction searching for his opponent. An outline of a man getting back up came into sight. Justin didn't wait for him to recover. Connecting to the water and wind elements, Justin reached into the sky, combined the rain droplets, slowed their vibration, and sent a barrage of hail the size of golf balls at Alexei.

The first volley of hail stones hit their target, knocking Alexei to the ground, but then a wind gust blew the rest of the oncoming projectiles back toward Justin. The white objects were camouflaged in the mist and Justin didn't see them coming until they were almost on top of him. He held up his arms to protect his face as the ice pellets stung his arms and stomach. One of them nailed his injured wrist. Justin closed his eyes for a moment while dealing with the pain. When he opened them again and looked through the fog, Alexei was gone.

Justin thought he heard the sound of steps running to his left, but it was hard to be sure over the roar of the wind. Bolting forward, pain erupted in his right ankle causing him to favor his leg as he pursued Alexei. Air Force One loomed above as Justin heard the hollow clatter of what must be Alexei running up the portable metal stairway to the front part of the plane. Justin hurried behind him and up the steps, but two-thirds of the way up the ladder Justin saw Alexei appear at the top of the stairs with a sadistic grin. "Enjoy the ride!" Alexei hollered over the storm.

Justin grabbed onto the railing as a blast of wind collided with the stairway. The portable staircase was pushed off its four stabilizer footings knocking Justin to his knees. He avoided falling down the steps, but before he had a chance to attack back, a twister collided with the staircase wrenching it from the plane and spinning it in circles multiple times. The stairway toppled over, slinging Justin down onto the tarmac. Justin lifted his hands, surveying the shredded skin and blood on his palms from the road rash. He felt other injuries beneath his clothes, but he didn't have time to worry about them right now.

Rolling over, Justin shot a volley of wind at the door to the front of the airplane but Alexei had retreated inside for protection. Justin picked himself up and hobbled over behind the nearest plane to avoid being an open target. While he could use the wind to lift him up to the plane, Justin wasn't confident in his aim and suspected he might miss and throw himself against a metal wall.

Justin was ready to end this. He closed his eyes for a moment to concentrate. Focusing the energy, he could feel it resonate within and all around him. It felt like the edge of his body had expanded to include the entire Air Park. He wasn't connected to the energy. It was a part of him. He reached out and ripped off the back emergency exit door of Air Force One. Then he amassed a ferocious gale and sent it blazing through the aircraft shooting out of the aisle anything in its path that wasn't bolted down. A typewriter, office chair, and other debris shot out the back exit door followed by a human body. Justin redirected the wind and dropped Alexei to the ground in front of him.

Alexei lifted up his head and tried to attack using his powers, but Justin cut off every attempt Alexei made to connect to the energy. Instead of hijacking Alexei's energy, like he had before with Rex and Steven, this time Justin was one with all the energy and simply blocked Alexei's attempts to connect.

"Is something wrong?" Justin smirked at Alexei.

A primal growl came out of Alexei's throat.

"You're done, Alexei. I'm not going to let you kill anyone else ever again."

"See. You're just like me. Forced to kill when necessary." Alexei glared and pushed himself to his feet, and as Justin took a step closer, Alexei launched himself at his opponent. Rather than flick Alexei aside with the wind, Justin reached back and swung his fist at Alexei's face with the help of the wind, sending Alexei sprawling to the ground.

"I won't be forced into being a killer. No one can take my freedom away. Not even a murderer like you." Alexei tried to get up, but Justin held him down with the wind. "But there are other ways to prevent you from hurting people." Justin opened himself to all four elements and shot the energy into Alexei causing Alexei's body to jerk and stiffen in resistance. Justin's anger at Alexei tried to take over and flood Alexei with more energy, but Justin refused to give the Council an excuse to try to extend their control over him. Especially since Henry was relying on him.

He tightened the energy flowing through him, creating something of a bottleneck to prevent overloading Alexei too much. But he could almost taste the energy pushing against him, wanting to be freed. A hint of honey saturated his tongue. The immensity of power seemed to almost sing to him, promising anything if he would let it wash over him.

Justin searched for his center like Anya taught him and found his focus. Once he overloaded Alexei enough, with great effort, he unplugged his connection to the elements. Letting go was similar to pulling on a thick extension cord that wouldn't disconnect from the wall outlet. The rush of energy flooded out of him and he felt an unnatural emptiness. He stood there a moment, aware of only the allure of the energy. It was like standing in front of a bowl of M&M's and eating only one. The energy called out to be consumed.

The ring of a phone jarred Justin out of his trance and in surprise, he scrambled through his pockets for his mom's phone. "Yeah," he mumbled into the phone.

"Justin. Are you okay?" It was Raven's voice.

"Yeah, I'm fine. It's done." Justin shook his head to clear his mind. "But now I have to figure out how to get Alexei out of here."

"I've already taken care of that. Just give me a minute and I'll be out there."

Chapter 47

THE FOG BEGAN dissipating and Justin smiled as he saw Raven's face emerge through the mist. But the next person he saw wiped the smile right off his face. Rex marched toward Justin with Grant at his side.

"You two are lucky to be alive!" Rex stopped right in front of Justin and glared at him.

"We're lucky? Alexei and Boris are the incapacitated ones," Justin said.

Rex stood over Alexei who laid still on the ground. "What did you do to him?!"

"I did a partial overload."

"You did what?!" Rex stepped toward Justin placing them nearly toe to toe. "You have no idea how to do an overload. You probably fried them."

Justin refused to back up in response. "They're just fine. I saw and sensed how you guys did it in the meadow."

"All four Elementers have to keep the energy in perfect balance," Rex said.

"Yeah, and for those of us who can use all four," Justin paused for emphasis, "it's easy to do. Besides, it's not like I had another choice. I needed to stop them from blowing up the factory and escaping again."

Rex took a step back, but didn't back off on his glare. "The two of you never should have come here on your own."

"Raven tried to convince you to do something, but you all said there wasn't enough evidence. If we had listened to you, over a hundred people would be dead at the Lannix factory. So don't tell us we were wrong to come."

"You have no idea what you're doing," Rex said.

"I beat Alexei, which is more than you can say," Justin said.

"Being able to access the energy and understanding it are two very different things. You're an impulsive, foolish kid that clearly doesn't grasp what he's involved in," Rex said.

"You don't know anything about me," Justin said.

"I know that you can't go around wielding this much power so irresponsibly."

"You, and the Council, can't tell me what to do. Alexei was wrong to think he can do whatever he wanted, regardless of its effect on others. But you and the Council can't decide how I live my life. Just because it scares the Council that I can access all the elements, their fear doesn't give them the right to control me," Justin said.

"You're not above the rules. You broke both of them," Rex said.

"I did not!" Justin was the one this time to take a step toward Rex. "I've kept it secret. I drew Boris into an abandoned building just to the north of the Lannix factory to stay out of view. You'll find him partially overloaded in that building. In addition, I made sure this area was cleared of people first and then created the fog so no one would see me fight Alexei."

"Even if no one saw you, you still overloaded two Elementers by yourself," Rex said.

"You guys did it to Alexei's friends. As long as it's necessary, which it was, and it's only a partial overload, it's allowed."

"No one is allowed to do it by themselves," Rex said.

"There's no such rule," Justin said.

"There hasn't needed to be such a rule until you came along," Rex said.

"I'll keep your powers a secret and not destroy life, but the Council has no right to do anything to me just because I'm more powerful than any of you."

Rex opened his mouth to argue, but Justin cut him off. "And if you try to control me, I'll show you what I can do."

"Justin?" Raven's voice interrupted. Justin turned in surprise because he forgot for a moment that she was there.

"What?" Justin said.

Raven nodded her head in the direction of the museum. Justin looked through the clearing fog and saw Nikki and Lewis walking toward them. Nikki halted when she saw Alexei lying knocked out on the ground. She looked up at Justin. "What did you do?"

"Nothing," Justin said. "He came up and threatened me so I ran and hid in one of the planes. He thought I was in Air Force One, but as he climbed the stairs into the plane the storm toppled the stairway. It looks like he hit his head hard when he fell. He's been out since."

"He's still dangerous and needs to be reported to the police," Nikki said.

"This is our patient," Rex said.

"Who are you?" Nikki looked up at Rex.

Grant took a step toward Nikki. "Miss, we work at a nearby

mental hospital. This man escaped while we were taking him to a medical appointment. We've been searching for him for the last couple hours."

"How did you know to come here?" Lewis asked.

"When we couldn't find him near the doctor's office, we finally came here looking for him. It's his favorite place. He normally isn't harmful. But he's been off his meds for the last two days to prepare for the lab tests and without the pills, it really messes him up and causes hallucinations. It's our fault he escaped and if you report it to the police we'll lose our jobs. My wife is fighting cancer and if I lose my job we'll lose our health insurance. She'll die without treatment. Please don't say anything. He really is harmless normally. We promise to take him away. This will never happen again."

Nikki paused and then slowly nodded. "Okay, then I'm going inside. This weather is terrible."

Lewis and Raven followed her, but Justin hesitated. Raven turned to wait for Justin. "Come on," she whispered. "Rex and Grant will take care of Alexei and Boris. They won't get away. Nikki and Lewis will ask too many questions if we don't go with them. Besides, it's almost time to meet up with Lewis' mom and go to dinner."

Grant stepped up and placed his hand on Justin's shoulder. "Justin, we'll make sure we get them both back to Bellingham. You can go with Raven."

Justin glanced down at Alexei knocked out on the tarmac. Alexei wasn't a threat anymore. But Justin knew that he needed to find and stop whoever was behind Alexei. Otherwise, Henry would never be safe out in the open again.

"Justin?" Raven gently called bringing him out of his reverie.

He looked up at her and thought that even if the Council

was against him, at least he had her to count on. "I'm ready," he said. He wasn't only ready to leave the museum. He was ready to find out who was behind the attempt on Henry's life and the sabotage of the factory. And once he found who it was, he'd stop them.

Thank You

Before you go, I'd like to thank you for reading *Power Revealed*.

If you liked the story, then I need your help! Please share the word with your friends and take a moment to post a review for this book with the online retailer of your choice.

I love to hear from readers like you. Stop by my website (http://leahmberry.com/) to learn more about The Elementers, take part in contests, vote for ideas for the next books, and share your thoughts.

Acknowledgments

My biggest thanks goes to my husband for supporting my writing even though the time I've spent writing this adventure has reduced the time we could spend having our own adventures together. I promise to plan a big, crazy adventure very soon.

My boys also sacrificed a lot of time with me, but at least they were able to enjoy each new chapter as it came into existence. Thank you for being the ultimate beta readers and giving your honest feedback. You didn't hesitate to tell me what wasn't working. The book is so much better because of you.

Thank you to my parents who always believed in me and supported me no matter what odd things I did. It is so much easier to take risks, whether it be traveling the world or writing a book, when you know you have people who will love you no matter what.

Krista Jensen, Carla Parsons, and Norma Rudolph welcomed me into their writing group when I arrived in Cody, Wyoming, and provided great support, advice, and friendship. I love and miss you. Melynn Minson and Stephanie Driscoll, my virtual writing group buddies, served as fabulous beta readers. The book is better because of you. Thank you also to my fellow writing group partners in Washington and Arizona.

Thank you to Abigail Michel for copy editing, and to Indie Designz for the cover design and interior formatting. I was new to this whole process, but they were patient, professional, and fabulous. Your help is greatly appreciated.

Finally, my thanks goes to you, the reader. Half the fun of writing a book is sharing it with others, so thank you for letting me share it. I hope you enjoyed this adventure and go out and live your own adventures too.

About the author

Leah M. Berry grew up in the-place-of-too-much-snow (also known as Canada). In her early teens, she decided she wanted to live all over the world and not simply because she needed to warm up. First, she went alone, later she married and conned her husband into coming, and now they drag their kids everywhere they go. Currently, they live in Arizona, but by the time you read this book, their location could easily have changed. Wherever they are though, their heart is always in the Pacific Northwest.

When she's not reading or writing about adventures, Leah is off somewhere experiencing them for herself. She loves hiking, backpacking, kayaking, traveling the world, and basically anything that involves exploring the wonders of nature. If she could have Elementer powers, she's currently torn between wanting to be a Wind or Tree Elementer.

.

Made in the USA
Middletown, DE
09 May 2015